Cardinal Synne

Cardinal Synne

David Lens

To all those with the courage to speak out

and act against tyranny of any kind

Cardinal Ignatius Synne placed or, rather, tossed the sheets of parchment onto the table in front of him. His exasperation not with the contents of the document but with the zealous ignorance of the Roman Curia that had assigned the writing to the Index of Forbidden Books. Material considered heretical, dangerous to the faith or morals of the Roman Catholic Church. True, the list had acquired the status of an historical document in the later part of the twentieth century but that would have been no consolation to the author of the script, tortured, tried for heresy, burnt at the stake in a Breton town, a few hundred years earlier.

He leant back, frowning, puzzled. It wasn't the first medieval script he had read in which unease about Catholic doctrine had been challenged. He wasn't surprised. What puzzled him was that this particular document had been allowed to exist. The Inquisition had stringent protocols. Protocols which, normally, would have seen the parchment not even assigned to the Index but destroyed. Why was it not destroyed?

The author was Gabriel de Tregor of Gwalarn, an Augustinian monk from a priory in Finistère, a priory that now contained only a handful of monks. De Gregor had travelled widely in the South West of France and was exposed to Cathar and Jansenist teachings considered heretical by the Roman church. He had also remained for some time at the priory on St Michael's Mount in Cornwall after a pilgrimage inspired by accounts of miracles said to have occurred there three centuries earlier.

A man, fitter than most half his age, Synne had one vice: a liking for tobacco. He pulled an old Meerschaum pipe from the back pack at his side, its bowl crusted up with the tarry residue of decades of pleasure. A leather pouch, plump with almost fifty grammes of Balkan leaf blended with a greater than normal quantity of Latakia, gave off a whiff of the fermentation process that characterised the mix. He took time filling the pipe, not looking at his fingers but eying the parchments that had angered him.

Ignatius stood and fumbled about in his jacket for a lighter. Not allowed to smoke in the library, he pushed his chair back and headed for the stone stairs to the terrace below. Outside, seated on one of the stone balustrades between the pillars of the cloister, he pressed newly ignited embers down into the bowl. Nodding mischievously at a passing nun, he smiled as she looked disapprovingly at the cloud of smoke.

'Good day sister'. His cheery, Irish brogue could not help but raise a hint of a smile.

'Ah, 'tis one of our own pollutin' God's good air.'

'No sister. Think of it as incense raisin' a prayer of gratitude to all the saints in heaven. Father Ignatius,' he nodded a greeting as he transferred the pipe to his left hand and put out his right.

'Sister Francesca. Scourge of Jesuits, small boys and smokers.' She took the hand as she said it and they both laughed.

'Forgive me Father, for I have grinned.' They laughed again.

'And which part of God's own Eden are y'from?'

'Kenmare but my convent is just outside Dublin.'

'Yourself?'

'Just across from the Aran Islands, originally but based at Trinity, Dublin. Here for three months.'

'Well, nice to meet you Father,' and, pointing skywards, 'may all the saints forgive ye.' She smiled again and walked away.

Ignatius watched until her black habit blended with the shadowed entry to one of the passages she turned into. He drew on the amber stem of his pipe and, a second time, pressed the bright embers a little more firmly into the bowl. A double stream of smoke exited his nostrils. He never inhaled. For him the taste and smell were sufficient. The buzz most craved from an inhaled, nicotine fix was not his passion.

His thoughts went back to the last section of the manuscript he had just read. There was no ambiguity in the Latin passage. Gabriel de Tregor had confidently written, "… they shall move around the sun and pass their faster sisters but with seasons longer." Other passages referred to the composition of matter. One observation alluded to formation of solids from liquids. Amber setting from resin prompted our monk to suggest that everything, at some time, must have a fluid origin. Plants needed water; pumice needed magma; the plaster in the Sistine Chapel needed a slurry of ingredients.

It was a reference to the 'divisibility of parts', however, that intrigued the cardinal. De Tregor had speculated that, with an infinite process of division, a solid should ultimately reach a particle that could no longer be parted. There was nothing profound in this conclusion. The Greeks had posited this centuries before. What was novel, what did pique the cardinal's attention, was the

3

comment, "… that each final part of one substance will differ from another, so divided, by way of brimstone from iron, a flame from its wick, blood from water." Elsewhere, a reference to attraction, "... lightning to a tree, lodestone to iron but not to gold, in the way the moon pulls the sea with no visible force." It was the latter that particularly intrigued him. What process of reasoning was going on in de Tregor's mind for him to make that observation? Further commentary alluded to what could only be a prediction of some form of atomic bonding, "... that tin will flux with copper because the two have the same affinity whereas water will not with oil even when much heat is given".

Synne sensed, from his knowledge of the parchment and a strange feeling of knowing the writer; that de Tregor's words represented more going on in his mind than just the pictures created by his thought processes. He stayed a while longer sitting on the low wall between the pillars. A clock, somewhere, chimed a quarter hour. Time to get back. He tapped the contents of his pipe, mainly ash, into his hand and scattered it into the earth bordering the grass in the quadrangle.

A Jesuit scholar and one of the youngest cardinals ever to be appointed by a pope, Synne had sought a period of rustication in a seminary. Following a distinguished, academic career in theoretical physics, he needed time to reassess both his vocation and intellectual interests. He was not old but training young priests at the seminary was merely a pause, a diversion in his spiritual life. He had other ambitions. Leave to spend a sabbatical in the

Gregorian University, Rome, now found him researching documents related to Cosmology.

In his early forties, he was experiencing a second conversion. Not like that of some dogmatic, evangelical Christian. No, this was a growing conviction that there must be some kind of cosmological theology - maybe theology was the wrong word - counter to his training, begging to be recognised and supersede it. For a while now he had concealed nagging doubts about his faith. His spiritual confessor had not detected this during their infrequent meetings, or so he believed.

It had seeded itself reading 'Hymn of the Universe', written by Teilhard de Chardin - Jesuit priest, French philosopher, trained palaeontologist and geologist. De Chardin, stimulated by a scientifically informed and intuitive perception of the universe, viewed the cosmos as something more profound and mysterious than that portrayed by the allegorists of the Old Testament. For him the account in Genesis lacked imagination - or too much, rather. Lacked some kind of undefined wisdom and, by its format and literary construct, smacked of patronising naivety. A perception that did the concept of a divine creator little honour. For de Chardin the magnificence of the cosmos demanded something more profound in its appreciation than sterile performance of the Mass. Something worthy of a mystery that had tantalised the mind of Homo Sapiens right from the start of human reason.

But this revelation met with opposition from de Chardin's superiors, opposition that forced him to cease, overtly, expounding his opinions. He was called to account and lodged in obscurity in some house of recantation.

A sudden insight into an area of quantum theory that had puzzled Synne for years, hit him during a wakeful period brought on by consuming too much coffee before the evening Office of Compline. Had it been brought on by some meditative, religious experience it would have been akin to a Pauline revelation. This it was not but it had the effect of reinforcing his doubts. It overturned decades of doctrinal commentary stored in his memory without erasing it. Different from hallucinations brought on by a low, blood-sugar count or excess, spiritual exercise in self denial, this was a eureka moment. Heuristic. Intuitive. Deeper, more cerebral than what he imagined some black Pentecostal congregation or other Christian or Hindu, Muslim or other mystic might have induced in themselves in some public show of undignified, spiritual excess, a kind of spiritual masturbation. It always made him cringe to watch pastors ministering to swooning members of their congregation feigning ecstasies of self-induced euphoria. Behaviour that looked so staged and so expected during the mass conditioning. The 'hallelujahs', the 'Jesus-be-praised' shrieks of the congregation psyched up to fill the collection plate.

He knew, now, that the basis of his Jesuit indoctrination was solely that: a form of benign conditioning that did not contradict or offend moral scruples. There was nothing ostensibly wrong with the teaching but, as always, when it became an inflexible yard stick it also became a rigid punishment stick. He was a cynic. It was merely a set of man-made rules influenced by the vocabulary and superstitions of the age it evolved in. Subtly but surely, formulated and refined over years by constant exposure to the drip feed of Catholic dogma.

2

Back at the table Ignatius opened his laptop, re-read parts of the manuscript and recorded content and location of certain passages. It was time to leave. He returned the document to the librarian and made for the main exit.

'Professor'?

The voice was from a mature student seated close to the door and, since no one was nearby, must be addressed to him.

Ignatius turned, 'Penny. It is Penny isn't it? What are you doing here?'

'Studying for a PhD.'

'Well, I'm impressed but it's a long while since your time at ...'

A ssh from the balcony above interrupted their conversation.

'Come on, let's a ... , let's go for a coffee. We can catch up at the café in Pisa Street. I've pretty well done all I want, for now. My treat.'

*

'So, what've you been doing and what are you reading? Not physics, I would have thought. Certainly not here.'

'No. Linguistic Philosophy. Want to get away from science. Worked for an electronics company for a while. Then oil industry on drill-bit telemetry to do with fracking but got disenchanted with the politics and ecological battles being waged. The public don't realise so-called carbon-free, energy generation is itself energy-dependant on non-renewable energy at various stages. Nothing is as simple as each side declares. Anyway, that's boring. Nice to see you again. You're still lecturing?'

'No. I've stepped down and have an emeritus tenure at the university, back at Trinity. I'm on a bit of a sabbatical researching early cosmology writings by Jesuit and other fraternities. Particularly from the Index of Forbidden Books.'

'One Americano, one espresso.' The waiter set the coffees down, took payment and went to a table newly occupied.

'You've not married and settled down then?'

'Yes, there was someone but I kept my birth surname. One of the mining engineers. Got killed. More than a year ago now. Stupid accident. A stack of drill shafts fell on him. One of those things which shouldn't have happened but did. I suppose that's why I'm here. Where are you lodging?'

'At one of the Jesuit houses. You?'

'Renting a studio apartment nearby.'

'What are you doing for income?'

'Teaching a bit of English here and there but was left a legacy by an aunt. That covers my costs here and I still have the house we bought when we married. The teaching provides for a few non-essentials, extravagances like dining out.'

'Look, I've got to get back but let's meet up for lunch. Tomorrow? That any good?'

'I'd love that.'

'The Green Olive restaurant. Do you know it? Only a couple of streets from the uni.'

'Yes. They know me. Will be surprised to see me turn up with a priest.'

'Not as surprised as when they see me turn up with a woman. An attractive one at that.'

'Well, let's give them something to talk about.' Penny smiled inwardly as she said it. Ignatius's compliment did not go unappreciated.

'Fine. We can meet up at, say, one o' clock outside the library. I'm guessing you'll be working through the morning.'

'Normally. I'm still surprised we haven't crossed each other.'

'I tend to get in very early and work until I need coffee. Usually skip lunch and go for a late bruschetta and antipasta at the Green Olive. Quite often skip dinner at the House.'

'One o' clock then.'

Coffee finished, they stayed a little longer, discussing one or two of the other students in Penny's graduation year, before leaving for their lodgings.

De Tregor's interests spanned astronomy and theology. Both led him to Italy where his prime interest was to find out more about telescopes and lens grinding. His ability to converse in Latin brought him into contact with Galileo and priests sympathetic to Galileo's heliocentric world. That and other radical views would get him into trouble with the abbot, a man jealous of Gabriel's superior intellect.

Gabriel had had an uncanny insight into the phenomenon of mankind in an infinite universe, through images he was privileged to see through one of the newfangled, Galilean telescopes. Images of galaxies, as yet not called such, that filled him with respect for the vastness of space and the phenomenon of creation.

Later, back in France, news of the censoring of Galileo had filtered through to remote regions of Europe. The mere fact of its topicality added to Gabriel's conviction that the Italian scientist was right. It reinforced his view that there was something mightier than a church that preached purgatory and redemption through the sale of indulgences. He was not to know, how could he? that later, the likes of Feynman, Dirac and Einstein would be subject to the same challenges a curious intellect in any age demanded of its imagination. For him dogma needed the authority of rational conviction if used as a means of censorship, particularly if the consequence was the stake. The universe demanded a creator or did it? Maybe its existence was spontaneous, like the bubbles from nowhere appearing in the sparkling wine sometimes served at the monastery.

*

Gabriel de Tregor crushed the oak galls. In the county of Cornwall, at the island Priory of St Michael's Mount, across the Channel, to the north of his Breton homeland, they were commonly known as oak apples by his brother monks. The Mount was a place of pilgrimage. The church and priory had been built in the twelfth century by monks from Mont St Michel in Normandy, who had acquired the island after the conquest of 1066. Its causeway, linking it to the ancient town of Marazion, was traversed at low tide by the faithful lured by accounts of four miracles said to have occurred in the recent reign of Henry III.

He tipped the fragments into a beaker and added rain water. The brew was a first stage in the preparation of ink for his manuscript. Twenty four hours later he removed the brown solution from its resting place on a window sill by the table he worked at. Filtering the contents through a cloth into a fresh beaker, he added an iron salt together with gum Arabic. The brown liquid turned black. Taking a goose quill from a pot alongside, he examined the tip and tested its flexibility. It needed trimming.

The thin blades on the knives in the scriptorium were honed to a degree where their keen edges could slice through live, human flesh without producing any sensation of cutting in the recipient. Gabriel laid the broad tip of the quill, flat, onto a small tablet of wood. Rotating the split, splinter-sized ends, he tested the angle of cut under the edge of the blade, pressed and removed a millimetre of the ink-stained tip from the pen. Any subsequent cut, if it ever came, would close the interval between freedom in this world and the fatal censure ahead his words would cause.

Gabriel lifted the cover from a pewter inkwell, tipped some of the newly infused liquid in and dipped the quill into it before seating the lidded top back into its snug-fitting rim. Charged with ink, the nib glided smoothly across a fragment of parchment, a piece discarded from a sheet trimmed earlier. He was pleased with the width of the line and the bold tone of the ink. It needed no refinement. Left-handed, he had crafted the slant of the cut to suit the contortion his wrist must adopt to avoid smudging freshly crafted letters as they advanced across the page.

He selected a new sheet from a precious pile of paper kept in a cupboard protecting it from rodent and other depredation. On a pilgrimage to the twelfth century cathedral at St Omer, just south of Calais, he had stayed at the Abbaye of St Bertin. The monks there had presented him, as a parting gift, with a small stock of their supply from the mill in the nearby village of Wavrans.

Before beginning, he contemplated the pristine sheet for a few seconds and crossed himself, more out of habit than devotion.

All this activity was being observed, surreptitiously, by a novice monk, one Francesco Fougères. Fougères was the nephew of the abbot, Luc d'Angers. His vocation motivated more by the prospect of an easy life than by religious conviction. No scholar and of a limited kind of animal cunning, he had been charged with reporting any action, oral or written, that constituted a breach of the rules of the Augustinian order to which he and Gabriel belonged.

Satisfied with what he had written, Gabriel read it through once, folded it, put it in the sleeve of his loose, brown habit and got up from the table. Ink and quill he put back on the window sill, glanced around and crossed the slate floor to the exit.

Fougères followed. Puzzled, the latter was surprised that Gabriel did not return to his cell but instead made for the chapel. It was not time for prayer or communal worship. The chapel was empty. One candle burned in a recess adjacent to a stone shelf accommodating the holy host, the wafer representing the body of Christ, deposited in an ornate, brass monstrance. Gabriel walked to the wooden screen at the back of the altar where it shielded a bare rock face forming the eastern end of the chapel.

Two irregularly shaped, perforated, side panels supported the screen against the slanting, un-dressed granite. The monk knelt before one of the panels. Through a gap Gabriel slipped the letter from his sleeve. Tomorrow he would pass it to the emissary who took post to the various monasteries and wider brotherhood dotted about the Catholic empire.

*

'The man is a heretic,' the abbot waved the sheet in front of his nephew.

Smug with the kind of attitude that went with a conniving mind, Francesco Fougères could already sense the job of cellarer to be within his grasp.

'Yes, that is my belief. He, it is also my belief, purchases our wine and provisions to the benefit of his own pocket and to the supplier's advantage.'

d'Angers handed the sheet back to his overweight nephew, 'Put it back. I suspect he intends to send it to Galileo's friends in Siena or to the man himself. We'll let him pick it up and confront him in flagrante delicto. Keep an eye on him after the night's fast. The messenger is due here before evening and will stay with us until midday tomorrow. On second thoughts, give it back. Put another sheet in its place.'

'Thank you Father Abbot,' Fougères addressed his uncle with a fawning intonation. He understood the power of flattery, 'I will take care of this.'

4

Before he had time to get off his knees the letter was snatched from his hand. Two monks appeared from the opposite side of the apse and joined Fougères as back-up. De Tregor was not a violent man but he knew the contents would have been read and considered incriminating. Knowing this and knowing the prevailing mood fomented by the Inquisition, he considered his life more important than loyalty to a corrupt abbot. Getting up off his knees he adopted an air of submission, dropping his shoulders, feigning defeat. His detractors, tense, expecting resistance, relaxed.

Gabriel grabbed the letter, pushed the nearest monk into the other two and made a dash for it towards the cloisters. There his way was blocked by d'Angers and two more monks. The three behind, by this time, were close. Turning, Gabriel darted across the aisle and circled back towards the altar. He grabbed the candle, put the flame to the letter and dropped the burning sheet into the cavity behind the screen.

Cobwebs and other flammable material were ready for a flame. Some monk, from past times, lazy and suffering from gout and responsible for decorating the screen with advent holly and pine fronds, had taken to disposing of the dry, incendiary material into the darkened space behind.

The sheet glided against the screen framing the altar, still burning. It dropped onto the pile of tinder-dry holly and resinous pine frond cuttings. A brief pause followed by a crackling noise stopped the advancing monks in their rush towards Gabriel. There was more flame than smoke. The flickering, orange flame, showing through the patterned cut-outs of the screen, cast weird shadows on the walls. It took merely a few seconds before the pile became a blaze. Gabriel looked in disbelief at what he had started. It was then, looking back at a route for escape, he saw the abbot with a look of triumph, holding up the letter he thought he had just burnt. Any thought of pinioning Gabriel held second place to dousing the flames. One of the monks made a dash for the bell rope to warn the other brothers, the remainder to fetch water.

Gabriel legged it to his cell. There he picked up the leather satchel that accompanied him on his journeys. It held a spoon, fork, knife, pewter cup and other sundries. The knife was in a leather sheath, although used for dining, it also served as a weapon should the need arise. Monk or not, some of his more unwelcome experiences travelling abroad governed his survival instincts.

The way was clear. All monks were formed in a chain, passing vessels of water from the well situated in the centre of the quad. He slipped through the arched entry to the stable block and headed for the forest at the edge of the monastery. There was a hermit's cell by the creek, used by the monks as shelter when tending the nets they shot from the shore. A path, wide enough for an ox cart, ran along the side of a stream running into the creek. It would take Gabriel five minutes to reach the cell. He could no longer hear the bell.

Two boats were riding alongside a narrow, wooden jetty. One was occupied by a couple of monks assisting another up to his waist in water, hauling a net. The net was full of thrashing mullet that trawled the inner reaches of the creek as the tide came in. Gabriel stopped at the edge of the trees and watched. The brethren would be at least another hour by the time they had beached and gutted the fish. He slipped back to inspect the cell. On the bench the monks had deposited a scrip containing half a round loaf, cheese and a flask of wine alongside. He pulled the stopper, a wooden peg wrapped in a piece of suede and took a swig. It only took an instant to use his knife on the bread. Cutting an equally modest piece of cheese, he transferred both pieces, with the knife, back into his satchel.

Outside he looked for a suitable tree to climb and wait for nightfall. A large, ancient oak with three primary branches emanating from its three hundred year old trunk, offered protection. Six metres above the dead leaves and acorns that littered the floor, he straddled the coarse bark covering the largest of the three, his back resting against a secondary growth of smoother, younger wood. Early autumn, too early for storms to have shaken the main leaf cover from the gnarled, old oak, he settled in for an unknown period of discomfort. For over an hour he fidgeted and repositioned himself as he waited for sundown.

The voices of the three monks receded into the background. Noises of wood pigeon, waves lapping the rocky creek and the odd tern foraging on the foam from the advancing tide, was all that he could now hear. He waited until he could barely see the traverse back to ground and made for the hermit's cell.

5

Ignatius bid the rest of the brethren good night. His mood, as he climbed worn, stone steps to the upper cloister, was one of exhilaration competing with a cautionary brake on his emotions caused by his encounter with Penny. He had, with great effort, maintained a celibate existence throughout his vocation but the meeting with his former student had left him disturbed. That they should meet for lunch had been more than just a social, friendly invitation on his part. He realised that now and knew, at the time, he'd been uneasy suggesting it.

'Guilt! Bloody, Catholic, destructive guilt,' he muttered to himself as he reached the door to his room.

The gradual change in mindset he'd been undergoing, since reading de Chardin, was understandable, justified. The medieval influences, the forces that had forged early Catholic doctrine were dated. Forces founded on loose interpretation of scripture and premisses now recognised as false.

They compared, almost, with the excesses and repetitive superstitions punctuating page after page of the Qur'an. There warning after warning, threat after threat of God's punishment of unbelievers, was described in terms of man-made images of hell. Sometimes repeated three or four times on the same page. Images forged at a stage of human civilization where goblins, jinns and other figments of imagination were considered to be real. A theology, if it could be called such, that described a god who was, by definition, indescribable. A god who, by contradiction, unrecognised by the imams in their reading of the Qur'an, does not need the intervention and interference of Muslim zealots to prosecute judgement against so-called sinners. Imams whose income depended on perpetuating myth.

The very need to assign written characterisations of their god was itself a form of idolatry no different from the painted images they were forbidden to create. Statements that were a form of blasphemy - by their definition - but unrecognised as such. It was an outmoded doctrine. Twenty-first century cosmology was not the home for such beliefs.

He had, in an earlier period, found himself increasingly appalled by the fact that modern, sentient beings could still be intimidated by the brain-numbingly, tedious ramblings of parts of the Qur'an. In Ignatius's mind an architect of the universe was a more profound and powerful entity than that of the descriptions voiced by charlatans who hoped to gain from their fiction. From soothsayers of the ancient Greek gods to the Caesars of Rome proclaiming their divinity; Mahomet through to Joseph Smith of the Mormons - history was littered with self-proclaimed 'messengers of god' taking in the gullible and weak-minded. But what was more evil was the discovery by these ministers of religion, imams, rabbis, pastors, priests and nuns, that innocent, gullible children - adults even - could be terrified into a crippling and life-blighting existence by threats of eternal punishment. The overwhelming relief he felt from an earlier, courageous rejection of such superstitious beliefs, was akin to the sensation he experienced from an earlier insight into an obscure field of quantum physics, an insight that earned him nomination for a Nobel Laureate.

But what did it matter? Cardinal he was and cardinal he intended to remain - for the time being - but on his terms and not those of the Curia. It was to mean conflict with centuries of Catholic tradition and with the even wider membership of the world religions he might later antagonise. He would not set out to destroy the civilising benefits of those structures. His mission would be to strip them of superstition, contradiction but, more importantly, reveal the harm they were never intended to exist for. Reveal the fact that all religion was opinion, not an immutable law of physics. But he was not yet ready. He knew, once started, he was likely to be hunted by extremists offended by his message. He didn't care. Fidelity to one's conscience came before any false duty to mass hysteria manifested by extremist mobs.

There was no key to his door. Leaving it ajar, he crossed the interior to a pair of double doors overlooking the garden and pulled both halves open. The heat of the Roman day had infused the evening with resinous scent from an Italian stone pine whose foliage was level with the balcony. Its naturally shaped canopy gave it the names umbrella pine and parasol pine. The scent permeated the current of air and carried itself through into the rooms beyond. Too early for sleep, he settled on an adjustable, mahogany, garden chair on the balcony. He leant back, lighted his pipe and enjoyed the first few draws with eyes shut.

The architect, commissioned to design the palace, for palace or such it must one time have been, must also have been chosen for his skill in managing the heat of Adriatic and Mediterranean climates. It was cool on the balcony. The chair faced down an avenue of Cypress trees. A wisp of filament from one of those exploding, party things - he didn't know if they had a name - was entangled in the nearest and caught his eye. Immediately he thought of Feynman's 'string theory' and then particle dynamics. Was there an infinitesimal delay in time between the creation of a particle of matter and its complementary antimatter particle or was it simultaneous? Were both particles close to each other or separated by non metric parameters of some yet to be discovered, quantum characteristic? The concept almost called for a third, associated particle condition. Or did the latter comment not make sense?

The issue had an analogy with arguments expressed by the pro-abortion movement the Church was wrestling with in Poland and, similarly, with bigoted factions of the evangelical wings of Democratic and Republican parties in the United States. This was another area where, emotionally, he was at odds with Catholic thinking. He had been too aware, in his diocese, of the trauma experienced by women raped and forced to carry a child through to birth. Aware of the distinction between wealthy Irish Catholics who could afford an abortion outside the Republic and those who were struggling just above the poverty line and couldn't.

The whole, damned argument seemed to revolve around the question of distinction between a foetus and the definition of the stage at which flesh acquires a soul. Matter and anti-matter. Miscarriaged foetuses, the mind boggled: was heaven filled with 'innocent' lumps of flesh with, as yet, no perfectly formed limbs or internal organs? At the instant of conception did the soul exist at the immediate point of penetration of sperm with ovum? Or did the soul inhabit the foetus at a later stage of development? Or was 'soul' merely a concept before the double helix and cell division was discovered? The latter was a process no different in the biological reproduction of little rabbits. Why, then, should little rabbits not have souls or any other mammal, fish, mollusc or tree, come to that? Or, rather, why should they?

This in turn brought his mind back to de Tregor. There must be something he was yet to read in the manuscript or maybe had read but at the time had not appreciated its significance. It was nagging at the back of his mind but he couldn't fix it. He stopped frowning, gave up and turned his thoughts to Penny.

6

There were three or four people queuing outside by the time Ignatius got to the university. The door opened promptly at the designated hour. He made for his usual table but faced in the direction of the entrance. This morning a new archivist was assisting the librarian. An intern he guessed. She was more engaging, eager to assist. He gave her the name of the document he was examining the day before. Returning a few minutes later she handed both the original manuscript and a second document to him.

'This was in the same box. Listed as 'Addendum'. I thought it might be important.'

He gave the new item a brief examination, 'Thank you. It might be significant.'

Back at his seat he quickly scanned the first document, hoping to resolve the previous day's riddle. De Tregor was an enigma.

'... you are justified by faith.'

This was St Paul, Luther in later context and now Gabriel de Tregor by conviction. But this was not enough to allocate a document to the Index or to condemn its writer to the stake. There had to be something more to have justified preservation in the Index and the stake.

Ignatius speed-read the unexamined later section of the manuscript. A red, ruled line - obviously put there by an Inquisitor - at the vertical edge of the script, in a final section on philosophical speculation, demanded inspection. A scribbled note alongside, also in red, referred to an 'Addendum'. Ignatius picked up the new document.

" ... *kosmos* ... ", the word - but written in letters of the Greek alphabet - stood out from the single page in contrast with the Latin script surrounding it. "The *kosmos* is God, not the Trinity."

Trinity was not in the vocabulary of the New Testament. Later adoption of the term arose from the single exhortation, "In the name of the Father, the Son and the Holy Spirit". Nowhere was the term 'Trinity' mentioned by New Testament writers.

'Got it!'

This was the heresy, as far as the Inquisitor was concerned. Our monk had committed the unpardonable in denying The Trinity. Ignatius now felt an even closer, kindred relationship to the writer. De Tregor was practically 'Post-Reformation' in his outlook. The writing concealed a no-compromise attitude to truth as he perceived it. He and de Tregor, in some sense, were the same person.

He added a few notes to those already written, photographed the single page of the Addendum and emailed it to the laptop. Time for a smoke.

Back from his break he checked his Inbox. There was one new message. The Subject line merely stated 'Philosophy'. The content of the email was nearly as brief, it merely said, 'Appointment confirmed. Formal confirmation and conditions in separate letter to follow. The Provost.'

This was good news. His appointment as a Fellow on the governing board at Trinity, attached to the Faculty of Philosophy, opened up a channel for publicizing his radical views. The transition from theoretical physicist to philosopher had been smooth. He frequently sat in on lectures offered by the philosophy dons and often joined their group in the Common Room. His standing amongst his colleagues was one unaffected by petty jealousies, factions or other controversies that infect university politics. The mischievous humour, which amused the nun, he also used to effect a genial relationship with any of his contacts.

7

The café in Pisa Street was not crowded. Ignatius found a table under a potted olive tree and waved away the waiter, signalling he was expecting someone. Spotting her weaving her way through to him, he got up and pulled the other chair away from the table. Smiling, she reached him and gave him a peck on each cheek. The brief brush of her lip and hint of perfume generated a frisson of experience long absent from his life. He responded, involuntarily, relishing a slightly longer period of contact. Both, now aware of the effect each had on the other, were momentarily distracted.

Ignatius pulled the chair a fraction further out, breaking the moment, 'The usual?'

'No. Espresso please.' Penny dumped her bag on the table and sat.

He didn't need to call the waiter. The latter was observing the scene with a knowing smile. Ignatius held up his thumb and forefinger about half an inch apart and indicated two cups.

'How's the research going?'

'Just wading through Wittgenstein at the moment and some of the French mob. I don't like Sartre. Camus? yes but Sartre? Nasty little man. What about you?'

'Well, just had some news from Dublin. Have been appointed to a Chair as Fellow at Trinity, in the Philosophy school. I've been edging that way for a while now. I didn't mention anything the first time we had coffee because it was still under consideration. Theoretical physics is getting a bit too messy and diverse. I want the freedom, now, of something a bit more subjective, something I can put to better effect in influencing opinion. Controversial.'

'Congratulations. I'm pleased and intrigued. That says you have an agenda in mind, I guess but how will that affect your pastoral responsibilities?'

'A lot I hope,' Ignatius added sugar to the little espresso cup and stirred, 'how long do you see yourself here?'

'Just another couple of months, if that.'

'I'm curious. What made you choose here anyway?'

'I just fancied a spell in Rome. Didn't need to come here but after Robert died I just wanted to get away and sort of rusticate. I've got the option of finishing back at Dublin. You start back there during the new semester?'

'Yes. The Chair has been financed by the media billionaire, Stephen Bokowski. The guy is an atheist, probably truer to say agnostic. Israeli. He sat in on the panel that shortlisted the candidates. I then had to meet him, in camera, as one of three final candidates. Interesting, very interesting character.'

'Any strings attached to the appointment? There must be if he's financing it.'

'Surprisingly few: speak from conscience; disseminate no untruth knowingly; challenge cultural mores; be fearless but constructive.'

'God, that pretty well permits open season on society.'

'I'm hoping so.'

Ignatius put the empty cup down, leant back and gave Penny a reflective stare.

'Look, I'm pretty sure you know I ...,' he hesitated, 'I enjoy your company.'

Penny laughed, amused, not cynically, 'Go on, it's pretty obvious and I don't find it an ordeal, you must know. Come on, we're both adults.' She knew how to handle him in a way that was un-patronising. 'If that's a euphemism for saying let's take it further, I have no objections. I thought you'd never ask. But, again, how will that square with your clerical responsibilities?'

Ignatius flexed his shoulders with the hint of a shrug and an internal feeling of relief, not that he was particularly tense, 'I'm not intimidated by Catholic strictures. Never was. That's partly the reason I'm where I am now, mentally that is. Let's have another coffee.'

Two coffees arrived.

'Just one thing, I'll find Professor a bit formal now we're seeing more of each other and Ignatius is a bit of a mouthful and Cardinal is out of the question.' Penny, it had to be admitted, was not intimidated about being direct, 'What do I call you?'

Ignatius smiled, 'Well, my middle name is William. Unusual for an Irish Catholic in its association with

William of Orange. So call me Bill. That's what my friends call me.'

'Where does the William come from? Must be a family name.'

'Yes. My grandfather. His family aren't Catholic.'

'Bill it is then. I like that.'

'Good. Settled then.'

8

The bench was hard. Gabriel had an uncomfortably cold night in the hermit's cell. Oyster catchers foraging in the rocky pools on an outgoing tide, woke him up. It was barely light. Thirsty, he hung his satchel across his chest and went to the stream flowing into the creek. There he knelt, cupped a few handfuls of water into his mouth and then refreshed his face. It was likely the abbot would carry out a search. He walked to the two boats tied to the jetty. The larger was a boat mainly used for dredging oysters, occasionally for supplies from the town of Morlaix, south of the monastery. It carried a single mast, lug sail and pair of oars. What to do? Make for the coast of Cornwall; sail up the river to Morlaix or travel over land to Paris? Whichever way, he needed provisions. It was risky to remain too long at the cell but he decided to finish the bread and cheese there. The monks might return to net fish on an incoming tide and it was pretty certain the abbot would search this area close to the creek and cell.

Checking the interior for signs of his stay, he decided to look for some dip or depression in the undergrowth, well away from the water's edge. Foraging for ceps and other fungi over the seasons and thus familiar with the terrain, he knew he would easily find a safe spot. There was plenty of bracken about. A pile of dead ferns would make it more of a resting place than merely an uncomfortable hide. Later, long after Compline, when the monks were asleep, he would return to the monastery and get provisions from the kitchen.

Settled. The plan gave him some peace of mind for the first time since his escape.

He peered out through the door-less, granite portal to the cell and listened. No unwelcome sounds. The mixture of willow and gorse, alongside, was fairly dense. He found a route across some of the older trunks that had layered themselves in the way that willow groves colonise water-rich soil to form little coppices. Groves where the monks harvested the withies from which to weave salmon traps and other basket ware. Some two or three hundred metres from the creek he found the remains of an entrance to an old badger sett. The soil around had long been covered in ground ivy. Years of badger activity had left a shoulder-deep depression that would make his concealment into a comfortable sojourn when layered with an adequate bed of dead bracken.

The hours dragged but it gave him time to reflect on the tangle he'd got himself into. He regretted the inconvenience he'd caused his brother monks but his contempt for the abbot's nepotism and even greater dislike of his overweight nephew, softened any guilt he might have felt.

In any case, the turn of mind that now informed his spiritual insight also informed his conscience. God was the *kosmos*, not the Pope. That brought his mind back to the letter. Should he attempt to find it when he went to obtain food? The Inquisition was brutally thorough but cunning. They preferred not to rely solely on oral accusation, if they could help it. Torture they might but, more often, capital punishment was only administered when heresy was confirmed beyond doubt. Heresy that was undeniably evident in testimony written in the hand of the accused. The Office of the Holy Inquisition, its full title, feared challenge on the basis of secular and doctrinal law - unassailably all-powerful though it considered itself. He could only decide whether to search when actually breaking back into the monastery and assessing the risk of discovery at the time.

*

There was no moon. Gabriel found his way to the main path leading to the monastery, more by instinct than sight. He waited against the wall before passing through the archway to courtyard and well. In all the years he'd slept in his cell or the main dormitory, he'd known little nocturnal disturbance. The abbot's chamber was off the chapel. A short, connecting passage led from his room to the vestry. A new candle was back in place. He took it and crept to the abbot's quarters. The letter was likely to be in a leather wallet or casket.

Gabriel placed the heavy candlestick on a bench out of direct line with the doorway to the abbot's sleeping quarters. A writing table, untidy with the paraphernalia of clerical study - a crucifix, an inkwell, a pot of quills and various documents - was tight up against the only window.

Our monk slipped across to it. His letter lay on top. Not surprising, since the abbot had done nothing clerical since the skirmish in the chapel. De Tregor picked it up and stuffed it into his satchel. The little chest, in which donations were kept, caught his eye. He hesitated. Accommodation on his journey to Paris would require payment. The box contained a sizeable sum. He picked up a handful of coins and quickly selected a few silver écus, some coins of smaller denominations and two gold francs. To heresy and arson would now be added the crime of theft but he felt no guilt. The Curia had forced the action on him. The Curia could pay.

Grabbing the candlestick, he left the anteroom to the abbot's sleeping cell and headed for the kitchen and cellars.

A bowl of raw dough was proving on a stool close to the remains of a fire in the inglenook. The leg of pork hanging from a hook in the chimney was of more interest. Gabriel took the smoked flesh down and brought it to the table where he had set the candle. It took just a few seconds to slice several pieces from the leg. A cluster of dry-cured saucissons were strung up under a wooden shelf, he helped himself to a couple. Under a wooden frame covered in smoked muslin, three or four hard cheeses were being stored, safe from vermin. He again helped himself to a few segments. Separating the lot into in two or three portions, he wrapped them in napkin-sized pieces of linen that lay folded on a shelf. He needed a water flask of some kind and looked about for one of the many animal skins, used for carrying wine, he knew should be somewhere in the kitchen. Finding two or three hanging from a bar suspended from the roof beams, he selected one with a firmly fitting stopper and a loop he could sling across his chest. Tempted to go to the cellar for wine he knew he was pushing his luck too far. Instead he filled the skin from a water jug. The haul of food bulged his satchel but was not over-heavy.

The candle back in place he took one last, sad look around the chapel.

9

The Provost's secretary picked up the phone, 'Yes, I'll send him in.' She looked across at Ignatius, 'You heard that. Just go straight in Professor.'

'Thank you.' The cardinal picked up the shoulder bag containing his laptop and walked towards the Provost's study. The door opened before he reached it and Michael O'Connor advanced to meet his long-time friend.

'Good to see you Bill,' he put out a hand, 'and congratulations, again.'

The red light on a filter-coffee machine and jug half full signalled that a brew was ready for drinking. O'Connor waved Ignatius to an armchair and went to pour a couple of mugs emblazoned with the university crest.

'I've got no appointments for an hour so we've got time to catch up. How was Rome?'

'Fine but it's good to be back.'

'Well let's get the official business over with then we can have a Bushmills and a less formal look at the brief. You would know, I guess, I had no influence over your appointment. In fact I declared myself an interested party and only acted to weed out obvious non-runners in the early stages. Senate gave them the once over and sorted the rest out with a more thorough eye. You need to deal with this. Another lot I'm afraid,' the Provost reached for a set of documents from his desk. 'In your own time. Just sign this top one now though, then I can witness it with my signature. The rest go to the Bursar. No witness required. Just your signature.'

Ignatius gave the document a quick look through, signed and passed it back to O'Connor.

'Anything significant happened since I've been away?'

'Depends what you call significant. A recent declaration of abuse claims in various schools but you must be informed of that I would guess. The Pope needs to abolish the rule of celibacy for your lot. I'm glad Trinity is a Protestant foundation otherwise it would be totally staffed by sexually-repressed intellectuals.' Their friendship, Michael knew, was robust enough for him to express his cynical opinions of the Catholic faith. 'But there's a more sinister issue that's going to affect the university, indirectly.'

'Can't think of anything likely to be more controversial than the abuse scandal. The uni, no doubt, has had its share of predatory dons but that's a periodic occurrence that plagues any establishment. So what don't I know?'

'It's just about to break. The press haven't got on to it yet. I heard only a couple of hours ago.'

'Come on, don't keep me in suspense.'

'You know the land we own, adjacent to the convent, well, it's passed planning and been released for development as a site for the new Robotics and AI college. Problem is the company preparing the site has uncovered a number of graves. Some twenty or thirty babies and a handful of women.'

'Recent corpses?'

'Don't know yet. Also, because the site is screened by trees, any interments carried out at night would have been unobserved over the years. It's bloody monstrous.'

'Look, you know I'm less than totally loyal to some church doctrine,' he paused, 'so what I have to say is only between you and me. When I'm up and running with the new appointment, I'm going to mount a major, reasoned criticism of the major faiths, amongst other controversial issues. Stephen Bokowski knows this. I told him at the one-to-one interview. That was an acceptance or rejection risk I gambled on when we discussed my provisional appointment to this new chair. Criticism will be coupled, for example, with an attack on religiously motivated, medical ethics committees worldwide that are opposed to abortion under any circumstance. It's a fucking disgrace, pun intended, that the men who father the foetuses don't bear any responsibility for the upkeep of the unwanted children. And another thing, these committees are mostly male dominated. It's a bloody outrage. Apologies for the explosion of expletives but I'm pissed off with the hypocrisy on all fronts - secular and sacred, government and gods.'

'Fair enough. From my point of view, as Provost, since most of that will be aired on the TV programmes you'll be chairing and the newspaper columns you're commissioned to write, it won't impact on Trinity as a liability to be handled under legal duress. You'll just have to manage content responsibly in any separate, academic pronouncements as a Fellow, as far as I'm concerned.'

'Don't worry; I think you know I'll be guarded on that score. In any case, whatever statements I make I will, as far as I can, leave no room for contradiction or, at least, flag up what is opinion, ring-fenced with boundary conditions that qualify the argument, just like for a set of partial-differential equations.'

'Good. Let's have a dram and drink to a successful tenure in the new appointment.'

Mike O'Connor fetched two glasses from a cabinet and produced a bottle of Bushmills from a cupboard below, continuing the conversation as he did so, 'I can't help noticing you're more relaxed despite your focus on the new role. Something I should know?'

'What d'you mean?'

'Well, remember that shelagh you were fond of in the sixth form? You've got a bit of a glow about you like you had back then.'

Ignatius laughed, 'You canny bugger,' he took the glass offered him, 'I met one of my old students in Rome. She was in the library and spotted me leaving one day. We've kept up since I left. In fact it's becoming more than just regular. She'll be here in Dublin, soon, to finish off a PhD in Linguistic Philosophy.'

'That's good. I understood, when you decided to go for ordination, it was possibly out of some kind of loyalty to your mother, your Catholic upbringing rather than conviction but, equally, for want of a way of putting it, I was surprised your a ...,' Michael paused, grinned, 'your more carnal instincts didn't dominate.'

'That's a quaint way of saying I needed a good screw occasionally.'

Both laughed. It was good. They still felt at ease and able to be blunt in each other's company.

'Anyway, that's the score. Emotions aside, I'm tiring of all-male company in an ecclesiastical prison - because that's what it amounts to - unnatural and as arid as just about any rigid, rule-based setting could be. Does have its up sides but no, I've had enough. I'll hang on to my clerical status for as long as possible, whilst I can still be an influence in certain quarters. If I become excommunicated then that, in some ways, will add authority to what I reveal.'

'Be careful. The Vatican is powerful but I don't need to tell you that. The present Pope seems one of the most liberal we've had but he has his enemies. There's big money and power tied up in connected agencies inside and outside the Vatican. As Provost in a Catholic-dominated republic, I have to tread carefully. The enlightened officers of the Garda are one thing. The religiously superstitious ones are another. Not averse to cow-towing to their local priest and condoning the excesses of the religious

40

authorities. They are about as bad as the police in the caste-ridden hierarchy of India. Little different to the medieval, 'honour-killing-type-of-mentality' or rape of a lower caste by a higher caste the Indian police turn a blind eye to.'

Ignatius finished his shot of whisky and picked up the documents required by the bursar, 'I know you've plenty to get on with so I'll leave you in peace and wander down to the Common Room to see who's there. Thanks for the drink and chat.'

'It's good to have you back. Look, come for dinner. Let's make a date. Bring your 'new interest'; Rose will be pleased to meet her. What's her name, by the way?'

'Penny, Penny Lane. Her mother was a Beatles fan.'

'Fine. Give me a call at home when she settles back here and we'll fix a date.'

'I'll do that. In fact I'm picking her up from the airport in a couple of days.'

*

The flight landed quarter of an hour early. Ignatius had arrived ten minutes before the scheduled landing but baggage and immigration formalities would take time so he bought a coffee and waited close to the Arrivals exit.

The first Rome passengers trickled through. Penny appeared wheeling one medium-sized aerolite case and carrying a duty-free carrier bag and her backpack. Ignatius ducked under the flimsy webbing, grabbed the case handle, stood the case upright on its four little wheels, gave her a hug then kissed her. Some priests, fresh from a tour of the Vatican, dodged around the pair and suitcase, eyeing the two with bemused expressions.

'Good afternoon Father Ignatius.'

Ignatius turned, 'Good afternoon brethren,' grinned at the group, 'I trust you enjoyed your visit to Rome,' then turned back to Penny, grabbed the suitcase handle and made for the airport car park.

'How was the flight?'

'Fine. I slept a lot. Was awake for most of the night, excited about seeing you. Been waiting long?'

'No. Got here ten minutes or so before your flight was due. I've got my father's car. We're going back to my parents' house. As you flew to Shannon rather than Dublin it was easier to stay with them and meet you from there. They're only a few miles west of Galway, about twenty. The way back to Dublin is a day's journey, really, if we were to travel by public transport this late in the afternoon.'

'God, I haven't anything smart with me.'

'Don't worry about that. My father will be charmed by you and my mother is a dogs and horses type who won't notice, particularly.'

'What will they say about you, a priest, being involved with the opposite sex?'

'Not any of their business. Mother is not a devout Catholic anyway. Grandfather Synne was Jewish but married a gentile of Huguenot extraction so my father is not Catholic and won't see it as a problem. Having said that, he was the one who sent me to a Jesuit school. Not at all religious but wanted me to have a sound education. He's as right-wing as they come so we'll be in for some quite controversial, non-PC polemic. Maybe it's from him I get my sceptical streak.'

'Good grief! What a mix.'

'You could say that. That's where the name Synne comes from. It's a corruption of Zynne or Szein, from Middle European ancestry. We don't know exactly. So my father won't have any objection, in fact he'll likely as not think I've come to my senses. Here we are,' Ignatius pointed the remote at a metallic grey, Volvo estate, 'dump your sack on the back seat. Too many dog hairs in the bay.'

10

De Tregor tossed the mooring rope into the boat and pushed off with an oar. Out in mid stream he raised the coarse, flax sail. Adjusting it to a north easterly wind he set off against a three knot current and made roughly a two knot gain towards Morlaix. Little more than a slow walking pace. The current he was fighting increased, in visual terms, indicated by the speed with which it rushed past the banks. As the river narrowed and either side came closer, the tidal fall accelerated the discharge of the river towards the Baie de Morlaix. He was glad he had not chosen to head for open water and the rougher seas beyond.

Although he had used the craft a few times, assisting a brother monk fishing or navigating upstream towards the various riverside hamlets, single-handed he found the effort tiring after the disturbed, uncomfortable night in the hermit's cell. Pen-an-Traon was off his port side. The church was a welcome sight and he knew he could tie up alongside the sturdy, wooden pier the inhabitants used to unload the larger merchant ships. Ships that came to trade goods like tin, brought from the Cornish mines, in return for cognac shipped up from the Charente.

It was well past mid day according to the sun. He knew any innkeeper would provide a cooked meal and wine in return for some menial service, leaving him to conserve his satchel of food and small pile of coins. It was a prosperous little settlement. The inhabitants were hospitable to the many strangers who crewed visiting ships. It paid them to show generosity, encouraging the many vessels to choose Pen-an-Traon to do their trade rather than the moorings on the west bank of the river. Gabriel wasn't known as a regular but his monastic garb marked him out as trustworthy.

Some urchins gathered to watch as he tied up.

'Have you come to take mass?' an older youth questioned in a local, Breton dialect.

'Bless you child,' Gabriel stood and turned, 'no but I can offer such service in return for fare.'

'Your boat will be beached and lower by evening. You best leave more slack or risk the line breaking if you intend staying overnight.' The warning came from a fisherman in a larger boat tied up the other side of the wooden jetty.

'Thank you brother,' Gabriel gave a slight bow at the same time gesturing with fingers together in a submissive greeting. He refrained from offering a Trinitarian blessing, knowing fishermen were superstitious where clergy were concerned. 'Where might I find lodgings?'

'There is an auberge by the church or the local priory will take you in, no doubt but it's a fair pull from here.'

Gabriel nodded his thanks again and slackened off the line.

The prospect of a full, night's sleep in a comfortable bed, was appealing.

'The boy's will take you to the auberge. You'll get a good supper. Fish has been plentiful. Where've you come from?'

Gabriel decided it unwise to name his monastery and quoted a priory he knew was situated at the head of a creek near St Pol-de-Leon. It was likely the fisherman had off-loaded a catch or two in the well-populated harbour of the town but would have avoided the creek as too shallow for the large fishing boat. It seemed to satisfy the man. He thanked him once again and followed the little group of children into the village.

The innkeeper, used to custom from the river, greeted the monk's appeal for lodgings, 'I can give you a bed and supper. Just get me enough fallen timber for a week's burning,' pointing in the direction of the large wood beyond the village. 'Here, take this length of rope with you. The sprogs,' he nodded to the children, 'will show you the path. There's plenty of fallen beech and oak to be had off the track. Just watch out for boars with young'uns, foraging acorns.'

De Tregor took the rope and followed the group now excited to be part of a priest's entourage. He enjoyed their banter. They plied him with questions about goblins and dragons and he was only too pleased to add colour to their vivid imaginations, knowing their minds would have been conditioned by tales from the various seamen visiting their small but thriving port. Plenty of fallen, dead branches, not too rotten and a few swung on and broken off by his enthusiastic helpers, soon formed a decent raft of fuel for the innkeeper's kitchen.

Lying in bed, exhausted, he put all thoughts of his next move out of his mind and slept soundly. His body clock, conditioned by the divine Offices of the monastery, would normally have disturbed him for the 2am office of Matins. He slept. Lauds at 5am, the same.

Breakfast was a few slices of dry-cured boar's leg, pickled onions, bread and dripping washed down with ale. It had been light for an hour or more when he left the auberge. Another tide, this time rising, had raised the boat's gunnel level with the top of the pier. He untied, pulled in the line and stepped down onto the floor timbers. There was no one about to see him off. Letting the boat drift out into mid-stream, without his assistance, he raised the sail and set off for Morlaix. The current, this time, worked for him. With a stern wind, he was making about eight knots. In less than an hour he was at the outskirts of the town and could already smell wood smoke and fresh horse manure.

A low, rocky shelf and a gap between branches supporting debris trapped by earlier floods, was just what he was looking for. He lowered the sail and took up the oars. When he was close enough to reach a branch, he dropped the oars grabbed it and pulled the boat into the bank. Hitching the bow mooring line over the thicker end of the branch, he sat in the stern and checked his position for cover. The boat weaved figure of eight signatures in the water as the branch flexed against the current. Another vessel would see him only if they were in a line of sight of more or less half a right angle.

The undergrowth above the ledge was dense but he could stand comfortably to peer through bushes bordering what looked like an animal enclosure of some kind. Up until now his decision had been to lose himself in the town but he was wondering if the abbot might be predicting his moves. Certainly the boat would be missed by now. He decided to cut a few, bushy branches to hang over the boat's gunwale. It would fool no one who was observant but for the casual boat man plying up and down the river, decided it was worth the effort. That done he set off to skirt the town. His ultimate destination Paris, he thought it safer to lay a false trail by being seen traversing north east on the road to Lannion. He would then make for Rennes, after some days sojourn, hoping, eventually, to reach Chartres and then Paris.

11

Gabriel knew a change of outer clothing might aid his escape but also realised the benefits his monastic garb conferred. He decided to stay dressed as a monk. New clothing meant either carrying his monastic habit or jettisoning it and he had no desire to burden himself with unnecessary possessions.

'Hello Cabo, who's dog are you?' De Tregor pronounced the French slang word, cabot, for dog, as it would be written phonetically in modern English.

The mutt had appeared from undergrowth not long after Gabriel had abandoned the boat. It then followed him, pleased to have found a human who did not try kick or throw stones at him. The monk made no attempt to discourage him, glad of its company.

He skirted Morlaix and made for Lannion, expecting to reach it well before evening. Clusters of hazel bushes, already showing immature nut growth, bordered the path close to the road he was avoiding. They sported straight, stout staves. Taking his knife, he set about selecting one that offered a staff of shoulder-height length. The dog, excited to be a welcome companion to this unorthodox human, stood ready to pounce on any imagined prey likely to be disturbed in the process. Gabriel trimmed a short baton, two or three centimetres thick and tossed it to the dog.

'Here Cabo.'

The dog leapt to catch the piece and brought it to his new-found master's feet. Gabriel picked it up but put it to the dog's muzzle, instead of throwing it, signalling he wasn't into the business of entertaining stray dogs. The animal took it and conveyed its understanding by walking off ahead of de Tregor as he followed whittling small side branches and other excrescences from the staff.

Lannion was another town at the last, fordable point of an estuary. Smaller than Morlaix, it nonetheless accommodated a number of auberges. This time Gabriel was obliged to use some of his money. The dog curled up outside the inn but de Tregor took him a few of the less choice pieces of cold mutton he was offered for supper. Breakfast was bread and cheese with cider. The monk still had most of the provisions he had taken from the monastery but replenished them with a fresh chunk of bread and a small slab of local ewe's cheese.

He left the inn at sun-up and made for Guingamp some twenty miles away but chose not to travel on the main highway. Cabo, still outside the tavern, followed. The two made their way south east towards their next destination along wooded tracks connecting small hamlets which, in turn, were connected by slightly wider bridleways to the main highway.

'I don't know where we'll end up boy but you're welcome to share the delights of good conversation and the food I have to offer.' Cabo, sitting at Gabriel's feet as the latter sat perched on a granite rock, watched knowingly as the monk cut a not ungenerous slice from the already started saucisson.

'There you are boy.' He tossed the morsel to the dog. Already adept at catching flies, the cur caught it and sat waiting for the next piece. 'That's your lot for now. If you're good you'll have some bread later.' The dog, again, seemed to understand from the tone of de Tregor's voice and set off exploring the bracken and heather around the granite outcrop. Gabriel finished eating, re-wrapped the remaining food, went down to the stream below and re-filled the animal skin. He gave his pewter mug a good swill out and scooped up a good draught of the refreshing water to wash down the meal.

12

The Synne home was up a short drive from the R336 main coast road from Galway. A modern house, it was surrounded by low, granite stone walls of much earlier build. The profusion of squares and rectangles of grass they enclosed testified to the traditional division of land amongst siblings, following the death of a patriarch. Sure enough, dogs were the order of the day. Dogs, two Labradors and a tiny terrier until then out of sight, leapt over a wall from one of the paddocks and jostled around the driver's door.

'Alright, alright, calm down, calm down.' Ignatius patted heads as Penny circled round to join the melee.

'Don't jump.' The dogs, even more excited by the prospect of a new companion, fussed around Penny, tails going furiously.

'You little beauty,' Penny bent to stroke the terrier and immediately had a damp, cold nose thrust in her face by one of the Labs.

'He'll take any amount of fuss,' Ignatius' father had come out, unnoticed, to greet the two as the jamboree with the dogs was taking place, 'I'm Josh,' he held out a hand in greeting.

'Hello. Penny,' taking his hand. She smiled, 'We've certainly caused some excitement with this lot.'

'Yes they're a friendly bunch. Always pleased to greet visitors but good guard dogs if we're not about outside.'

'Bill, car run alright?'

'Yes. Smooth as ever.'

'Right, let's get your gear in. Kathleen's put you in the back room, downstairs. She's just nipped to the shop to get some stuff. Should be back any time.'

The group, led by the dogs, made their way to the open door. Josh showed them to their room and went off to make tea. A fresh ruckus from the dogs signalled the return of Kathleen.

'Hallo! I'm back.'

The uproar from the dogs eased, 'We're in the kitchen.'

Penny got up as Kathleen came through. Ignatius gave his mother a brief kiss on the cheek then introduced Penny.

'Lovely to meet you at last. Let me put this lot in the fridge. Then we can talk over tea.'

The encounter lasted for two or three cups.

'I'm cooking mussels for supper and will shove a bread and butter pudding in the oven for after. Not allergic to them I hope? Mussels, I mean.' They laughed.

'No. Love them.'

'Now, I don't know what your plans are but I've booked the Aran ferry for Inisheer, if you want to spend a few days in granny's house on the island. If you don't, Josh and I will use it. It's just that it can get pretty busy this time of the year. Not crowded but sometimes a bit difficult to get a convenient departure time. Anyway think about it. No hurry.'

'Might be an idea. We'll discuss it tonight.'

'Bill tells us he's changing horses at Trinity. I gather you only knew recently.'

'Yes.'

'And you're completing a doctorate there, we gather.'

'Yes. I'm looking forward to it. Trinity is an old stamping ground anyway. But you'd know that, as I was an ex-student of Bill's.'

'I'm sounding like an interrogator.'

'Yes Kat, you are.' Josh grinned at Penny as he said it.

'Right. Leave the cups. I expect you'd like to freshen up. Dinner at seven?'

Penny looked at Ignatius, 'Fine by me.'

'Yes. I'm guessing there'll be drinks.'

Josh nodded, 'You bet, son. A bottle of Roederer in the fridge. Let's say six thirty.'

13

A cloudless sky gave way to a gradual build up of clouds brought in off the Atlantic by a south westerly wind. Sunset was a spectacular display of pink, then flame-coloured cumulus.

'Galway Bay is famous for its sunsets and from Aran there are few sights to compare anywhere in the British Isles. I hope you take up Kat's ferry booking. The weather's going to be fair over the next few days. It'll be worth a stay on Inisheer.' Josh spoke to Penny as he waved his glass in the direction of the islands visible through the living room window.

'We've just discussed it and we'll take up the offer but let me know the cost.'

'Forget it.'

'No. I insist.' Penny, when she was determined, rarely backed down.

'Tell you what then,' Kat spoke, sensing resistance, 'book us a one-way crossing for the first week next month. Is that OK? I'll give you the date.'

'Fine.'

'So,' Josh pushed a dish of olives across the low table in front of the group, 'how did you find Rome?'

'I loved it. Second visit, but this time I spaced out my research so I could visit a few of the lesser known galleries and museums.'

'What have you got, another year before submitting your thesis?'

'Less, if I get it finished. I intend to but a lot now depends on what Bill and I decide to do. Bill won't know how his tenure will pan out. At least he has his experience in the physics faculty as a yardstick but the additional media work load and copy deadlines make for a whole new regime of activity.'

'Children?' This was Kat.

Penny laughed. Ignatius gave a burst of air through pursed lips, part embarrassment, part amusement at his mother's bluntness, a touch of the Princess Anne.

'If I'd wanted them I would have had them with Robert but neither of us wanted children.'

'Just my sentiments, now, in retrospect.'

'What d'you mean?' Ignatius affected mock offense.

'You were no trouble, child or teenager. A bit of a rebel occasionally but no real trouble. I just wouldn't bring a child into this world the way it is now. Too overpopulated, 'specially third world countries. God,' she hissed, 'look at some of the conditions of their own making they live in. Open sewers. Dirty water, quite often shown with an ox or other animal standing in it where some woman - it's always a woman or child - is filling a water container. Where are the bloody men and why don't they keep the animals out of it? They could readily separate off a clean area. They seem to have mobile phones, some of them. For god's sake, if they can afford that they could afford to rig up some kind of barrier to protect their drinking water from being shat in by some animal.'

Josh, used to his wife's outspokenness, gave Penny a discreet wink and refilled the glasses.

'This new appointment, which television company has this man Bokowski acquired that you're going to be involved with?'

'It's a small setup in Dublin that FONT - *Fibre Optic News Transfer*, an Israeli company - has bought. FONT are international and the station will be re-branded as a new cultural and political force. Controversial. I'll be hosting a panel of selected speakers, different each week. The weekly newspaper feature will also be along the same lines. It'll be independent of my university brief which is to set up a new degree course and to oversee some doctoral candidates in the Philosophy Faculty. Stephen will have some minor input in the BA course but,' Ignatius paused, 'he won't have a controlling influence, generous though he is with the terms of the foundation.'

'You won't have time, surely, with that kind of workload?'

'I've got a generous expenses budget, controlled, of course, to employ a secretary, research and office staff. So I aim to interview and appoint an executive officer to oversee and assist production.'

'How'll Bokowski find funds for that? Surely he'll want advertising revenue?'

'No. He wants to attract finance from similarly minded CEOs. He's providing the premises, cameras and technical staff for the panel. Already he has a million

Euros from just one donor and there are at least half a dozen others, one or two who voiced similar proposals without his prompting. They are rock solid offers. He has other sources that will be self-financing but I don't know what they are. He didn't say.'

'Knowing you, content will not be quite in keeping with your pastoral image.'

'Look mother, I've long since given up on pedalling 'Catholic opium'. I don't intend to be callous but it's time blind altruism recognised that what might be good for one or two sections of society might, in the long term, cause more harm of a kind different from that which it is attempting to alleviate. Charitable attitude to immigration from third world countries is a case in point. Already some areas of larger, European and UK cities are becoming festering sores of unregistered, insanitary, single-brick-skin dormitories built illegally at the back of other premises. I've seen it in my capacity as a priest visiting parishes at the invitation of the local bishop.'

'So?'

'Politicians and local authority councils will need to be goaded - that's one of the areas where FONT comes in - to take action to seek enforced demolition of such disease-incubation centres, because that's what they are. The owners, very often from the Indian subcontinent, are exploiting these tenants. Usually hiring them out at slave wage levels, because they are illegal immigrants and can't complain to authority. These owners should be prosecuted and repatriated to the lands of their ancestral origins - India, Pakistan, Bangladesh or any of the rogue African states some hail from.'

'God, you'll not get that happening.'

'Maybe not. But people, usually novelists of third world ancestry or PhD arts graduates of colour, commissioned to write articles in colour supplements - pun not intended - about inequality BAME and BLM, bang on about overcrowding when what they should be criticising is over-breeding, overpopulation. To complain that a family from some third world Commonwealth country, with five, six or ten children in a two-bedroomed house, is disadvantaged and should be given a three- or four-bedroomed house, is ignoring the fact that families of the indigenous population have been waiting years on an oversubscribed housing list for some kind of adequate, affordable accommodation. The UK government should rescind the 'passports-for-Commonwealth-citizens' rule. Student visas are another example. Fifty thousand issued to Nigerian students who are, under the rules, able to bring in their dependants. A lot of the many students from those countries then, conveniently for them, go under the radar because there is no effective way of keeping tabs on their location. If something isn't done to allay public anger we'll get an AfD type reaction.'

'What's AfD?' Kat broke in to Bill's rant.

'A German, right-wing, mainly anti-immigrant party and I'm not sure there are those who wouldn't welcome it happening over here. Population pollution - because that's what it is - is leading to seriously degraded levels of an overloaded, civil infrastructure. Overburdened health and social services. Population control, radical control, has got to be implemented. If it isn't we'll end up with cities festering with disease because a population used to third world sanitation - or, rather, lack of it - will convert their neighbourhoods into shitholes, literally, like the back streets of Delhi and Nairobi or like the Lagos swamps teeming with shacks built over filthy, faeces-infested water. I've seen the open sewers, the leprosy, TB, cholera and other serious diseases when I've travelled to these places. We're now getting TB strains resistant to antibiotics in this country. After more than half a century of complete eradication we've allowed it to be imported again. Diphtheria and scarlet fever the same. Birth control, this is yet another area where I'm at odds with Catholic doctrine.'

'Jesus, Mary, mother of God, where is the loving shepherd of the sheep? Father Ignatius of the flock?'

'Mother, these frustrations have been building up over a long period. I've been suppressing them, ignoring them. I can't, any longer, subscribe to universal love and the 'everything-in-the-garden-is-lovely' mentality of evangelical, happy-clappy, guitar-playing, narcissistic, bearded wonders and starry-eyed virgins believing in the second coming. Christians have a duty to recognise the evil as well as the good in people and organisations - St

Paul's teaching. Christ said, "Love your enemies," he didn't say, "love evil."

There are too many contradictions, too many inconsistencies. Blind attachment to religious fiction; outdated dietary laws; culturally-related rules that lead to honour-killing or the barbaric practices of FGM or circumcision. The problem is that these very real concerns are being dismissed as exaggerated by those who benefit from saying it. These kinds of issues are what Bokowski is passionately concerned about. For example, he feels the Knesset, the Israeli parliament, is held back by the Hasidic influence. Tensions between the Ashkenazi Haredi and Sephardic Haredi Orthodoxies need to be held up to scrutiny and are why he empathises with my take on wider, similar issues.'

'Yes but isn't it the content of such socially curated, religious practices that hold ethnic groups together? Isn't that the reasoning behind the attitude of the Orthodox, rabbinical cadre? The reason that Judaism has survived the Holocaust and, before that, centuries of pogroms, because of its adherence to the commands of books such as Leviticus? Adhering to these identity markers are what preserve the character, perhaps that's not the right word, the very essence, the very core of Judaism.'

'I understand. I am aware of that argument. But if one examines certain claims logically in a wider, global context, such as: If God exists and, by definition, is all-powerful and the Jews are his chosen people as the Old

Testament claims, if he is all-powerful and wants the best for them why didn't he give them Devon, for example, which is a more fertile, more appealing tract of land than the heap of sand and rocks called Palestine? I know that's a facetious comment but think about it. However you look at it it boils down to some account written by some scribe claiming authority from some anthropomorphic god who doesn't actually exist.

I am, I've always maintained, not advocating abandoning the religious structures that bind society or groups or nations together. That framework is necessary, maybe, until it could be replaced by something better, if that were ever possible. But there again let the religious, the atheists, the agnostics and the humanists coexist without interfering in each other's life with the caveat that all are on guard against any one of the religious movements seeking to impose their version of truth, laws or practices on the rest. I'm asking people to be realistic. I don't want liturgy or dignified ritual to disappear but I do want undignified, embarrassing exhibitions of so-called worship to be abandoned. The value of the Psalms, as examples of devotional study, is of immense importance to so many of faith but is of no less importance to non-believers whose interest only extends to the literary, the poetic and non-religious character they manifest.

No, what I deplore is savage action based on some atavistic, medieval interpretation of the Qur'an, of so-called 'god's will'. I want people to recognise such action as the product of primitive, sexually repressed and limited intellects such as that exhibited by Qur'anic extremists. Look at the tyranny the Taliban exercise over girls' education and women's' lives generally. Iran the same, with their Religious Police. Primitive, medieval societies in spite of their twenty-first century smart phones and computers. Their Allah is an insult, an offence, to the concept of any god of divine or spiritual purity, by whatever metric you assign.

It goes too, in a similar way, for the voodoo-intimidating hold that African, whether Caribbean African or continental African witchdoctors have over their gullible, superstitious victims. We need to be aware of the insidious growth in alien populations here that will eventually, if unchecked, obliterate refined, civilised, Western culture that stable centuries of industry and intellectual scholarship have created. There's a whole load of purging to be done, not just religious but political, commercial and cultural as well. Cultural in particular. We are becoming a civilisation of low standards and poor taste, especially in the growth of low-brow entertainment being trafficked on television.

Politically and commercially we can't use the example, say, of the popularity of Indian curry houses with the British public to justify, by extension, the growth in power of heads of large Indian industrial conglomerates here. Powerful names that are associated with corruption and graft on other continents. Corporations involved with hostile third parties that, in the long term, will be able to exert the same damage that Russia subsequently has with EU dependency on Russian gas supplies. We cannot allow the short term commercial benefits of these alien influences to justify further growth that will eventually become a malign influence because these heads of corporate commerce wield clout amongst our politicians. Heads who stand to gain, individually, from taxpayers' subsidies, to the tune, literally of hundreds of millions of pounds. Wives of these people who, in some reported instances, accurate or otherwise, have syphoned off tens of millions of that money into 'safe' bank accounts or property in places like Monaco. We've been too blind and accommodating to perceive the eventual threat posed by these vultures in doves' feathers.'

Josh shook his head pursed his lips and waved his glass as if to an imaginary audience, 'Well, you've got your work cut out, that's all I can say. But I can see it'll be a stimulating challenge rather than a work burden. Anyway, let's eat. I'm ravenous.'

14

Cabo rushed at a hound that appeared from the doorway of a hovel on the outskirts of Guingamp. Gabriel shouted. The two dogs paused and fight avoided as a man from the same dwelling shouted at his dog to return to the reed-thatched home it belonged to.

'God be with ye.'

'And with you.'

'There is an abbaye or monastery close by?'

'Yes Father. Below the hill. Benedictine.'

'Thank you,' Gabriel with palm open at right angles to his body, made the sign of the cross, 'In nomine Patris et Filii et Spiritus Sancti.'

'Thank you Father.'

Cabo and his new master walked on in the direction of the hill. It was barely light. At the entrance to the abbaye, de Tregor pulled on a rope. A bell somewhere above his head alerted a monk who arrived in the time it would take to recite the Lord's prayer.

'Yes?'

'A brother monk seeks admission.'

There was a delay of only a few seconds. Gabriel heard the sound of a bar slid from a bracket and the door in front of him was pulled back. The monk sized him up then invited him to step through. Cabo was also allowed through.

Simple admission protocols were completed and Gabriel led to a guest dormitory.

'Ablutions are down through the cloister to the first door,' the monk pointed in the direction of a short flight of stone steps, 'a plate and flask of wine will be waiting in the refectory. I will come to show you in a short while. The dog, is he a good ratter?'

'I don't know but he catches rabbits so I would think that a rat would interest him.'

'Good. We are troubled with the vermin. He can rest in the kitchen at night.'

'Where are you from?' The abbot sat down by Gabriel as he ate the supper left for him.

Our monk again hesitated and named a monastery some distance west of St Pol de Leon. 'I am making a pilgrimage to Rome.' The lie didn't trouble him.

'You are an Augustinian I see. Feel free to fit in with our services. Stay as long as you wish. We can find work for you, particularly if you are a learned disciple of Christ.'

'Thank you father. I would be grateful to stay for a short term. My calling is not urgent.'

'Good. Matins are at midnight. We retire at the hour of nine. Peace be unto you.' The abbot rose, uttered a further blessing with the familiar sign of benediction and left.

Gabriel wandered back to the dormitory. Cabo had been installed in the kitchen and had settled by the heap of smouldering ash in the huge fire place. A novice monk had taken pleasure in feeding the animal a few scraps, sufficient to win the dog's affection and ensure its stay as rat-catcher designate. The cur had never known such luxury. It was just as well. He would be separated from Gabriel when fate would catch up with the outlawed monk.

The following morning, after the Office of Prime at 6am and breakfast, Gabriel was taken to the library and scriptorium. The abbaye was large and rich. Its facilities reflected its prosperity.

'We are producing a copy of the Revelation of St John. If you will, you may assist Brother Peter in illuminating the capitals at each of the new chapters.'

Gabriel looked down at the work being done by Peter and then around at the array of desks and seated monks labouring on various chapters of the last book of the bible.

'I will be pleased to assist. My draughtsmanship with a quill is competent but skill in colourful embellishment of capitals untested.'

'That is easily rectified,' Peter greeted his newly acquired apprentice - a term that exaggerated, by irony, the obvious lack of youthfulness evident in the years written on Gabriel's face, 'you can start by in-filling the profiles of the signatory animals that I draw.'

Gabriel nodded and followed his guide around the hall as he was introduced to the various clerics. Artisans though they were, scholars they were, also. The quantity of gold paint and pots of blue, lapis lazuli pigment scattered around the desks, further reflected the opulence of the monastery. Blue pigment was a rare colouring and a costly one. Brought from Afghanistan, it fetched high prices in the western hemisphere. The stone was crushed, then ground to a fine powder, mixed with oil and used mainly to colour robes on the figures of the richest clients able to afford to sit for the most accomplished artists. Often, robes of the virgin Mary were blue, signifying a subject worthy of the most costly pigment. Here, in the abbaye, it embellished flowers that intertwined the architecture of the primary letter leading the script or, in another instance, the jewelled collar of a minute mink peering out from the letter O beginning chapter 17. Gabriel was fascinated and looked forward to his first session of wielding a brush instead of a quill.

15

Days went by. Gabriel was beginning to feel comfortable and disinclined to move on. He was enjoying his new-found employment as a colourist. But the risk entailed in staying outweighed comfort. News travelled: a fire in a monastery would excite interest, particularly if connected with some scandal involving one of the monks. Time to move on. Maybe one more day. But one more day became one more week. He would make for Rennes, via St Brieuc, when he was ready.

Gabriel secreted a small portion of hard cheese and a saucisson ready for departure. Cabo, he decided, should stay. The dog had settled, proved to be a good ratter and was popular with the brothers. He would miss him. This time he would seek accommodation at an inn in St Brieuc before journeying on to Rennes. If Luc d'Angers was in pursuit it was likely he would discover Gabriel's stay at the monastery and assume his next sojourn to be likewise. Rennes was a different matter. Much bigger than St Brieuc, it boasted a cathedral: La Cathedrale St Pierre; a basilique: St Sauveur and a number of smaller churches. There would be various religious orders supporting these. He could find accommodation similar to his current lodgings but he would avoid that of an Augustinian order and seek out, again, a Benedictine priory or abbaye.

'I bid you well brother,' Peter, the colourist who had supervised Gabriel's art work, gave him a hug at the open door of the monastery. 'Come back this way and tell us about your Rome experience.'

'I will. Look after Cabo. I am sorry to lose him but he is in good hands here with you all.'

Gabriel said no more and set off towards the main road below the monastery.

Sometime later, at the edge of a small hamlet, he sat against the smooth bark of a large sycamore, ate some cheese and filled his mug from the animal skin. Again, it was children, always curious and on the lookout for diversion, who engaged him in conversation. It occurred to him to tell them he was going to visit the priory at Mont-St-Michel. They, like the others, were pleased to listen to frightening tales of somewhat exaggerated experiences he had met with in his travels. Leaving them stimulated with a fresh set of anecdotes, he knew their parents and neighbours would be informed of the monk they had met on his way to Mont-St-Michel.

'Cabo! What are you doing here?' The dog was all over him, jumping up, squealing and wagging his tail with excitement.

Gabriel put down the staff he had with him, knelt and hugged the dog.

'Come on then boy, let's get going. If you must follow me, then you must.'

The two set off. Gabriel now with a lighter step. He hadn't realised how much he'd missed the dog until then, even in just that short time on the road. They arrived at St

Brieuc just before sunset. Larger than St Pol de Leon and a busy port, he had no problem finding an auberge. One night was all he needed to stay. At daybreak a small breakfast of hot milk on stale bread set him up for the next stage of his journey to Rennes. As usual he had managed to cadge something for Cabo, a small shin bone. It would take them another eight days, at least. This time he set off south instead of going along the direct road to his goal. There were no monasteries that he knew of, along the route. A small hermitage but he'd had his fill of discomfort. He would seek lodgings at any farms until he reached a main road leading east to Rennes.

16

The week at Inisheer passed smoothly. There were no moments of tension. Neither partner was particularly dogmatic by nature - strong willed maybe but not self-centred. Both had used the time in a variety of ways. Leisurely walks, pleasant lunches at the pub interspersed with reading and work sessions on their laptops. Bill, known by islanders since his visits as a child, had made friends over the years with some of the boys and girls. The population didn't seem religiously offended by the fact of his need of a companion. Surprised or amused perhaps but no animosity was shown towards the pair from any quarter. Both were sad to leave but encouraged by good wishes and exhortations to 'return soon'.

Josh insisted on driving Ignatius and Penny back to Dublin. Kat took advantage of the opportunity for a shopping spree in the Capital. The four went to lunch and the parents returned after inspecting accommodation Penny was renting close to the university.

Ignatius left Penny there and looked in on the Common Room. A few postgrads were floating about but the campus would remain quiet until the freshers arrived for the beginning of term. His new office was situated not far from the main library. There he checked a few items in boxes on a long table set against a bare wall. The centre of the floor was occupied by a round table. Eight chairs were spaced round its periphery and each allowed its neighbour plenty of arm and leg room.

A university laptop sat connected to a large screen on a twin pedestal desk. In front of the screen lay an envelope. He hadn't noticed it until now.

'Welcome. Suggest we meet when you have settled in.'

The card was signed by the new Dean of Studies, Janet Hicks.

'Hello', Penny's voice announced her arrival, 'I had to come to see your new setup. I've brought you a coffee maker, filter. It was for me but haven't even unpacked it from its box. Pretty sure you'll find a use for it.' She wandered across and dumped it on the table with the other boxes then turned and glanced around Ignatius's new den.

'What d'you think of it?'

'Great. I'm surprised how spacious it is.'

'Stephen Bokowski has been generous with the foundation and insisted he wanted a room in which he felt comfortable, when he visits. It's possible I might be moved into the new premises. They're almost ready. Quite a major conversion. Bokowski is fitting out a complete television studio which will be made available to all faculties.'

'Why is he so generous towards Trinity?'

'His daughter came here. Read English. She died in a terrorist rocket attack in Israel, four or five years ago. She was very happy here. According to him it was the happiest time of her life. Made a lot of friends. One of them was her tutor. Stephen married her, later - much later - after his wife was killed in the same rocket attack. Partly the reason he has become so actively hostile to religious extremism. Pathologically hostile. That's why he identified with my sentiments at the interview and why I'll be pushing a lot of non-PC comment.'

She picked up the card now open on his desk, 'How soon d'you have to get moving on the new degree course?', waving the card in front of him.

'I want to get going on that before setting up the Panel project. But I can't leave the latter for too long. The degree won't be running, anyway, until the next academic year, at the earliest so there's time to play in both camps and some of the content will be existing, faculty modules.'

'Your tenure in the Philosophy faculty, will it affect the assessment of my PhD?'

'No. I'll be mainly concerned with students offering a thesis with a strong mathematical bias - like, say, mathematical logic - or a speculative, cosmological bias. There'll be assessors appointed who'll be specialists in Linguistic Philosophy from other universities. I'll be nowhere in the frame. Anyway, enough of that. Let's get into town for a coffee. I can buy some ground coffee for my new machine, for which I haven't thanked you.' He gave her a peck on the cheek, 'It'll get a hammering, to be sure.'

'Bit late in the day for coffee and lunch was pretty filling. Shall we go for a pub snack and decide what we're doing over the next few days? I've got to stock up. What about you? You still intend to stay at the diocesan house or with me?'

'Difficult one. I'd rather be with you but it might be wiser, for the time being, to stay at the rectory and gradually withdraw from diocesan responsibilities in a less conspicuous way. I'll cite pressure from Trinity as an excuse, which won't be quite untrue. We can set up something more permanent, together, once we've got through the next few months. The SJ haven't commented on my Bokowski appointment. There might be some flack, I would guess, for getting involved with the media.'

'"Won't be quite untrue", that's a good one,' she laughed, 'but maybe that's the simplest.'

'That will be the simplest until we figure where we're heading with this. Let's get going. We can discuss a few things on the way down.' Ignatius followed Penny, locked the door and both made for the road to town.

Ignatius broke the silence that had settled on them for the first part of their walk, 'I'm wondering if I buy something between Dublin and Tullamore, you keep the house in England and we have a joint pied-à-terre close to Trinity.'

'That'll be a bit extravagant but it'll be a solution. What's the likely outcome with the Jesuit authorities? I mean, will there be some kind of censorship once they cotton on to my existence? Excommunication? They'll be increasingly aware of your absence from Daily Office.

Can't see how you'll hide it or will you just let it 'fall out', so to speak and take it from there?'

'I don't know. Even before the Rome trip I was moving further and further away from the whole pantomime. I'm getting more and more hostile to embroidered chasubles, silly hats and genuflecting spinsters. It's not the idea of 'no need' for a religious ministry - people take comfort from a sympathetically conducted burial service or reassurance from a baptism - it's more a matter of moving away from an ostentatious display of ritual. Pomp. In a sense, for example, the mass should be conducted around a simple table with real bread and not these ridiculous wafers but with glasses of wine, not a silver chalice. I know, in terms of practicalities, it's not as simple as that. But it would have greater significance as a spiritual act done infrequently as part of a real meal, not a mechanically symbolic performance acted out at specific times of the day or week. Still, let's forget that and enjoy what's ahead.'

17

'Bonjour,' the oldest boy continued in Breton, 'are you from the monastery where the other monk came from.'

'Bonjour mon enfant, which monk was that?' Francesco Fougères stared down at the boy, from his horse.

'The one who came in a boat,' he pointed down the street towards the jetty, just visible from where the group of children were standing.

'Yes. Where did he go?'

'Up to the auberge but he sailed up river next day.'

Fougère grunted, reined his horse around, dispensed no blessing and turned East.

The children were unimpressed.

Fougères spent a number of days visiting various taverns, priories and monasteries. He wasted a considerable amount of time searching the area around Mont-St-Michel, having been fed the false lead de Tregor had told the children at Guingamp. Frustrated, he decided to head for Rennes and a rest at the Augustinian monastery he had visited sometime in the past. His piles were troubling him and hours each day in the saddle were not helping any. Food there was rich and plentiful but, again, it didn't help the gout that was also playing him up. As nephew of the abbot of the monastery in Finistère, he could be sure of a welcome from the abbot at Rennes.

Cabo pricked his ears, sniffed the air, growled and shot off into a low tunnel of undergrowth. A few seconds later a fox emerged further down the track and turned to face the dog. There was a momentary pause as both adopted a defensive stand-off. Cabo, the hairs along his spine erect, slowly circled the animal. The fox showed his teeth, turning with a wooden, almost clockwork, motion to keep the dog at its front. A faint slick of saliva dripped from its jaws. Both held their ground until Cabo, the larger of the two, leapt in. Mouths clashed. The two parted and again went for each other. This time the fox, a mangy, unhealthy specimen turned, gave a scream, typical of its kind and shot off with Cabo attempting a bite at its flank.

Gabriel shouted. At that distance he had not noticed the animal was now frothing at the mouth. Cabo halted, not from the shout but instinctively, now repelled by the unhealthy odour given off by the animal. A drop of blood fell from a small wound in his gum. The fox was rabid.

'Come back. Come back boy.'

The dog obeyed, the muscles in his back relaxing, hairs flattening. There was no longer any sign of blood. Cabo had snorted, sneezed and licked his muzzle clean.

'Good boy,' Gabriel patted the dog and both set off again towards Rennes.

18

'Come on through,' Mike O'Connor welcomed Ignatius and Penny, 'Rose is in the kitchen. She'll be out in a minute. Let me fix you a drink.'

Rose appeared pretty well immediately.

'Nice to see you again. Some time, Bill, since you were last here and Mike has told me about Penny. Welcome to the establishment.' She held out both hands to Penny and brushed cheeks, quite informally, as though each had been long-established friends.

'Glad to meet you. Bill says you all go back a long way. Since well before Mike was Dean.'

'Yes. School through to university and after. The friendship has lasted. We knew each other well before uni. Anyway let's sit and enjoy a drink. I've prepared savoury nibbles as a starter. We'll move to the table for the main course. It's wild salmon. Mike's been fishing and caught something for once.'

'Sarki bugger.'

'Well, it's true.' Laughter set the mood for the evening.

*

Mike brought out a box of cigars, 'Fancy one of these? They're from La Palma. A quarter the cost of Cuban.'

Rose opened a window and a sliding glass door that led to a conservatory, 'I enjoy the smell of a cigar but don't like the smoke hanging about overnight. Stale in the morning.'

'So, your new media project - sounds exciting.' Rose sat on the sofa by Ignatius implying she expected more than just a yes or no.

'Well, we're hoping it'll raise some hackles. Not for the sake of causing annoyance but to challenge self-appointed authority. In fact any authority with a sense of unearned entitlement and the means to enforce their opinions on a captive public'.

'You must have had something in mind when you were interviewed. There are any number of options that come to my mind, not least politics.'

'Politics, no doubt but I want, particularly, to tackle theocratic tyranny. The kind exercised by the Taliban or the Iranian religious police. What a shower. I really have lost any sense of Christian charity towards practitioners of evil. Love thine enemy? Forgive them that trespass ... ? Love them that practise FGM; that stone women on trumped up charges of adultery; that behead members of NGO charities? Redemption for them? No! Not bloody likely. We had a similar conversation with my parents a few weeks back. I believe very much in distinguishing between evil and unintended harm. Even though I'm now challenging Christian, so-called wisdom, I have to acknowledge St Paul's counsel not to tolerate evil, to give 'no quarter to false prophets' as the rubric runs. The problem with religion is the more plausible ones are founded on mythology posing as reality, as substance.'

'You'll have a job with the PC brigade.'

'They're one of the sets I want to get at. Too many of them with blinkered vision. Particularly the ones who make excuses for the inexcusable. Street crime is getting worse. The police are damned by the public if nothing is appearing to be done and damned if they do. If they challenge certain ethnic minority individuals or groups with known histories of crime, through stop and search, they get castigated for racial profiling when in fact a significant percentage of crime is carried out by such people. Particularly knife crimes by such gangs. Those thugs, in some respects, are no different from any white ones except they seem to have a blood lust common to their counterparts elsewhere. I have, during part of my vocation on missionary furlough, witnessed the most savage acts of violence committed in some African states. One tribal adversary hacking the limb off an opponent with a panga, with no shred of human revulsion that would prevent you or I from doing such a thing. The kind of primitive mentality that can commit such an atrocity is totally beyond the imagination of any civilised culture. Can you imagine the sight of blood spurting everywhere, a limb hanging from a length of exposed sinew and muscle before finally being severed from its socket? And this occurring over an obscene number of seconds, the perpetrator unaffected by the act.' Ignatius shook his head, the others grimaced.

'Now we've got the 'woke brigade'. Police officers are not supported by some of their senior officers. They are expected to 'take the knee' and, if they don't, are seen as not being in line with policy promoted by their less courageous superiors even if the latter are in the minority.

What is an officer to do in trying to restrain a violent criminal who has been observed carrying out county-line drug activities or found to be carrying a weapon? These thugs should be deported. But then you get hue and cry from the human rights crowd. The same for illegals here on the pretext of claiming refugee status. Some genuinely seeking sanctuary but there are too many others who are not; economic migrants or worse, terrorists.'

'Yes but we can't turn into a kind of European Guantanamo Bay.'

'Why not? 9/11 was an evil, horrendous act. Some said Mecca should have been nuked immediately. The US should open every daily news programme with, say, an eight second shot of the two planes hitting the Twin Towers and one showing victims leaping from windows. Horrendous. Where are we? We're well into the twenty first century and still we're getting murders committed globally since 9/11. We're forgetting this continuing history of religiously motivated madness.'

'You can't stigmatize the whole of Islam because of that. There are well-intentioned Muslims who condemn the act.'

'If that were sufficient grounds I'd agree but, as in Afghanistan with the Taliban, the passive majority is intimidated by extremist bigots. Misogynistic, extremist bigots. Men who believe in scientifically disproven statements in their religious canon and the priority of their own sexual urges. They're an evil, self-righteous bunch of bastards. Well-intentioned Muslims? No. They're about as effective as sheep trying to influence wolves. A religious canon interpreted by barely educated jihadists needs to be assessed by the threat it poses and not by any benign aspects it seemingly professes. Love thy neighbour might be a beautiful concept but if thy neighbour is evil he needs to be excised. I loathe and detest these people. They're evil. They're not led by any god, they're led by their own misguided, self-righteous arrogance, blind allegiance to imams and mullahs unwilling to expose the Qur'an to its contradictions, to the wider disciplines of critical comparison, logic and ethics. They need to read modern, critical philosophers.'

A brief silence followed Ignatius's anger.

'What are you both going to do about a home? You can't forever lead semi-detached lives.'

'Leave the poor devils alone,' Mike waved his cigar at Rose, 'they've come to enjoy themselves.'

She ignored him.

Penny took a sip of Cointreau, 'Not sure. I've got a place in England but want to settle over here. Bill's in a slightly different position. We're wondering about a property somewhere outside Dublin. Towards Tullamore but not exclusively. Anywhere within reasonable travelling distance from the city.'

'Not a bad idea. Not good to be on top of the shop, so to speak. Some nice countryside to the west, particularly if you can find a spot sandwiched between the road and river. Pricey though.'

'Yes but I've got a pot of money more than enough for a deposit. My salary or salaries, rather, will command a good mortgage. I've got a collection of rare books and manuscripts that would fetch a fair price at auction.'

'Not filched from the Gregorian University I hope.' Mike laughed as he said it.

'No. Pinched from Trinity College Dublin. Joking aside, I picked up a lot of stuff in shops and bazaars during travels on Jesuit business. My time at Stoneyhurst, the Jesuit school in Lancashire, as a pupil and a year there teaching, gave me time to spend in the school's museum. They have collections of Jesuit memorabilia going way back. Missionary journeys to Japan and South America. I got a feel for genuine artefacts. The difference between authentic and fake. I know the market, particularly the American collectors so can put one or two pieces up for auction, if I need to. A lot depends on the reaction of the SJ in the coming months. The Superior Provincial is a friend but I won't be a hypocrite. I won't try to pull the wool over his eyes.'

'As a Jesuit, how d'you see your future? At gut level.'

'Positive. No guilt whatsoever over my relationship with Penny. You must have an idea of my outlook from what I've said already. One of my few misgivings, though, is damaging any worthy structure during televised debate, structure based on what I would argue as sound, Christian principles. Sound in the Cartesian sense. Not New or Old Testament narrative embracing dubious accounts bordering on some quasi-supernatural superstition or happening. Walking on water? Water into wine? No! Absolute fiction. I think all a person can do is live as though a holy spirit exists, if they don't want to deny its possibility but they need to get on with living free from preoccupation with trying to influence it. If it does exist, in the sense of Pauline theology, it doesn't need us to monitor its activity. If it doesn't exist, no problem anyway. There's no way of testing consequences of believing prayer, supplication or wishful thinking has influence on any outcome. All one can do is believe in the sincerity of one's own conscience.'

The mellowing effects of alcohol slowed the conversation.

'Bill, I think we ought to be making tracks. It's been a lovely evening. It'll be a pleasure to return the hospitality once we've sorted ourselves out. In fact, let's fix a date now so we can take you for dinner somewhere, first.'

19

The Benedictine monastery at Rennes was larger than the one at Guingamp. Gabriel expected the income, generated from the town and well-cultivated countryside, would be higher and give the monks a better standard of living than that at the previous abbaye. Again, as an educated, well-travelled brother, he was welcomed with enthusiasm, offered ablutions, given a meal and assigned a cell. Cabo was provided with a rush mat in a dark corner of the kitchen, vermin were as much a problem here as in the previous monastery. He manifested no sign of rabies. Not an exceptional outcome in a dog exposed to the virus. The disease would lie dormant but lethal in his body for an indefinite time. He would reach a good age and die gently but not before evening the balance between good and evil in favour of his master.

'So,' the abbot, one Pascal Bezier, sat on the bench alongside de Tregor, 'you have met the illustrious Galileo Galilei, our brother the cellarer tells me?'

'Yes Father. Stayed for a time in his workshop, making lenses.'

'That is what I want to talk to you about. We have a facility for casting glass here but for the making of flasks, jars and the like, not lenses. It has been out of use for some time. Our artisan went to Murano, to learn more, as you did to Padua but died in a plague outbreak. Would you consider instructing one of the novices in the skill and science? Our main concern would be to make spectacles.

We have a ready supply of ox bones that can be cut and formed to hold pairs of eyepieces but we would expect you to commission the materials and instruments to give us the shapes. Can you do that?'

'I would Father but glass for spectacle lenses needs a higher melting temperature than a wood-fired furnace can obtain. We would need a supply of coal in order to achieve the purity and clarity that comes from higher melts.'

'No problem my son. The good people near Châteaubourg, digging a well, have uncovered a plentiful supply. It will be easy to ship it by boat along the Vilaine. So you will assist us in the enterprise?'

'That would give me much satisfaction, Father Abbot. It would also not be difficult to build a telescope once an atelier was set up to make spectacle lenses. Would you be agreeable to let me experiment on that as well? I would need the use of a lathe, a supply of brass and seasoned timber.'

Gabriel sensed the abbot was progressive, his uninvited, favourable reference to Galileo encouraging. So Gabriel decided to push for all he could get on the basis 'if you don't ask you don't get'.

'I will see to it, my son. Give me a list of your needs. There are foundry workers and artificers in metal in Rennes. I would very much like to scan the heavens with one of these new spy glasses, myself. The bodies that cross the sky have always been an intrigue and I hear the planets are coloured.'

'Thank you Father and thank you for letting the dog stay. An excellent catcher of rats and obedient about cats so your mouser won't be tormented. In fact, he is likely to curl up for warmth against Mila, I think that is your cat's name, if she will let him. The monks at Guingamp thought highly of him. It was there he was trained to respect the cat. Together they will help protect the victuals stored about the abbaye.'

'Good. Enjoy your wine. We shall talk again.'

*

Francesco Fougères reined his horse in front of the Augustinian abbaye. He liked the look of it. It should prove a worthwhile place to spend some time – waste being, perhaps, the more accurate word - before going on to enquire at other monasteries in the region.

Welcomed, he soon found a job that gave him satisfaction as a slaughterer and curer of pigs raised on the monastery farm. The monk he was assisting suffered from poor eyesight and arthritic joints. The aged celibate was glad of company; the pigs were getting heavier and more difficult to handle. Between meals Fougères helped himself to slices from some of the older, salted hams maturing in the stone, curing house. Discovering that Gabriel de Tregor had not called at the abbaye, he decided a stay of three or four weeks would do no harm. Using the monastery as a base, rather than a short-stay dormitory, would allow him to indulge his appetite for the butter-rich pastries and sauces these monks produced daily. De Tregor could wait.

A novice assisted in the processing of entrails. Intestines were cleaned and treated to be filled with coarse-cut pork, garlic and herbs and aged to produce saucisson. Always greedy for food, Fougères could not resist a morsel of some intestine or other offal even before it had cooked thoroughly. He bullied the novice and maltreated the pigs, enjoying the squeals of anger as he prodded them with whatever tool or stick might be to hand.

His appetite for sex was becoming an obsession. He visited inns where women offered their services and a bed could be provided for a few sous. On one such visit he overheard a snippet of conversation regarding a monk who was setting up a spectacle-manufacturing atelier in one of the monasteries. A sixth sense told him this might be his quarry. He guessed it would be amongst the progressive, Benedictine brotherhood that he should look. Brothers who bordered on heresy with their insatiable curiosity for probing the mind of god.

Returning to his lodgings he decided he would make a visit to these scholars to see if the renegade monk, he was hunting, was the artisan in question. But there was plenty of time. Life here was too pleasant to rush things.

20

'So, what do you think of Rocky Valley Drive? Do we go for it rather than the place between Dublin and Galway?'

'I like the area. It's the closeness to the Wicklow mountains that appeals to me. Plenty of walks and not far from the N11. Quick into town. We can get to the M4 easily if we want to get to your parents. Ideal weekend retreat if we keep the little flat in Dublin. The only problem is where we park the Discovery.'

'No problem. We can park it at Trinity if we walk to and fro the flat.'

'Settled then. I like the house. There's room in the garden for a studio and the two extra en-suite bedrooms will come in handy if Stephen Bokowski decides he'd like to stay with us rather than use a hotel. He seemed pretty keen to give us the once-over in a domestic setting, I thought. The flat really is a tight fit.'

'Right then. We'll put in an offer. I want us to have a base away from the city before the new series starts but not too far to get to if we want to escape on the spur of the moment.'

The move took little time - few possessions to move. It was the legal paperwork that dragged the process out but they were in place before the first planning meeting for the new series was scheduled. Both had ideas for interior improvements. Ignatius was content to leave decisions on decor to Penny. His main interest lay in creating a comfortable study that he could retreat to, more Zen in nature than clinically academic.

Penny had designs on clearing a site adjacent to a granite outcrop in the garden. She sketched plans for a generously-proportioned, two-storied, oak-framed studio complete with light catering and washing facilities and containing an area she referred to as a 'hell hole' for messy projects. The design featured a small, covered veranda facing the mountains. All this, she had decided, would be partly financed by letting out her house in England. The upper floor would contain a clean, comfort area furnished with a desk, a couple of easy chairs and convertible studio couch-cum-bed. No television! If she needed to, she could watch programmes in the house or 'catch-up' on her computer.

Ignatius suggested a few modifications. One was a major, structural addition of a small, rotating observatory. They found an architect with a good reputation for what might be termed boutique designs. He produced 2-D and realistic, computer-generated 3-D plans for the project. The light-free zone, benefitting from proximity to the wildness of the Wicklows, made exploration of the night sky a draw both couldn't resist. The two, because of their physics background, were fascinated by the sheer spectacle of a sky dotted with a 'tapestry of astronomical delights' - as Penny was apt to describe the pleasure.

'I like this idea of an overhanging gable sheltering the veranda.' Ignatius gestured to the folded A2-sized drawing and pushed it towards her, 'The exposed oak is more like an exoskeleton. Solid stuff.'

'Well, it's got to support the upper bit and it gives a bit of character to the gable frame.'

'Can I come to visit you, because I'll be pissed off if you intend to sleep out there all the time?' Said with mock concern.

'If you're a good boy I might let you but don't worry, I want to sleep in the big house, in the same bed as you, Holy Father.'

'Cheeky devil!'

They both erupted in a peal of laughter. The tension, generated by the uncertain period leading up to acceptance of the offer, released.

'Right, I must get to it and organise the line-up for the first screening. Stephen wants a star showing. If the first broadcast doesn't meet with the critics expectations but more, the viewing ratings, it'll be a long haul to redress the balance.'

'How're you going to play it? Opposing personalities or like-minded sceptics?'

'Dunno. Mixture of both, maybe. Depends on the pool of willing participants.'

'You're going to need names. Names with a capital N. It's a question of whether they sympathise with the tone of your subject choice or object to it. Whether seeking confrontation or trying to edify. From what you've said, way back, Bokowski is more likely to settle for the former I would guess.'

'Mixture of both, I would guess. He would appreciate an informed discussion between like-minded people so controversy doesn't, necessarily, need to set the agenda.'

'What about a mixed panel of well-known English-speaking, French and German journalists or philosophers with left and right wing tendencies, male and female, balanced by one or two British,? It would set the precedent of an international line-up and set the stage for future, international, celebrity choices.'

'Bokowski's Israeli connections with the Hebrew University would throw up some interesting names. There's no dearth of stimulating talent to draw on. I would also arrange it so they give a lecture, in their specialised fields, to undergraduates in the new degree. In fact, make it an open, inter-disciplinary invitation.'

Their conversation was interrupted by the sound of a vehicle crunching on the rough chippings on the drive. Ignatius went to what was now the library window overlooking the front lawn.

'Who the hell is that?'

A well-built man was getting out of the driver's seat of an SUV. Another from the passenger's side. Both were muscular and looked as though they could be capable of handling a net aboard a trawler or playing forward row rugby. They were not roughly dressed. The older one was wearing a good quality, Galway tweed jacket and looked prosperous.

'Trouble!' Ignatius looked back at Penny, 'Leave this to me and act friendly. I'll explain later. IRA. I'll let them in.'

Ignatius went to the door and opened it just as the men reached the raised step fronting the porticoed entrance.

'Just heard you boys as you drew up. What can I do for you? If you're here about tarmacing the drive we're not in the market.'

'No Father. We hear from a source you're wantin' a studio built at the back and you, being new to the area, might need a bit of guidance.'

It was obvious that the 'source' had disclosed Ignatius's clerical role. The older man held out a hand, 'Patrick Ryan.'

'Come on through. You've time for a whiskey?'

The two nodded knowingly at each other, as if to confirm a previously anticipated response and moved through the door after the cardinal.

Ignatius introduced Penny, with no explanation as to her presence, invited the men to sit down and went to a table with a bottle of Tullamore DEW sitting on a tray with glasses and jug.

'Water?'

'As it comes.'

'Penny?'

'The usual. I'll fill the jug with fresh.'

Glasses charged, Ignatius sat in the window seat and raised his glass, 'Slànte Mhath!'

The four raised their glasses to the traditional Irish greeting for 'Good Health'.

'So what kind of 'guidance' are you able to offer?'

'Site levelling. Foundations and services from plumbing and electrics through to IT. Structure, roof and glazing. Fittings? We rely on you to source same but we can install them.'

Ignatius looked in his glass, gave it a reflective swirl, nodded affirmatively and faced the two entrepreneurs.

'I appreciate your interest. You're quick off the mark. You would be offering the same with some kind of manager fronting the project?'

'We have a number of similar works, successfully managed, goin' back a decade or two.'

Penny, mindful of Ignatius's warning, motioned her glass in the direction of the back garden, 'I'm the one wanting the studio. Bill,' she used her regular address for Ignatius, 'wants it to have a small, rotating observatory. How difficult would you see the construction to be?' Her tone of voice was friendly and conveyed a hint of acceptance of the status quo.

Ignatius signalled a faint but sure sign of approval towards her with a slight pursing of his lips and barely noticeable nod of the head, as if to say, 'Keep it up girl'.

'To be sure, our team is professional. We would refer to you and your architect at major stages of development and you can obtain references from past clients. We've dealt with the church and local authorities on all sorts of projects. We're not cheap but we're not rip-off merchants. Good workmanship comes at a price.'

Ignatius took a sip of whiskey, 'We haven't approached any company yet. It's still early days. We might change our minds over the final design but so far both of us,' Ignatius inclined his head towards Penny, 'seem pretty well in agreement over layout. You would expect us to get two or three quotes as you've been in the business some time and know the drill. If you leave us contact details we'll forward the plans and spec for major, internal installations and conveniences. So far, as you can see,' Ignatius pulled the plan from a side table and opened it, 'we've only outlined the major interior partitions without locating the type and placement of a heating system, for example or other basic services. Although it's meant to be a studio we also want it to double as a bit of a retreat, a place where we can relax.'

'No problem. As I'm here, can I look at your site anyway? Might have some suggestions that will save you some early headaches.'

'Don't see why not. Can look now. We'll finish the drinks after.'

Ignatius led the two through to the back garden.

'That sheep fence needs lookin' at. Where'll you run a cable from? From the house or the pole out front? What about a covered walkway? Weather can be pretty wild out here.'

'House'll be simplest. Don't intend to use any heavy-duty, electrical stuff like an industrial kiln,' Ignatius was mentally flagging up detail and beginning to be irritated, 'but maybe a covered passage between the two is a good idea. I'll think about it.'

'If you're goin' to have a rotating observatory, even a small one, you'll be running a motor of some sort. Have you thought about that? The power system and runners might be way out of proportion in cost to the rest of the building.'

Ignatius was not going to be deprived of his observatory. He didn't need to be told going about it the wrong way could result in a costly headache.

'I've had one or two ideas since that plan was drawn, as to how to engineer it. I'm now not into anything complicated but I want three-sixty degree access. So, maybe, just nothing more elaborate than a slide-off cover that allows a telescope to poke through on a small, internal, rotating platform, hand-operated. We're not talking Jodrell Bank.'

That put a stop to any further comment about the studio.

'Well, site access down the side of the house will be no problem.'

'Right, let's get in and finish our drinks.'

21

Gabriel inspected the interiors of each of the separate, mating halves of the clay moulds for surface irregularities or stray particles. There should be none. He had prepared the surfaces with all the care and precision that any master craftsman would take over his work.

The glass was now fluid. Gabriel set one of the moulds on top of the upended log that served as a work surface for manipulating or forming the various glass artefacts produced in the past by the monks. He poured the molten silica from the crucible and tapped the shell to release trapped air, holding the shell with a thick, double layer of hessian. The other five moulds he treated likewise. Each of the three pairs slightly shallower in thickness than the other planar, convex/concave spaces formed by the lens-shaped, wooden blanks used to give them form. He was watched by a group of monks excited by the prospect of relieving the deterioration of sight that time brought with age.

A second set of moulds contained concave and convex spaces. These would provide object and eye-piece for the new telescope he had drawn plans for. Plans adapted from accurate drawings he had made during his time with Galileo in Padua. The combination would permit the image not to be inverted, a characteristic of earlier telescopes. In the past, upside down images were seen, by the superstitious, as portents of evil. Some malign force distorting God's true world.

Each of the setting moulds he placed on a bed of dry sand in a tray. There they would remain overnight, cooling, ready to be opened carefully the following morning. The blanks inside would be washed. ground, polished and inspected with the same attention a lapidary might give any gem stone in his care. Those moulds producing unsatisfactory lenses would be destroyed but their patterns kept and modified for further experimentation.

'Marcel,' Gabriel held a half mould up to scrutiny, 'see this speck? It will burn and taint the glass.'

The young novice took the half and examined the cavity.

'Yes.'

'Blow it out. It's from the coal or from the melt additive.'

Marcel handed back the mould and was given a pair of tongs. Gabriel added a small quantity of manganese to a crucible of molten silica and gave it a stir with a long, glass rod of a higher melt temperature.

'Right, you pour the glass. Be careful not to nudge the mould.'

The boy, for he was not much more than that, lifted the crucible of molten silica from the hole in its sand-stone platform. Glowing coal, from the aperture sealed by the crucible, sent an immediate wave of heat onto the faces of those nearest. Marcel tilted the vessel over the aperture in the mould. The intense heat penetrated the coarse material of the long, loose gown he was wearing. It wasn't uncomfortable to begin with but his hands, uncovered, began to feel the skin-hardening temperature radiating from the deep red, baked clay container as the molten substance slipped noiselessly from this alchemy that was liquid glass. It was a sight few present had ever witnessed. The amazing spectacle of this incandescent trickle of intense heat and light never ceased to fascinate even the most seasoned of glass workers. The gloom of the darkened premises intensified the glow emanating from the very depth of the magical substance. Its properties, unlike static light refracted through a passive material from an external source, had a dynamic that added to the spectacle. For the assembled monks it was a treat, a performance that gratified even the most cynical of the order.

'Stop. That's it. Rest the crucible back in the furnace. Tomorrow we shall inspect our work and you shall be introduced to the pleasures of lens grinding.' Gabriel spoke partly to Marcel and partly to the monks now in animated conversation at their first encounter with glass of clarity superior to the tinted material used to make their flasks and goblets.

22

The journey across town, to the other monastery, took Francesco Fougères longer than he'd intended. A stop at an auberge, for light refreshment, developed into a full blown halt. A litre of wine, a whole saucisson, half a mallard, a large portion of loaf, cheese and crayfish from the Vilaine, blunted his resolve to reach the monastery by mid afternoon. Besides, after a bladderful of wine, the female company looked enticing, even if he didn't match their impression of a lucrative client.

Fougères became quite aroused as the wench, serving him a portion of apple and suet pudding, leant over his table. Her cleavage and ample bosom made him draw in a breath and stare in unbelief at the voluptuous offering in front of him. On impulse, he leant forward and buried his face into her cleavage. She, putting her hand on the back of his neck, pressed it further into her flesh. Letting him go, she stood back and nodded towards the stairs. He pushed the plate of food further onto the table and lurched to his feet. The wrong side of being sober, he followed her, none too steadily, on a pair of gout-ridden legs receiving yet another dose of inflammation from the rough, red wine he'd drunk.

As he approached the stairs a surge of acidic, undigested food rose into his throat. It burnt. The pain made him pause and he steadied himself with one hand on the nearest table. Before he had chance to swallow, it turned into a full-blown flush which he regurgitated over the shoulder and neck of a forest worker just raising a bowl of milk to his mouth. The smell was not unlike some kind of corrosive, metallic reaction to an acid. Milk and vomit coalesced as the forester jerked the bowl up and away from his face.

'You son of a papist whore.' The man rose from the bench, thrusting it away with the backs of his legs, grabbed our unfortunate monk by his tunic, threw him on the floor, knelt and proceeded to wipe the filthy, glistening coating of slime from his clothes with the skirt of Fougère's habit.

By this time a small audience was assembling around the pair hoping for further entertainment from the tree-cutter. They weren't disappointed.

'Right, your holiness, let's see if you can wash clothes as well as you can soil them.'

The cleric was yanked to his feet and frog-marched through the inn out into the lane. The crowd followed. Our forester shook the protesting monk, 'Stop struggling or I'll cut your ears off,' and led him to a covered lavoir, a cascade of troughs where local women washed family garments.

There he handed the monk over to some friends, 'Hold on to this wretch whilst I think of a suitable reward for his efforts.'

The muscular tree feller removed his belt and tunic and tossed the latter into one of the lower, stone tanks. He then rinsed his neck and shoulder, leaning over an upper trough, with a ladle used for drinking. Satisfied the coating of stinking reflux was totally removed he turned back to the now apprehensive monk. The crowd had, by this time, doubled, trebled in size as local urchins, always on the look-out for a bit of excitement, had shouted invitations to the surrounding dwellings to come out and take part.

'Holy father, seller of indulgences, indulge thyself in the cleansing of garments, rather than of souls.' The forester lifted the end of the monk's cowl and propelled him towards the trough. The edge of material topping his chest cut into the folds of Fougère's many chins and forced him to gag yet again. Guillaume, for that was our forester's name, warming to the attention of his audience, let go and pushed the monk into the channel below the trough and then over the edge, into the water, with a thrust of his foot. The crowd cheered. Guillaume pulled the bedraggled monk from the water and pointed to the soiled tunic floating in a film of greasy-looking detritus. By this time Fougères had vented all the food his stomach was going to release and had found his voice.

'The god of Abraham will punish you.'

'Abraham has nothing to do with it, you farting wart hog. Hear that?' The forester turned to the crowd, 'What shall we do with him when he's done?'

Some wag with an imagination suggested, 'Circumcise him, if his sympathy lies with Abraham.'

'Hear that, you warted pig?'

The indignant monk knew it best to keep silent. He retrieved the half submerged tunic and began to agitate it in the constantly replenishing flow of water. Gobbets of duck, saucisson and cheese continued to surface and floated over the spillway. Unused to sustained exertion, puffing and wheezing noisily, Fougères eased off and leant forward, supporting his bulk with arms submerged up to his elbows.

The crowd knew Guillaume as an orphan and grandson of Huguenot grandparents killed in the St Bartholemew's Day massacre in Paris, 1572. The massacre was history to most of them but it roused sympathy for the tree cutter. Protestant though he might be, his normally good humour and generous character had demonstrated the madness that allowed a populace to respond to blind, religious intolerance. This time, however, his long, buried anger with Catholic ignorance erupted in the performance he displayed in tormenting one of the instruments of that intolerance.

'Perhaps you have need of restoration and encouragement.'

The forester removed a knife from its sheath. The crowd became instantly quiet wondering what was going to happen next. Guillaume seized the white rope that functioned as a belt around the monk's torso. He slipped the point under the loop and sawed through. Replacing the knife, he doubled the length of knotted cord, gave it flick and then whipped it across the monk's ear. The cleric howled and put a hand up to the red, now swelling ear. The crowd cheered. The forester prodded the cleric in the back, 'Get on with it or I'll remove the ear to lessen the pain.'

Now fearful of further punishment, Fougères plunged and agitated the garment in the water until it was free from stain. Guillaume pointed to the higher trough and pushed the monk towards it. After further rinsing, he indicated his satisfaction by instructing him to wring out the garment and lay it flat on grass to dry in the sun, alongside other garments left by the washerwomen.

'Time for payment. We shall return to the inn. You can clean up the floor and settle your debt and pay for the inconvenience you have caused me and my friends.'

The crowd followed the bedraggled monk waddling with legs as far apart as his water-sodden habit would allow. At the inn Guillaume extracted some coins from the monk's scrip and laid them on a table in front of the innkeeper.

'And here's extra,' adding a few more, 'for fresh victuals and wine. Serve me and my friends another bowl and make this pig clean up the floor.'

The innkeeper nodded, sent his wife to fetch a pail and mop and a servant to get food and wine.

Fougères completed his tasks and decided he should seek accommodation elsewhere but not before returning to the lavoir to give his habit a thorough clean and retrieve his rope belt. He was tempted to hide

Guillaume's tunic but knew he would be hunted and punished again. His experience led him to a greater resentment of Gabriel de Tregor. In his mind De Tregor was the cause of his humiliation.

Approaching the Benedictine monastery, his earlier goal, he dismounted. As ever, his innate guile prevented him making direct enquiries at the gate of the abbaye. He looped the reins of his horse over a branch of yew. The tree, one of an avenue carefully tended as a source for manufacturing long bows, already showed evidence of careful husbandry. The bright red berries, attracting a variety of birds, ensured the propagation of its species further afield. He stalked down the blind side, hidden from windows and other vantage points and stood watching for some while, getting a feel for the community.

23

Ignatius and Penny watched as the two men exited the drive on to the back road.

'We're going to have to deal with them. Little alternative. But they'll do a good job.'

Penny nodded, 'I knew as soon as I saw them get out of the car they were IRA. I understand. Three years at Trinity and you can't fail to pick up on the drift of *'local commerce'* - for want of a euphemism.'

'Yes, if we don't oblige we're in for obstruction. Alternative outfits might prove a cheaper but poorer bet than that lot anyway. I'm having another. You?'

'A small one. Why did they pick on us? There's plenty of development going on around Dublin. I should have thought having to transport materials out here was a bit of a hike when there could be plenty of lucrative work closer.'

'More to it than that. The suggestion of a covered way means they want privacy for them not shelter for us.'

'What d'you mean?'

'They see this as a possible safe house, of sorts. Being set amongst expensive properties here on Rocky Valley Drive, screened by trees on boundaries and convenient to the Wicklows, it's an ideal spot. There's nothing we can do about it.'

'Wait a minute, I'm not sharing my house with terrorists. I don't have a high regard for the likes of Mountbatten. A man who achieved senior naval rank and influence more from an accident of birth; his privileged, royal connections rather than merit; from a pushy sense of entitlement and an inflated opinion of himself, by all accounts. Any man who chases titles and god knows how many knighthoods, what? upwards of fifty honours of some kind or another? must have been excessively self-promoting and possessing aspirations beyond his intellect to achieve them. But his death was murder despite his royal connections. I don't have a lot of time for the extended growth of a royal lineage but I am a monarchist rather than a supporter of a plurality of royal hangers on, if you can distinguish between the two, not a bloody anarchist. Elizabeth did a brilliant job over her seventy year reign - she and Philip, together.'

'It won't come to that, sharing the house with terrorists as you put it.'

'It bloody better not,' Ignatius and Penny rarely antagonised each other. This was just one of infrequent expressions of character that occasionally erupted between the two, 'and you can't tell me you agree with recklessly executed, extra-judicial killing can you even if the Fenians feel justified in other acts of opposition? The children who died had no reason to be a butt of the bombers.'

'Who said anything about killing? You're the one who mentioned Mountbatten. All that is likely to happen is their wanting it for meetings when we're not here.'

'How'd you reckon that?'

'Because of my connection with various *'threads in the diocese'* - for want of a euphemism. Touché.'

They both laughed at Ignatius echoing her earlier use of the term to defuse the tension.

'We'll face the situation when it comes. I've listened to confession, as a priest, a number of times, from some pretty senior operatives. They won't be a problem.'

'Bokowski's on the phone.' Penny shouted to Ignatius unloading the car.

Ignatius came in, took the phone and put it on speaker mode, 'Hello Steve.'

'Bill, good to hear you. How're you settling in?'

'We've got the place ship-shape and comfortable. Come and see us when you're over next. In fact bring Judith and stay a few days, if you can spare the time.'

'That would be good. Judith is eager to see your retreat but I'm warning you, she'll try to sell you her interior decor expertise. Anyway, why I've rung, I'm pleased with the proposal for the first show: *'Religion, Superstition and the Gullible'*. Who've you got lined up on the panel?'

'Richard Hawken, Michael Levison, Melanie Kerr and Faisal Sayyid.'

'Holy Moses! Hawken and Sayyid will generate some heat. The 'stralian is one of the most acerbic critics of the Qur'an you could wish for. Sayyid's a Qur'anic scholar of some note, School of African Studies at one of the Russell Group unis isn't he? Levison? I've encountered him once. Balanced guy. Secular Israeli. Kerr? A real cold fish. Sharp. Tongue like an acetylene lance. Good mix.'

'I'm pretty certain it'll attract positive comment from the critics.'

'One thing's sure, it won't be dull. The guy you've got as executive producer, has he got the experience to handle Hawken?'

'The 'he' is a 'she'. Robyn Fraser is a woman. Robyn spelt with a y. Scottish. Won't put up with any nonsense. She's reputed to have savaged that bolshie character presenting MNM, *Mid Night Marque*, the independent, late-night chat-show put on by *On Time* media group. Talked down to her. Told her she was hormonal. Told her to start a family or get herself a dog. She got up from her chair, stepped in front of him, bent down with her face six inches from his, smiled, grabbed him by the balls, pulled and twisted.'

Steve laughed, 'God, I'd liked to have been there.'

'So would I. It's still doing the rounds on YouTube.'

'OK. Well, thanks for the invite. I'll let you know well in advance when I'm over with Judith. Love to Penny.'

'See you. Thanks for calling.' Ignatius put the phone down.

'What'd you think of that?'

'Genuine. No hidden concern as to your choices.'

'Yeah, I felt the same. Anyway, with a two year contract, he's unlikely to want to start challenging my agenda. The Israelis have a reputation for being focused - perhaps forceful is the better word - in their dealings. If they're not happy with outcomes they'll tell you with no reservations but he's square. I have that feeling he'll go along with my decisions. We had that kind of rapport right from the start.'

'I think he actually likes you. Doesn't see you as a flunky. You're direct with him. Getting back to the Royals, I often wonder how they distinguish between flunkies who suck up to them and those who 'speak truth to power', for want of a way of putting it. The saga with Harry and Megan, didn't anyone in authority or with influence offer comment? I wouldn't use the word advice but didn't anyone assess the situation and visualise the outcome? Knowing normal interest, the relationship was bound to raise comment of a racial kind amongst some, benevolent or malicious. Particularly and unsurprisingly, the allegedly racist remark about the likely colour of the baby, innocently made or otherwise. Racist from one viewpoint. Disinterested curiosity from another.

D'you remember that quote about one of Winston Churchill's ministers? An aide is reputed to have cautioned one about challenging Churchill over some decision he'd made. The minister replied, "The time that I say yes to him, when I should say no, is the time when I am no longer of use to him," or words to that effect. Salient point.'

24

'Welcome. I'm Bill Synne bringing you the first edition of *Polemic*. For watchers at home the audience here in the studio will be posing questions relevant to this evening's theme: *Religion, Superstition and the Gullible*. We welcome comment by email and our website gives contact details. We have a panel of speakers whose skills and achievements may be known to some of you. For those who don't know them, I give a brief introduction.

Richard Hawken: Aussie - war correspondent. Covered conflict in Iraq, Syria, Lebanon and Nigeria and, earlier, non-combatant assignments for the media in other Middle Eastern countries. Just back from a different assignment covering the drug wars in Central and South America.

Michael Levison: Professor of Philosophy - Hebrew University, Jerusalem. Prior to that a colonel in the Israeli army.

Melanie Kerr: CEO Kerr Hotel Group - Vice Chancellor, Falmouth university.

Faisal Sayyid: Visiting fellow, currently School of African Studies. Professor of Qur'anic Studies, Cairo University.

I also take this opportunity to thank our producer, Robyn Fraser. An ex Royal Marine bands-woman/paramedic, she has firmly but kindly got this show on the road. Sometime crew member of Falmouth's All Weather Lifeboat, ALB as they are referred to by the

RNLI but now a volunteer with one of our Irish stations. Recent graduate of the School of Journalism.

Myself, I am, or was, professor of theoretical physics but taking up a new post in the School of Philosophy at Trinity.'

Ignatius did not mention his clerical role.

Right, the first question is from David Smith. Mr Smith.'

'Good evening. Faith is a matter of choice based on wishful thinking. Should state law be dissociated from dubious inferences derived from any religious text? I'm thinking particularly of the clamour, by Muslim activists, to establish Shariah law over in the UK and elsewhere.'

'Thank you. Melanie, will you kick off?'

'Where do I start? I think 'dubious inferences' is the crux of the question. Much civil law relates to ownership. Ownership of property. Ownership of rights to action. Ownership of copyright, patents, intellectual property and so on. A lot of criminal law derives more from religious canon, justifiably so. But a religious canon has no monopoly over Humanist belief, atheist belief or tribal mores. Both Humanist and atheist would, I don't doubt, have formulated fair laws similar to present Roman Law had religious sources such as the Qur'an or Old and New Testaments never existed. The moralistic aspect of the major religions compares with secular messages from the likes of Confucius, Buddha, various notable philosophers and others and has no monopolistic precedence over their

115

so called 'sacred' laws. Convenient but dubious interpretation of certain texts, merely to justify savage bloodlusts, capital punishment or man-made rules purported to have been 'received' from god,' Melanie shook her head as she sounded her disapproval with an audible cross between a sigh and a hiss, 'is the action of tyrants.

Tribal influences I'm less happy about. The Taliban and other groups such as Kurds and Indian sub-continent nations, for example, are narrowly tribalist in outlook and this is what blinkers their interpretation of the Qur'an. In fact a lot of Shariah law would appear to be influenced more by sexual urge than an impartial consideration of basic human rights, gender rights in particular. Sexual gratification. The undeclared obsession Muslim men everywhere seem to be preoccupied with. Look at the nonsense of *'Forty virgins waiting to greet the suicide bomber in Paradise',* not, the greatest mystery of all (in their book): *'Look at the prospect of meeting the very source of the mystery of creation, Allah himself'*. But even without a tribalist influence I would question the 'wisdom', in fact I would rather not use that word, let's say the 'scientific veracity' of so-called Qur'anic revelation used to justify their barbaric practices. The problem with most religions: It is possible to fabricate a plausible mythology that plays on the fears of the naïve. Mythology that poses as reality, as substance. Yes, I would support the questioner's proposal.'

'Faisal?'

'I have to challenge the first speaker's comments regarding the Holy Qur'an. In the name of God, the Lord of Mercy, the Giver of Mercy. *Alif Lam Mim.*

The Qur'an gives us the basis of Islam: justice and equality. Shariah law is determined from its wisdom. Allah has created men and women as equal but each with their prescribed responsibilities. Islam means peace. This is why Islam is the fastest growing religion in Europe of the twenty-first century.'

'I would take issue with that.' Richard's distinctive Australian accent and assertive but calmly voiced intrusion cut short Faisal's comments, 'Conferring the definition 'peace' on a label doesn't confer the truth of the claim. Proof of substance lies in its manifestation. Islam dispenses summary execution, I was going to use the phrase 'summary justice' but there is no justice, certainly not by the standards of civilised, refined behaviour accepted globally. When you watch postings on the Internet by members of ISIS and Al-Qaeda, the obscenity of their actions is only too evident in the swaggering, militaristic theatre of their performance. They are motivated by pleasure in violence and bloodlust, puerile pride in brandishing a knife or displaying possession of an AK47, to them the badges of manhood.

As adults, their immaturity reveals their lack of education, their narrow upbringing and gullibility in believing the fiction fed them at the mosques and madrasas they attend. The executioners even have the nerve to upload videos of their barbarous actions onto the media, proud in their narcissistic - because that is what it is - theatrical display of bravado, filmed 'bravely' slitting a shackled victim's throat. Evil. Primitive. Obscene.

On the other count, Islam is growing not because of doctrine superior to any other religion but because Muslim families have five, six, eight, ten or a dozen children. Growing because Western civilisation is accommodating more and more economic migrants and refugees whose countries are failing to provide them with security - economic and physical. Countries long established as predominantly Muslim and long known for levels of corruption and oppression well above those of their Christian or Jewish counterparts.'

Richard Hawken continued, 'During my time covering assignments in the Middle East, bribery, graft, achieving any kind of progress in a transaction depended on greasing palms every step of the way. So spare me the mantra that Islam is the panacea for curing all ills, the religion of justice and equality. Shariah law hasn't done a very good job of protecting its adherents, particularly fifty percent of its population, the girls and the women. Equality for them? No. Shariah law in the British Isles would mean a return to a medieval way of life. Burning witches; fear of jinns. A religion relying on a book that promotes a phenomenon such as fear of an 'evil eye' is a religion that has ignored reason and progress. It is a religion that has relegated that kind of belief to the same category as belief in fairies, pixies and goblins, magic spells and witchcraft. Such a book, at its inception centuries ago, is the equivalent of today's fake news. Oppression of those in Arab countries seeking justice and equality under the tyranny of a powerful, dynastic elite supported by a biased judiciary and a military recruited from that elite and an equally culpable, corrupt police force, is further 'sanctified' by the seal of dubious Shariah law, law derived from the texts of such a book. So, no to Shariah law.'

'Michael, your floor.'

'Without wishing to be seen as offensive, as a secular Israeli I have to challenge aspects of any religion that still, in the face of reason and scientific evidence, supports outrageous claims that verge on the ridiculous. Walking on water, as Christ is reputed to have done? Transportation to paradise on a horse, as Muhammad is reputed to have been? Who saw him go? Had the Inuit had a prophet would he have gone to heaven in a kayak or on a dog sled? No. Ridiculous.

Commentary in the Talmud, on interpretation of the Torah, is equally questionable. For example, pushing a switch on the Sabbath constitutes work. What? To me a ridiculous inference. And as for the multitude of gods in the Hindu religion where the morphology of some of their deities - a god with human body and elephant head, Ganesh. Another with two? three? pairs of arms, Vishnu -

defies anything the most extreme reaches of imagination sci-fi writers can produce,' Professor Levison shook his head in disbelief, 'the existing Hindu, Nationalist government is preaching the sacredness of such deities and appealing to the rabble-rousing, illiterate majority in its campaign against the Muslim minority. The new, techno-minded, middle-class, intellectual cadre coming along cannot, surely, believe in such gross distortions of human fabrication. I'm all for ensuring the security of a nation's population but ...,' Michael Levison shrugged in a characteristic, Jewish manner, 'the framing of law or government policy based on such nonsense, scripture or oral traditions derived from such gods is anathema to me. It's the rabble-rousing, toxic device that unfailingly appeals to a majority populace of mediocre intellect by cunning tyrants wanting to divert attention away from serious, government shortcomings.'

He continued, 'So-called sacred literature written by any man claiming divine authority, should be treated with scepticism. There are so many. I don't understand why. Over centuries, each era has thrown up a messiah who has been discredited but who has not persuaded subsequent generations to be sceptical. Authority and divinity claimed by various Roman emperors. More recently emperor Hirohito of Japan whose oaths of loyalty forced onto the suicide pilots of WWII, spawned a record of carnage at Pearl Harbour as well as their unnecessary death, for want of a description: as gullible martyrs.

Muhammad in the seventh century. The Mormon, Joseph Smith in the nineteenth century and the angel Moroni bringing him the Book of Mormon inscribed on tablets of gold - which, incidentally, no one else viewed - and all other quacks and charlatans, leaders of cults who know there is a gullible public ready to finance lucrative, global organisations of 'faith'.

American Baptists believing the creationist myths. The earth, what was it, four and a half or was it seven, thousand years old in their book? Come on, time for the media to promote common sense – no, that's wrong, common sense, so-called, is the problem. No, promote reason and scientific evidence in pushing for a denial of emotively formed attachments to un-reason, myths and magic. I've diverged, maybe but care needs to be observed when formulating any law canon. Bill, you have a viewpoint?'

'As a Jesuit I'm supposed to agree the tenets of Jesuit teaching but I am also guided by my reasoning, by unprompted thoughts just surfacing as and when. If one argues from a 'god-gave-us-a-reasoning-brain' standpoint one has to ask why we were given that faculty if it allows us to challenge revelation received from a cursive source. I know all the comfortable, establishment responses to the question, eg, Doubting Thomas in the New Testament; Job in the Old being tested by god. Various other caveats included as a crafty insurance clause, for want of an expression, in the Qur'an, where threats of hell and eternal punishment await the fate of apostates. What better imposition to place on the gullible? What better terror to subject naïve subjects of a theocratic state to? How do you combat that kind of superstition when a significant proportion of the population is semi-literate and has been conditioned, in their ignorance, to fear a whole load of pernicious indoctrination? Reasoning is either a faculty that shouldn't have been licensed to us, in which we are then capable of challenging god's wisdom or it is a faculty that has evolved as a consequence of Darwinian selection and empirical knowledge. I'm inclined to favour the latter two.'

'As a practising Muslim I find the foregoing remarks offensive. Muhammad, blessed be his name, was chosen by God to enlighten the world. It is not his opinion that is revealed in the Holy Qur'an but God's word. God chose the Prophet as his messenger. Look at the cultural degradation portrayed on television. Degradation that goes against the purity of God's laws. Is it no wonder that sexually transmitted disease, abuse and violence are so prevalent in society when drama and other kinds of entertainment would seem to portray it as the social norm? Your *Eastenders* is a typical example. Domestic abuse and physical conflict features so frequently in weekly soaps that, in real life, perpetrators are so conditioned by constant exposure to such scenes as not to consider it wrong or certainly not to see it as abnormal. The irony is they are portrayed as 'good ol' Cockney sorts, salt of the earth who wouldn't hurt a fly'. No, don't hold up proletarian, Western culture as a paradigm.'

Richard Hawken leant forward in his seat and glanced at Faisal Sayyid, 'I agree that there is a lot of lowbrow crap on television and would love to see some form of 'clean-up' implemented. Half the population, by definition, must have IQs at and above a hundred. I should have thought half or two thirds of the remainder must have an intelligence quota at or not too far below the norm so why they put up with the vacuous output demanded by the lowest ten or fifteen percent, delivered by equally vacuous comedians, celebrities and chat-show hosts, is beyond me. Comedians particularly of immigrant descendancy, sneering at our culture, denigrating, belittling our way of life when they're lucky to be here rather than the sinkholes – I use the latter word out of respect to viewers rather than a more appropriate two-syllable expletive - their forebears escaped from. Otherwise, why are they here rather than the 'Utopia' their forebears came from?

But getting back to the former comment, Islam doesn't have a monopoly on moral rectitude and who is going to be the arbiter of censorship because censorship is what we're talking about? As for Muhammad being God's messenger,' Hawken shrugged and lightly slapped both thighs, 'that's a self appointed claim written by the biographers of the Qur'an. It's almost a case of 'the premise being the conclusion' or do I mean 'the conclusion being the premise'? Anyway it's something like in the realms of circular argument.

We know there are statements in the Qur'an that are patently untrue. For example, one of the suras states 'the sun in its orbit' when we know it is the earth in orbit around the sun. So why would god, and I use that word not as a proper noun, deliberately, if he exists, mislead the man? The Muslim's prophet has got that wrong. It just confirms the narrative is the product of a man's mind. God doesn't come into it. Total nonsense.

As for violence, Islam seems to dominate the league table in that regard. Suicide bombers are totally indiscriminate in their choice of victims. Indoctrinated tools of a brutal, bigoted mindset and it's no good their referring to past excesses by the Crusaders, seven or eight hundred years ago. We've come a long way since then. By common, global consensus we have recognition of war crimes, abuse of human rights, all acknowledged by the ICC, The International Criminal Court of The Hague, all subscribed to, even if not practised by, most civilised countries.'

'Richard, I'll stop you there. It is probably an ideal time to come to the next question, concerning laws of blasphemy, since we've received a number of emails from Muslim listeners regarding same. It comes from Maria Delgado.'

'Maria?'

'Good evening. Are laws of blasphemy outdated?'

'Melanie.'

'Laws of blasphemy, by implication, anticipate that any human with an imagination, will challenge the tenets of a religion - be they scriptural, doctrinal, tradition or ritual - sometimes doing it from a sense of mischief merely to stimulate consideration of the crassness of such claims. Is this an admission that the founder, or founders of and subsequent guardians of that or those religions, are responsible for fabricating an untenable code of belief? Formulating a body of fiction that, in the light of civilised progress, does not stand up to scrutiny particularly when it carries the whiff of superstition and myth in its assertions? If anybody's god is as powerful as their holy texts claim then he doesn't need to fear the attacks of puny humans. Vengeance, there's a lovely word, seems always the ultimate prerogative of the all-powerful god who exists in their scriptures. For me, on that score, a blasphemy law is superfluous. God is perfectly capable of looking after himself – or should I say herself?

There is an issue of 'giving offence' to adherents of a particular belief, political mindset or religion. As a woman I find any religion that relegates women to a second class status, offensive. Judaism and Islam both demean my gender. By saying that am I being blasphemous because, in effect, I am challenging the so-called word of some god or certainly the various rules or protocols derived from religious texts purportedly revealed by this god?

Blasphemy means disrespect for God, with a capital G or matters of a sacred nature. I can't, on a sort of sliding scale of belief in fairies through to that in a divine creator of the universe, subscribe to a reverence for some nebulous, ethereal figment of superstition that will punish me if my thoughts and actions deviate from some man-made canon of belief. I would be interested to hear Michael's take on this.'

'I can guess where you're coming from in regard to Judaism. I'm assuming you are offended by the segregation of male and female in orthodox synagogues and the lunar, for want of a euphemism, cleansing rituals imposed on orthodox women. As a secular Israeli I fully sympathise. I can offer comment that experts and lay-public, variously, will and will not agree with. The issue of honour killing amongst the observers of primitive social protocols is, perhaps, a more serious matter that needs addressing. Those people need educating. The stoning of apostate Muslims is a vile practice in parallel with the same punishment meted out to so-called blasphemers. How you 'educate' these people, people who have been conditioned by their parents, elders, imams, I don't know, conditioned by centuries of hocus-pocus.

Superstitious people, I can't emphasise enough, are gullible, not only to ancient superstitions but to every modern 'Age of Aquarius', hippy, cult affectation that from time to time inflicts itself on society. Comets that foretell disaster? There are disasters every week, somewhere so why aren't there comets every week? Why not? One might almost suggest every pebble-sized meteorite that penetrates the Earth's atmosphere also spells a lesser disaster for some more minor event. The logic - or lack of - is just as valid. So the nonsense of associating a comet with the portent of disaster is an answer looking for a question.'

'I think Faisal has sufficient comment there to expand on before we go to the next question.'

'Thank you. Stoning of apostates is strictly defined in Islamic Law. It cannot be carried out without testimony from two honest Muslims. The Qur'an errs on the side of mercy.'

Hawken uttered a cynically audible 'Jesus' but allowed the speaker to continue.

'There are many interpretations of the book but there is only one God. Interpretations that give us Wahabbi, Sunni, Sufi and Shia followers for example. You have Catholic, Protestant, Greek Orthodox, Ashkenazi and Sephardic divisions and any number of offshoots deriving from the Judeo/Christian religions. You are no different. Your Catholic followers believe in the healing properties of relics, relics that have dubious provenance. That is tantamount to superstition. The sale of indulgences, a practice eventually seen by the Vatican as wrong but under the rule of Papal Infallibility was, at the time, sanctioned. As for blasphemy, the Qur'an does not sanction the death penalty for such.'

'I must come in there,' the camera focussed on Ignatius, 'Asia Bibi, a Roman Catholic woman, was convicted by a court in Pakistan, in 2009, of blasphemy. The charges were trumped up but that is not the point. Muslim prejudice permitted prosecution. She was on death row for eight years. When Pakistan's Supreme Court eventually overturned her conviction there was a backlash from extremist religious groups. They forced the government to reverse the decision. Are you telling me we are safe in accepting a religion like Islam with its Shariah Law and allowing it to grow and dominate in Western Civilisation? A religion where, not only in Pakistan but in probably a dozen or more Arab and African countries, excitable mobs of barely literate peasants can inflict the consequences of their medieval mindset on innocent people not of their faith. Worse, in Nigeria, those very mobs are armed kidnappers of girls and young women. Kidnapping in the name of Islam but motivated, I suspect, more by sexual lust than by religious fervour. No! I don't buy it.'

'We're getting inundated with emails, some threatening,' Robyn Fraser signalled Ignatius through his earpiece, 'just make a mention that they will be read and dealt with in a follow-up session on our radio slot.'
The session continued for the remainder of the hour.

25

'Here Cabo,' Gabriel threw the dog a small sliver of rich, Breton cheese, 'I think we must look to moving on before too long, old boy.' The dog had taken to searching him out at different times of the day, locating him from the direction of his voice or, more often, when Gabriel went to the refectory for food.

Back in the atelier Gabriel wiped the object lens and passed it to Marcel, still holding it in the small strip of linen.

'Fit it into the cylinder hard up against the shoulder. Push the annulus in to keep it in place but keep your fingers off the underside. You won't be able to remove finger marks once it's down inside the barrel.' It didn't need to be said but Gabriel took no chances.

'Now the eyepiece.'

The apprentice took the lens. A perfect fit. Gabriel smiled at the boy, 'You are a quick learner. I have been severe with you as was my time under my own master but you have excelled.'

A brief expression of pleasure flashed across Marcel's face, but he knew better than to bask in a lengthy interval of pride, 'Thank you Brother Gabriel. You have been a good and fair teacher.'

'Take the instrument. Let's see what we can spy from the bell tower. Later, before evening, we can fit it to the tripod and hope for a clear night's viewing. Our brother abbot should be invited to be first to view the sky.'

Up in the tower, resting the new telescope's end on one of the four observation walls encircling the walkway, master and apprentice surveyed the terrain beyond the town's boundary.

The young novice was thrilled with the outcome and swivelled the barrel of the instrument to and fro across arcs of observation that took in fields, birds in flight and the occasional oxcart on the highways intersecting the countryside.

Gabriel watched his young companion. The boy would make a worthy scholar. His many questions around the finer points of optics and a thirst for accounts of Gabriel's time spent in Galileo's atelier, indicated an intellect capable of a creativity beyond skill in hand and eye. The older monk felt the heritage of monastic life in the making would be safe in the hands of brothers such as Marcel. The boy was progressive in his thinking. Unbiased. Already questioning received doctrine.

'Time to get back for divine office. Are you pleased with your handiwork?'

Marcel straightened up, nodded, 'I am astounded at the capture of images so small. It must be possible to construct an instrument similar in principle to examine objects not visible to the unassisted eye.'

Gabriel smiled, 'Yes. But another time.'

*

'Brother Gabriel.'

'Yes?'

'You seem, if I may not be thought impertinent, to be preoccupied.'

Gabriel looked up from fitting a leather cross piece to a pair of ox-bone sections waiting for lenses to be fitted. He put the pieces down on the table, inter-clasped his fingers, as in submission to prayer, rested them on his tunic, across his waist and took a long breath. Over his weeks with Marcel he had developed a rapport, no, deeper than that, an understanding that his young assistant could be trusted.

'I am thinking of moving on. It is not safe for me to stay. My abbot is accusing me of heresy and there is other unintended conduct I am guilty of. He will have sent someone to search for me so I have to dwell not too long in one place.'

Marcel shook his head and hesitated before answering, 'I would travel with you but wish to complete my novitiate. Where do you expect to find refuge? You cannot run forever.'

'If I don't tell you then you cannot tell an untruth should you be questioned by any who might arrive here. I had thoughts of Paris but now consider even there unsafe. I have another destination in mind. If I leave Cabo here will you look after him?'

'Gladly.'

'Good. I am relieved. He's taken to you and he's an affectionate dog. Your vocation here is assured and you know as much now as I about lens making. Your abbot is enlightened and sympathetic to science and reason. He will be a good mentor. I would commend Italy to you should you wish to make a pilgrimage to Rome but, if you go, try to visit the university of Pisa. Galileo, since you have shown so much interest in him, was professor of mathematics there. I suspect now incarcerated somewhere for his views on the movements of planets advocated by Copernicus. Last I heard, he was up before the Inquisition and condemned by a committee of cardinals. But wherever your curiosity leads you do not go against conscience. Be informed by reason and logic which explains, without contradiction, the natural laws of divine order. I carry in my satchel the writing that is the making of my own undoing but it is a testament to truth. Truth as I believe the Holy Spirit has revealed it to me. Now, enough. I will bid you but you only, a personal farewell before leaving. You must not admit to pre-knowledge of my departure. That way you will profess but a minor sin of concealment, should you be questioned.'

'Have no fear. I trust your motives. I will miss you, we will all miss you but perhaps we will meet again.'

Gabriel picked up the assembly of bone and leather, 'Let us hope so.'

26

'Penzance.' The answer was given but in the Celtic language of Cornwall.

'Can I travel with you?' Gabriel spoke down to the brig's owner. The vessel was resting upright in the mud of the river Rance, close to Dinan. She was tied to a low, stone pillar projecting up and sandwiched between a rim of other granite stones protecting the bank   and waiting for the tide to refloat her.

A conversation of sorts carried on in the vernacular. A mix of commonly understood words in Breton and Cornish. The stored vocabulary of his earlier pilgrimage to St Michael's Mount, began to reassert itself, 'You'll have to make your own comfort down in the hold. I've been carryin' tin and I'm loadin' up with coal, wine an' Calvados from further east. There won't be much room but you're welcome as long as you can hold your stomach in a rough sea.'

'What's the tariff?'

'For you? bring food. Enough for a day, a night and another day and two salted hams as payment for passage. You'll be expected to lend a hand with the rig if the wind gets up.'

'Done. I'll be back at high tide.'

'Before that boy. I shall be castin' off as soon as she's afloat. A candle burn of two inches an' I'm away. I'm Zeke England. This here's my son Janner.'

Gabriel shook hands with both the men, 'Right. I'll be there.'

All of this was observed by Fougères who immediately hastened off to summon assistance. His search for Gabriel had paid off.

Gabriel passed two hams and a hessian sack of food down to the ship's master already preparing to embark. He hadn't paid much attention to the group of three men watching from a table under a huge plane tree. The tree fronted an auberge adjacent to the mooring. One of the men, the oldest and biggest, stood and nodded to the others. Before Gabriel could step down into the boat, he'd strode across, put the monk into a bear grip, lifted him and banged him down on the bank. Winded, Gabriel was unable to put up much resistance. A sack was forced over his head by one of the other two as the third lay across his legs.

The master of the brig started to clamber up on the gunnel of his boat.

'No you don't. This one's wanted for heresy. So keep the hams and mind your counsel, you and your crew or I'll summon the watch.'

Wind and salt-burned, hardened to the worst of what weather or man could throw at him, the captain wasn't having any of this. Shouting to a crew member to untie, he grabbed a belay pin to use as a cudgel and led two other members up onto the quay.

'Right, which of you spalpeens want a taste of this?'
He advanced on the three men who now backed off,
snatched the sack from Gabriel's head and instructed the
monk to leap aboard. Zeke backed up to the edge of the
bank and glanced sideways, down at the boundary stones
protecting the bank. Sure of his footing, he twisted round
and jumped onto the deck.

The brig, freed from its mooring, slewed out into
the river, aided by a push from a stout, ten foot boat hook.

'Get yourself down below. That motley lot won't
give up easy.'
A favourable wind took the brig up towards the estuary.
Not far from Dinan a crowd had gathered on both sides of
the river.

'Don't like the look of that.' Zeke spoke to his son.
'You and the rest slacken the main reef, I'll take tiller.
There's a chain across. That mob have got ahead on
horseback and called the watch I reckon.'

The brig, sails lowered, continued a short distance,
halted and started to reverse under the incoming current.
By this time Gabriel had registered the change in motion
and appeared on deck.

A spokesman from the crowd shouted across, 'Give
up the monk and you'll be afforded safe passage.'

'No fear. You are obstructing right of passage.'

'And you are in no position to argue. Give up the
monk.'

Gabriel turned to Zeke, 'This is not your fight. I thank you for your support but put me ashore. I will take the consequences. I cannot have your wellbeing and that of your crew on my conscience. Go on. Do as I ask. I have no fear.'

Zeke could see the situation was dire and knew his responsibility for the crew, over that towards Gabriel, was his priority. He signalled compliance, guided the boat to the side, shook hands with Gabriel and helped him up onto the gunnel.

Hands stretched forward to grab the monk. The chain was released and the brig freed to continue on its journey back to its home port of Padstow, on the Camel estuary.

27

'Now we're somewhere like ship shape would you like to invite Mike and Rose for dinner? They could stay the night.'

'Good idea. Stephen Bokowski phoned today. He's over for a few days with Judith. Needs to check out a few issues and sign some documents. What say we invite them too? It would be interesting to see how Judith and Rose react to each other.'

"You can't resist a skirmish can you? But it would make for a lively mix. We can put Mike and Rose in the guest bedroom. It's a fair drive back and if they've had wine they won't do that and Bokowski will expect to stay too, I would guess.'

'We could put them in our room. We could bed down on the air mattress in the small room.'

'Settled then. I'll sound out Mike and we'll fix a day.'

*

The four piled out of Mike's Discovery. Stephen Bokowski had hired a chauffeur-driven car for his stay in Dublin but elected to travel to Rocky Valley with Mike and his wife. Ignatius introduced Penny to Stephen and Judith, picked up the overnight bags and led the group into the house to wait whilst Mike parked his car alongside Ignatius's vehicle.

'Enjoyed the drive here. Some great scenery this side of Dublin,' Judith Bokowski addressed the other four, 'can see why you've chosen to move this way. Saw a bit of it when I was here working but didn't get down this far.'

'Yes. Bill and I fell in love with the area as soon as we came to see the house. If you haven't got to rush back we can go for a drive into the Wicklows tomorrow. Weather's supposed to be fine. Anyway, we can fix that later and as the 'boys' want to talk business, it'll give them time on their own in the library. No interruptions. Dinner's at seven thirty. Drinks at seven.'

Mike returned. Ignatius grabbed Rose's overnight bag, 'Follow me up and I'll show you your rooms.'

'So, your first broadcast was a success. Good reviews.'

'Yes, but we got flak from the, how shall I put it? from naive, liberal, left-wing elements. The woke mob that can't see society is, little by little, being debased by a tide of vacuous comment, low-brow, public entertainment, insidious religious influences and all the LGBTQ crowd and the gender lobby mob. Too many people, I've said it elsewhere, who like to dismiss valid concerns by attaching the label phobia to issues they don't agree with. Issues that need to be confronted.'

'Like what?'

'Well, accusations of xenophobia from minorities. Minorities who ridicule claims by the indigenous population that their jobs will be taken; claims that the situation is exaggerated, that jobs are not being taken. Enoch Powell was vilified for saying it but it is happening.

No one can be justified in assuming it's false news, just take account of the number of positions openly held in posts of authority. Numerous lucrative positions in the BBC, for example, presenters and commentators, talk-show hosts – it's self-evident, if you want proof just switch on your TV - non-native politicians holding ministerial jobs, voted in by an increasing, alien population who should, historically, have never been given a franchise. It seems to me half of India is governing our country – Home Office, Foreign Office, Prime Minister. Positions that white, Anglo-Saxon or Celtic candidates should be holding and who are well qualified to hold but who are passed over as a result of earlier, government, affirmative, inclusion policies. God knows what insidious influences are being brought into play favouring Indian nationalist interests, financial sleight of hand subsidising financial bailouts to the tune of tens of millions of pounds here of dynasties accused of corruption in South Africa and elsewhere.

These minorities aren't the originators, visionaries and entrepreneurs who, over centuries, created the theatres of opportunity that provided those jobs. Originators who built a civilised Western Culture whilst ancestors of those minorities were still living in squalor somewhere else on the globe and whose descendants still are.

In fact one recent investigation discovered that forty four percent of candidates selected for a BBC post was biased in favour of minorities merely to satisfy pressure from the woke community. But they're now presuming some sense of entitlement, some expectation of rights to the birthright, so to speak, of the native population. Worse, indigenous woke supporters are banging the drum in their favour. They're a minority with a loud voice and influence out of all proportion to their number in certain media channels.'

'Yes but if a non-native candidate is better qualified, shouldn't they be awarded the post? You want the most competent person available to do the job.'

'I understand your point, Judith but in a clutch of applicants there is bound to be an indigenous applicant who won't be that far from satisfying the requirements of a suitable candidate. Outside of the specific, operational skills demanded of a particular job, any appointment is also going to depend on a subjective appraisal of competing applicants. Surely a suitable, short-listed, native candidate is going to emerge from, literally, the hundreds who are eligible. Some graduate with a mountain of university fees to repay.'

'I'm staggered, I don't disagree with you but I'm staggered that you hold an opinion that is in total opposition to your original vocation.'

'Well, it's almost in the category of insight, if we're going down that road. Insight prompted by experience rather than prejudice. It's not some populist, bigoted reaction, some knee-jerk response to social or political policy. I've seen too much of the evil side of human nature, as a priest. I've become sceptical - not cynical - although I have to admit to making comments that verge on the cynical, sometimes.

No. Compassion needs to reflect the cost to those equally worthy of assistance but denied it by the very government they've paid their taxes to. Overseas aid, for example. I know all the arguments that justify such largesse but we're using taxpayers' money to assist other countries - not always in the field of alleviating poverty but on show-case, infrastructure projects. Aid not always being used for the intended purpose but being surreptitiously siphoned off into illegal, overseas bank accounts despite procedures in place to ensure that doesn't happen. But try justifying that to a homeless family here living in squalid conditions, which desperately needs a decent house over its head only to see some illegal boat immigrant treated to hotel accommodation. Or have waited too late for hospital treatment only to die because equipment is not available or worse, broken and awaiting repair because funds have gone elsewhere.'

'We've debated these issues for decades now,' Mike looked across at Stephen and Judith, 'but it's got to the stage where right-wing Populism is beginning to become acceptable in social strata where it was once denigrated. People's fears are justified. They are tangible. They are not imaginary phobias.'

'I'll give you that. But with close relatives and friends whose parents were Holocaust victims, I can't warm to the present mood that is giving it a voice. Having said that I wouldn't block it as one of Bill's next *Polemic* topics.'

Freshly charged glasses brought a brief pause.

'Populism or no Populism, demand for amenities, to service the floods of refugees and immigrants wanting a slice of an increasingly diminishing Western cake, is alarming even the most compassionate of viewers watching skirmishes reported at European borders,' Rose shook her head, 'why can't the UN sort out the causes that lead to these problems? Surely a neutral, international force with armed powers of compulsion, freed from any risk of legal suit, can be assembled to compel governments, particularly dictators, to take remedial action. It should be possible for a fifty one percent vote, with no waiving veto, to sanction action. A case in point is President Assad. The bloodshed in Syria over appeals for democracy might then have been averted and the resulting refugee problem avoided.'

'Easier said than done. You'll still get your rebel factions attempting to gain power. How're you going to identify the source of and stop the flow of arms to these groups? and how're you going to decide which group takes over as a new government?'

'What do you do for relaxation?' Judith decided a change of subject was merited as she looked at Mike, 'Provost of Trinity must make for some quite stressful demands.'

'I fish. Some good salmon rivers here in the Republic. Once a year I go to a fishing lodge, for a week, up in Connemara. Rose takes a couple of good books and a tapestry to work on and we also do a walk or two.'

'But you don't fish all year round.'

'I enjoy doing the occasional water colour but Trinity takes up a lot of my time. Not all work. Now and again there's a faculty dinner or some other function in the city. They're enjoyable and foreign visits, not too often, maybe once or twice a year, to continental universities where there's some kind of exchange going on.'

'Well everybody, breakfast at eight tomorrow.' Ignatius pushed back his chair. The later part of the evening had seen everyone mellow and ready for sleep. 'If Penny is running you out into the Wicklows,' he spoke to Judith, 'it'll pay you to get away early and come back for a late lunch. I'll stay here to see Mike and Rose off. Mike has to get back to organise some material for a meeting on Monday. It'll give Stephen and me time to sort out some business before lunch.'

28

The library was more a gallery than a book repository. Penny had installed a few low tables displaying various pieces ranging from modern, African bronzes to Inuit, soapstone carvings all collected during her travels rather than from local, English dealers. Ancient navigational and other aids collected by Ignatius, over the years, ranged along a broad shelf at chest height. The pieces, mainly ship's compasses, theodolites, sextants and astrolabes, sported a fair element of weathered brass.

'That's an interesting piece. May I?'

'Go ahead.'

Stephen Bokowski lifted the astrolabe from its mahogany display base.

'Picked it up in South Africa. Portuguese. Fifteenth century or thereabouts. Not many of them about but not exactly rare, either.'

'The detail's precise. Engraving fine. My grandfather was a maker of scientific instruments. Had his own setup. I've got some of his tools, his drawing board and tee-square and a number of technical drawings of the stuff he made but no actual instruments. Used a lot of brass.' Bokowski put it back.

'You appreciate engineering precision.'

'Yes. Because of him I went for an engineering degree at the Hebrew University. In these days of computer aided design, engineers aren't exposed to the pleasure of taping a sheet of detail paper onto a board, sharpening a 2H Staedtler pencil and constructing an accurate scheme of whatever piece forms the next component in the assembly they're designing.'

'Said with feeling.'

'Too true. I was fascinated by the novelty of watching him, seeing engineering drawings done in the flesh, so to speak. There's something engaging about a hand-drawn image that modern graphic design doesn't convey. Something conveying experience, insight, skill, human creativity. A feel for metal. Our perception has been blunted by the deluge of colour magazine and television images we're exposed to. So many created by software. So many accompanied by a blitzkrieg of noise - I won't dignify it with the word music - blasting our senses into a state of numbness.'

Ignatius picked up the astrolabe by its hinged link, 'It has a nice feel to it. I always imagine some mariner, some master of a trading vessel dangling it between his thumb and fingers. Raising it. Doing a latitude measurement. Sighting up on a clear night, fixing on the Pole Star, his second in command holding a lantern alongside.'

He handed it to Stephen, 'Here. Take it. It's yours to enjoy. Particularly to conjure up memories of your grandfather whenever you look at it.'

'No. I can't possibly take it.'

'I insist. It'll give me a lot of pleasure to know it's appreciated by someone with a feel, an empathy for the skill and calculation which went into its design and manufacture.'

Bowkowski took the solid little assembly of plates, pointed it at a lamp hanging from the ceiling and centred the pointer on it, 'Fifty three degrees. That's a coincidence. Can't be far off the latitude of where we are at the moment. Thank you. I'll treasure it. I'll keep it on this setting. It'll remind me of my visit.'

'Take the base as well.'

'Thank you. I know exactly where I want to display it. The base will blend in with Judith's idea of balance. She's a bit of a feng-shui advocate.' Stephen put the two objects back on the shelf, then held still for a few seconds, staring unfocused on some undefined point lower down the wall, 'Look, I'm glad the others have gone. There are one or two things I wanted to talk about which can't be risked in an email.'

Ignatius pulled his mind back into sharper mode. Bokowski's tone signified a measure of trust in what he was about to say but Ignatius was unprepared for what came. He was expecting some disclosure of financial risk or some other issue to do with big corporation politics.

'Your designs for the property have attracted the interest of the IRA.'

'Who told you that? I've had a visit from a couple of, let's say, entrepreneurs who pretty certainly have IRA connections but it hasn't been overtly declared.'

146

'I can't say. But you will have your own answer to that and won't be far wrong in associating my time in the Israeli Defence Force, the IDF, with other organizations connected with it.'

'Mossad?'

Bokowski just smiled, briefly.

'So what's the significance, since you appear to know more about my affairs than I do?'

'Palestinian links with the same weapons manufacturers that provided the IRA with kit.'

'Well, I can't exactly not sympathise with the problems the Palestinians are experiencing over colonisation of the Left Bank but you know I understand the motives behind Jewish immigration and don't oppose Israel's defence of that right.'

'It's not the IRA, per se, we're interested in. It's the weapons suppliers we want to infiltrate or, rather, their communication links. Their network of global servers. What goes to the IRA can also find its way to other terrorist groups.'

'I can't see how my connection with the two who turned up will achieve that and we haven't actually engaged them yet, anyway. Although it's pretty certain I'll have to.'

'What I thought. It's a long shot but if you establish an email link with them and let me know, we have IT specialists able to navigate undetected through to various sources even your two men aren't aware of.'

Ignatius felt his neck and stretched his chin upwards at the same time, 'Can't see a problem with that, if it's true. But if you know so much already why aren't you able to bypass me and establish the link yourself, through your IT specialists?'

'We can but I need a seemingly innocent link through a source unconnected with Israel. That's you. Also, if the hack is subsequently discovered and they close it down, it'll be too late for them anyway. We will have achieved discovery of at least one or more pieces of intel and your IRA contact will be regarded as an innocently duped mule by the terrorists.'

But it was not the IRA, the Palestinians or the weapons manufacturers Bokowski was interested in. A bigger, worldwide organisation was his target. Mossad had, long since, infiltrated numerous channels, suppliers and chains of command backing most of the Arab world. No, it was true, Bokowski needed access through a neutral network of servers unconnected with any Israeli influence. But it was not Hezbollah or any of the ISIS offshoots he was interested in, it was the Vatican. Ignatius's connection to Vatican intrigue, through the bona fide Jesuit Order, was his target. It was a devious move but in his mind, justifiable.

He, like many at political level, was exasperated that significant sums of money were being generated from tourists in Israel, at holy sites belonging to the Vatican. This income was not declared to revenue and taxation ministries overseen by Knesset authorities. Also, hotels and shops belonging to churches and schools - particularly the yeshivas belonging to the Ultra Orthodox Haredim - were exempt from tax and putting the burden of state funding on the rest of a secularly-minded, Israeli population. The former numbered fewer than fifteen percent of the ten million or so inhabiting this biblical land and contributed even less in terms of gross, domestic product.

The Haredim lived as a separate community where men were encouraged by rabbinical leaders to devote themselves to studying Torah - the sacred Jewish scriptures - at *yeshiva* seminaries, instead of working. Their young men were also exempt from compulsory, military conscription. This generated further resentment. They drew a lifelong monthly stipend for attendance at such seminaries, small but nonetheless a drain on revenue. As a political force, the minority Haredim exerted a powerful, unbalanced influence in the state parliament. They pushed for restrictions on all Israeli, public life. Restrictions based on extreme interpretation - or misinterpretation, rather - of biblical passages, accompanied by demands not incomparable with those of extremist Muslims pushing for distortions of Qur'anic text.

'Well, I'll have to depend on you to deal with it. I'll be too tied up here at the university to facilitate any kind of action. Just make sure I'm not landed with a can of worms. I'm already persona non grata with some of the hierarchy.'

'No problem. The whole exercise will be seen as yet another exploitation of an innocent by an untraceable hacker if or when it is detected.'

Ignatius kept quiet but was not convinced.

29

Gabriel was taken, trussed, in a cart, back to the abbaye. The abbot helped the captive monk down from the cart and untied his hands leaving the rope around his neck in place. Cabo came from the kitchen, attracted by the noise and activity. The dog's excitement, on catching sight of his old friend, was accompanied by canine shrieks of joy and a mad display of jumps and runs around the inner courtyard.

Francesco Fougères' slovenly appearance and shallow manner had not impressed the head of the monastery. Fougères, displeased with the lack of hostility shown by Father Pascal Bezier towards Gabriel, slapped the undefended monk across the back of the head. The blow was heavy. Gabriel stumbled and fell onto hands and knees.

'Stay there you heretic.' All Fougères' latent rage expressed itself in a display of vindictiveness. Struggling to kneel, Gabriel was given a shove in the small of his back, sending the monk onto his face. Fougères, raising a sandaled foot, was about to stamp on the figure stretched in front of him.

'That's enough of that,' Pascal Bezier shouted at Fougères but hadn't reckoned with the dog's intervention.

Cabo's pack instincts were triggered. As the monk steadied his balance, at the point of delivering the kick, the dog leapt in and sank teeth into the gout-ridden ankle of his master's assailant. Fougères screamed. The dog let go then leapt for the monk's face. Before he could be stopped his teeth had torn loose a sizeable chunk of cheek and jowl, exposing raw jaw bone.

Marcel, watching all this, rushed in and grabbed Cabo by the loose skin at the back of the dog's neck. He managed to subdue the animal whilst other monks dealt with the heavily bleeding monk. Another assisted Gabriel to his feet.

The abbot signalled, with a slight head movement towards Gabriel but with eyes on Marcel. The signal, a nod in the direction of the living quarters, conveyed an unspoken request to follow, bringing Gabriel. The three, accompanied by Cabo, made their way to the dormitory.

'You will stay here for the duration. But have no fear. I have leanings towards the convictions of our German brother, Luther. There is a way out of this I am sure.'

'I hope so, Father Bezier.'

The abbot unlocked the door of a secure cell.

'You will be provided with the comforts of a welcomed visitor. The dog had better stay here with you. I do not blame him for Fougères' misfortune. I do not like the man. He is not one of us.' Like Marcel, he had taken a fatherly liking to the renegade monk during his sojourn at the abbaye and was disgusted with the violence shown by his Finisterre brother, Francesco. Cabo trotted into the cell, tail wagging.

Fougères was carried moaning to the infirmary and put to sit in a specially constructed wooden chair used for dental examinations. The apothecary in charge of treating sick brothers was also the resident surgeon. He did his best to disinfect the wound before attempting to administer a measure of archanum, a form of laudanum, an opium based tincture. Some of the medicine went down the monk's throat but the remainder oozed through the gap between torn tissue and bone. Blood and tincture coalesced to form rivulets of mucus-like fluid. These seeped down Fougères' neck to form a sticky ridge on the folds of his habit.

The surgeon left his patient and went to a cupboard. Taking a small chest from it, he extracted a needle and length of catgut made from sheep's intestine. He nodded to the brother assisting him. It was an unspoken instruction, born of long association, to get ready to restrain the injured patient.

Fougères eyed the needle. He had, with sadistic pleasure, watched various acts of surgery performed on others at his uncle's monastery. Now it was his turn. The pain killer, he could feel, had not dulled his senses. Anxiety turned to fear and he urinated into the thick material that formed the skirt of his habit. The brother assisting the surgeon took up a position behind the chair and held the top of the tonsured head in both hands.

'Hold still.'

The needle had plenty of flesh to penetrate on one edge of the cheek but little left, at the ragged edge of jaw bone, with which to join the flap. Fougères let out a garbled screech, choking on a residue of blood that had collected in his mouth and seeped into his throat. The surgeon had witnessed the injured monk's behaviour towards de Tregor. Having benefitted from Gabriel's skill in making spectacles, he felt no sympathy for the pain experienced by his patient. His only concession was to mop up some of the blood freshly seeping from the wound. The sutures of catgut were placed, if not with a lack of skill, certainly not with care over any long term scar that would result.

Face repaired, the surgeon turned his attention to the swollen ankle. He could not suppress a smile as the puncture marks in the flesh showed, with a kind of graphic intention, the symmetrical pattern left by the rows of teeth, once the flesh was cleaned.

'I am going to dress this wound with a poultice. You will need to rest the leg for a few days so that means staying here in the infirmary. Your face will give you pain. I can only prescribe tincture of opium. Both wounds, your face and leg, will need daily cleansing with sour wine and powdered kelp. You should partake only of broth for five days and five nights. And no wine.'

Fougères grunted. The pain from torn nerves in his face suppressed any sensation of throbbing in his leg. Bacteria, from Cabo's teeth, were already colonising the mass of tissue surrounding the wounds. But a more deadly colony was migrating into his bloodstream. The rabies virus.

His incarceration in the infirmary did not stop him requesting paper, quill and ink. A letter to Cardinal Rochefoucauld, at the time resident in Paris, requested his attendance at a trial of 'the heretic', Gabriel de Tregor. The venue, the monastery at Rennes. Accompanying the letter, the original script retrieved from Gabriel's satchel. Francesco Fougères had deliberately chosen to bypass his uncle's monastery, expecting to curry favour with a more eminent authority and a chance of further advancement in the Augustinian Order.

As the infection from the bacteria started suppurating, the fever, that was now raging, masked any rabies symptoms. The infected monk became delirious and incoherent.

30

'Hello. We're back.' Penny called through from the hallway.

'We're in the kitchen.'

The two women made their way to the back of the house.

'How'd you get on? Expect you're dying for a cup of tea.'

'Penny took us to a nice little tea house, on the way back but I think we're expecting something a bit stronger.'

'So what do you think of the Wicklows?'

'Beautiful. Stephen, we should think of finding a place here.'

Stephen grinned at Ignatius, 'She falls in love with anywhere there are mountains.'

'Well, I'm glad she likes our 'backyard'. It must be a refreshing change from ...'

'You mean the 'sand and rocks' of Palestine.' Stephen Bokowski cut in on Ignatius.

'Well, I wasn't going to be as rude as that but I thought it.'

'No, you have a point. That's why I spend a lot of my time elsewhere. It's good to go back there from time to time, to remind me of my roots but the world's a big place.'

'Right then, back to drinks. Gin and tonic? Wine?'

'We were thinking Champagne. One of the bottles Stephen brought. It can chill whilst we have a shower.'

*

'You know,' Judith waved her glass around the living room, 'this doesn't need much alteration. What you were suggesting on the way back, I can see, would make it ideal as a formal reception room if the studio is designed more as a den. What d'you think Stephen? That window removed and replaced by a door into an enclosed, glass walkway to the studio.'

'If that's what they intend, seems a good idea to me. But why the covered walkway? It's only a tennis court's length to where you say you'll site the studio.'

Ignatius looked at Penny, hesitated whether to fabricate a reason but then thought the truth an easier option.

'Our IRA contact, for want of a title. His suggestion.'

'Yes and I'm not happy about it.' Penny frowned as she faced Stephen and Judith.

'So why then?'

'Complicated. They would only want to make use of it, if at all, for infrequent meetings and screened so the glass sides would need to be frosted. They know I practise as a priest.'

'So what?'

'Well, the Roman Catholic Church in Ireland, how can I put it delicately? is not known to be unsympathetic to the Fenian cause and, as such, any priest of Republican domicile is expected to lean that way, for want of an answer. Not all do, of course but a number hail from families with hostility towards Westminster.'

Each one, briefly, reflected on Ignatius's comment and tried to figure where his sympathies lay.

Stephen broke the silence, 'It could be to your advantage.'

'How'd you mean?'

'You could have the property bugged. Pick up some useful intel.'

'Risky.'

'Just suggesting.'

'God, this is getting into the realms of fantasy. I'm not living here under those sorts of conditions.' Penny slammed her glass down onto the coffee table.

'It won't come to that.'

'It bloody, better not. As it is, it's one thing to give shelter to unknown people quite another to start an espionage ring. We'd, surely, be putting our lives at risk.'

Judith laughed, 'Rather exciting, I'd say. There's always an 'escape' clause' somewhere, for want of an answer.'

Ignatius, until now accommodating and tolerant, asserted some kind of ownership of the situation, 'Whatever the outcome is, we're having a studio and it will be to our taste, under our control and under our ownership.'

The character that had inspired a pope to confer the status of cardinal on this Jesuit was the character that now asserted command of the direction and ownership of the conversation.

'I can dictate terms without relinquishing goodwill. The IRA is still superstitious enough, in a Catholic kind of way, to fear upsetting the church with a capital C. Subject closed.'

The other three chastened, to a greater or lesser degree by his words, sensed a lack of anger projected by Ignatius but with equal insight, recognised their obligation not to trespass, not to assume an entitlement to further opinion they didn't merit.

'Let's change the subject. Time for a refill.'

'I was fascinated by your choice of title for the first *Polemic* programme. What are we getting for the remainder of the series? I gather a number of critics are pleased with the non-PC aspect of the debate.'

'Well, the right wing element is but the left-wing intellectuals, for want of a description, are hostile. They're anti-establishment. Anti the media barons, anti anything that isn't in blind thrall to woke culture. We have a policy of selecting panel members, where we can, who are in positions not vulnerable to cancel culture.'

'Organizations need to be more bloody stubborn against that kind of blackmail.' Penny spoke with a glare and a frown.

'Your next one,' Stephen interjected, 'is *Immigration,* isn't it? That'll raise some hackles.'

'It'll be controversial, that's for sure,' Judith shook her head, 'too many plausible arguments for and against. Sometimes the price is high but, in the long term, worth paying.'

Penny waved her free hand quizzically, 'Price high? Like what?'

'Putting a curb on it, creating a dearth, a shortage of cheap labour in your country to service care homes, the NHS and other low-paid work.'

'You can't exactly say the NHS is low-paid work. It's on a par with the teaching profession. Where do you draw the line? Are you suggesting an unqualified, third world cleaner or care assistant in a hospital should be paid the same as a nurse who has spent three, I dunno, five years training?'

'There will always be a teacher and a nurse in any of your audiences or, at least, someone closely related to either or both even, who would argue nursing and teaching can't be compared. Shift work for a start.'

'True. But both professions, rightly or wrongly, have comparable rating in the public's eyes. Both have their share of stress-related illnesses. Both their share of members leaving the profession for different reasons, maybe but the net result is the same. The police could also merit the same rating. There are vast differences in aspects of the training in each of the three. We know that. Undeniable but there is also an overall, structural similarity in their makeup. They're all civil servants of a sort just like Bill at Trinity and all the other lecturers. But immigration covers illegal entry by economic migrants. There should be some kind of immediate, unchallengeable, repatriation mechanism. Repatriation protected from woke protocols that clog up the appeals system or from demonstrators gluing themselves to roads outside airports, preventing criminals being flown back to the Caribbean, for example. Protestors crying 'racism' or some other variant of hate speech.

But that raises another aspect: hate speech doesn't discriminate between what is instinctive and what is malevolent. I find obese people obscene. Some, I know, are so because of some medical condition but only a tiny fraction. Those I can sympathise with and accommodate but I find certain societies which place a high premium on surplus flesh or which manifest physical characteristics peculiar to their racial strain, similarly repulsive.'

'You can't condemn someone for a physical trait which is characteristic of their race. That's totally unreasonable.'

'Yes, I can't argue against that but I also can't ignore my physical reaction to what I instinctively find repulsive. Sometimes to the point where I actually want to vomit. What can I do about it? All I know is it's totally instinctive, a Pavlovian response almost. One day at a restaurant a woman swept past our table, her skirt barely covered her enormous buttocks. She had folds of fat hanging from her thighs. I had to push my food away from me. Couldn't face another forkful. I actually gagged. Just managed to prevent myself from throwing up. I'm not exaggerating.'

'I sympathise with that but no one can help their 'racial strain' as you put it. Obesity doesn't discriminate on a racial basis. White, black, brown, yellow, they all have their share.'

'Maybe but why should I deny it? It's also an aesthetic thing in the same way I am repulsed by some works of art, some of Francis Bacon's or Freud's work, for example and that has nothing to do with hate speech. The fact that an involuntary reaction might have a racial context, in a certain instance, is an accident of circumstance not premeditated malevolence.'

'I'm not sure that argument would stand up in a court of law. Anybody could argue, if accused of hate speech, that they can't help their feelings.'

'There's a difference between experiencing an involuntary reaction to a phenomenon, giving sincerely held, innocent expression to that feeling such that it gives unintended offence as opposed to deliberately uttered, hate-filled provocation. Don't you agree Bill? I'm not condoning racial attacks. I'm expressing an emotional view, if emotional's the correct word. Maybe I should state it another way and say expressing my distress at what I perceive as happening to my world. A reaction to unwelcome symbols and alien practices invading my cultural space. In fact, what I am is a culturalist, not a racist. I am beginning to have a sense of Western Civilisation being swamped by invasive, lowbrow, cultures. Noise from the latest concession to BLM inclusivity, emanating from some pop artist, being passed off as singing. Flattering rappers by according them the status of poetic genius. If I were a less robust individual I think I would succumb to some kind of self-destructive mental state, some kind of depressive illness.' Penny gave an exasperated sigh and sank back against her chair.

'Interesting you should say, 'gives offence' rather than, 'given in an offensive way', Bill turned to Judith, 'an ocean of difference in meaning. What might be totally inoffensive to one person might be objectionable to another. In the first *Polemic* programme any critical comment on perceived inaccuracies in the Qur'an, by any one of the atheists, would not be seen as objectionable by the speaker but to a Muslim unwilling to test the claim against verifiable evidence, it might. But why should an atheist refrain from expressing a logically held, reasoned opinion merely because it might give offence?'

''Logically held'' is the operative phrase. We're back to opinion as opposed to reasoned, scientific fact. Back to exactly the same kind of reasoned arguments that we had in the first programme and the religious contentions that bedevil the Knesset in my own country.'

'What I don't understand,' Judith opened her hands with a typically Jewish shrug, 'is why so many, in fact all the people I mix with and other random groups across all strata of society, don't have a voice when it comes to concerns about the Islamisation of Europe. It seems to me that the BBC and other media organisations are dominated by a minority who do not see the threat it poses to human rights and civil liberties. There are a few, new, TV channels beginning to champion those viewpoints but, so far, precious few. But what annoys me more than anything is the label phobia attached to Islam, Islamaphobia. It's not a phobia it's a threat just in the same way we were discussing issues previously. The word is being used to dismiss a phenomenon which is an insidious growth in Western civilisation. Used to belittle anyone giving voice to their concerns by implying they are neurotic, racist or xenophobic – there again, use of the word. We've been burdened with a recent slough of legislation, of ill thought-out laws that have introduced more problems than they set out to solve. Laws that give protection to evil.'

'True. I find the same,' Penny nodded, 'the people in the village where my parents live all voice the same concerns. Too many illegal migrants from Eastern Europe, North Africa, the Middle East and the Indian sub-continent. We can't forever keep choking our cities with more and more of these people. As they predominate so they become more and more proprietorial, more and more demanding. When you pass through security now at major airports you are increasingly subject to baggage searches by foreign security personnel with a hostile, vindictive attitude. By staff for whom it is obvious one is of indigenous origin and at eighty plus, as my parents are, so obviously non-terrorist as to present no threat to anybody. By more and more foreign Border Control officers and other staff, foreign for god's sake, controlling me coming back into my own country.

The last Labour government facilitated any number of socialist measures that sent taxpayers' money abroad to dependant families. This Conservative government is little better in a different way. Offering visas to 300,000 Hong Kong Chinese because they own some kind of British Passport and easing entry restrictions to god knows how many Indian nationals and their dependants merely to enhance commerce. It was because of commerce we got landed with slavery and god knows how many Windrush immigrants and their gang-culture offspring engaging in knife crimes and drive-by shootings, county line drug dealing and who knows what? And another thing which goes unreported in the press is the epidemic of gang rape being carried out by these gangs of black youths and others, against under-age girls. Girls who report it but are afraid to testify in court, their parents likewise, because of fear of further, physical violence. Limp, liberal do-gooders try to down play such stories for the sake of Political Correctness. They can argue these boys are criminal because they are denied opportunities open to their white counterparts. But that ignores the fact of the overwhelming numbers who are offspring of multiple fathers impregnating one, single woman. Absent fathers not present to act as a control or as suitable mentors when they themselves are a product of the same, promiscuous cycle. It has to be acknowledged. You can shout, 'Hate speech, hate crime, racist,' as much as you like but it's a depressing feature of black culture - black tribalism might be a better description.

We need to concentrate on SMET and direct it into entrepreneurial channels and not this shopkeeper mentality – selling cheap stuff made by China, Pakistan or India. People talk, disdainfully, about the Industrial Revolution as though it was carried out by men in blue overalls with an oily rag in one hand and an oilcan in the other. No. Our technical prowess developed over the decades from really brilliant engineers and designers with scientific insight and analytical skills in mathematics. Men who understood what the likes of Newton, Leonardo da Vinci, Euler and Bernoulli were all about.'

'What's SMET?'

'Science, Mathematics, Engineering and Technology. For too long we've relied on politicians with arts and humanities degrees dictating policy. Although, having said that, Margaret Thatcher, with a chemistry degree from Oxford, pushed questionable policies or, at least, listened to management gurus who advised her on trade and finance without considering manufacture and industry. And that 'ambassador', for want of a word, who fronted trade delegations and used it to further his other interests, spent taxpayers' money on his overseas jaunts

166

leaving us with dubious gain … .' Penny shook her head, closing her eyes in an expression of exasperation. 'I think I've vented my frustrations. Time for me to get going in the kitchen. I'm starving.'

31

Ignatius picked up the phone, 'Hello Robyn.'

'Hi Bill. We've received intel from MI5. It seems there is a cell advocating storming the next programme. They've picked up messages on social media that hint at disruption. 'Hint' is rather understated.'

'Any idea of the mode of attack?'

'Well, to complicate matters there's also a separate, totally unrelated group they're more concerned about.'

'Don't tell me. One's to do with immigration and non-violent. Am I right? And the other further threats from Islamic sources. Yes?'

'Near enough.'

'The civil liberties group *Beacon* is pissed off over further, intended deportations of criminals back to the Caribbean and anticipates biased support for The Home Office and CPS from whatever panel we've selected for the immigration debate.'

'Security should be able to handle any interference from them but what's the picture with the Islamic crowd? They're the more sinister mob. I wouldn't put it past them using suicide bombing tactics. Security isn't equipped to cope with a bomber turning up at their check point.'

'MI5 liaise with the HO, the FO and their Irish counterparts. They propose putting armed officers in the vicinity of FONT's premises.'

'OK. So what are you expecting from me?'

'Nothing. But you needed to know the present score. I'll deal with MI5 and advise FONT to notify members of the panel that there is a security risk. I'll get 'legal' to do that. That'll eliminate one aspect of any potential action against FONT for non-disclosure of risk, separate, of course, from normal insurance liability. We have the usual substitute choices should any one of the nominated panel pulls out.'

'Right. Thanks for letting me know. I don't think any of the selected panel will back out but we're covered. So that's fine. What about the audience? We've got all their contact details on file – no loopholes?'

'Yes. They'll be asked to sign a statement to the effect they have been informed of the risk. As far as we know, none of them are members of *Beacon*. All of them have been scrutinised, vetted as suitable for audience participation. I've taken the precaution of hiring two of my ex-Marine colleagues on floor security. We can't really do much more.'

'Good. See you then when we take the platform.' Ignatius made a mental note to arrive earlier to FONT to try to get some idea of how the covert, armed security detail might be deployed. 'Hang on, sorry, before you put the phone down, what's the position on the next topic?'

'Panel choices?'

'Yes.'

'We've got Professor John Baltry, Imperial, on the chemical aspects of Lithium. Michael Roberts from the

Vehicle Manufacturers Association. Sarah Constantine from one of the Green constituencies – South West England, fiery. We're waiting a reply from Amilie Foxx from the CBI. Should be a broad enough mix but I'm wondering if we shouldn't go back to our original title of *Transport 2030* instead of *Electrification.* I know we debated the wider aspects of energy use and generation at the time but it's occurred to me that the hybrid topic of sail and propeller propulsion is worth expanding. What d'you think? It'll provide a balance against controversy when disposal of lithium car batteries is aired, as it's sure to be.'

'I get your drift. It's been niggling at the back of my mind every so often. The wider topic of energy generation – hydrogen, gravity for example. Everybody's fixated on wind and solar. Let's stick with our original decision, see how the discussion develops and consider a further programme linked to the topic, at a later date. We won't have to issue a flurry of emails to researchers and admin then, saying we've changed our minds.'

'Fine. That's all. I'll get back to you if anything more serious on the security front happens.'

'Thanks. Just one thing, you might not get me here. I'm due to have a meeting with a senior cleric in Rome, next week. Best you email me unless it's really urgent, in which case use my mobile but I can't guarantee contact. If it's really serious and you can't get hold of me contact Stephen.'

'OK. Will do.'

32

Father James Dolan, the senior cardinal's secretary shook hands with Ignatius, 'Follow me. The Monsignor will see you in his office.'

The two men traced their way through a series of passages in a tourist-free area of Vatican City. The office, more private living room than office, overlooked a small courtyard sporting a central fountain.

After the briefest of ecclesiastical greetings Monsignor Joseph Morelli waved the two to a robust, chestnut-coloured, antique table. Ignatius stared at the unusually shaped top. It would have been a rectangle but for the fact that the two parallel ends were of slightly differing lengths. But the feature which dominated was an inlaid cross, a rich crimson-coloured cross of Saint James.

'A piece of history. It belonged to Rodrigo de Borja, Pope Alexander VI otherwise known as Rodrigo Borgia and is reputed to resemble the top-sail of his favourite galleon. Shaped to fit into the captain's cabin. Sit there. Father James will sit in on the meeting to record our discussion.'

A nun arrived with a tray of coffee and biscuits. She poured three cups. Strong, black, Italian coffee and put a bowl of sugar onto the table. No milk.

Morelli said nothing as he stirred sugar into his cup. He tapped the spoon, loudly, over the rim, rested his fat wrist on the edge of the table and peered at Ignatius over the edges of half-lens glasses.

'Your spiritual advisor tells me you haven't had contact with him recently. I took the liberty of calling him. He also makes disturbing comment about certain remarks you made in a recent television broadcast when I questioned him about it but, I am a little concerned to say, did not seem, himself, to share my concern.'

Ignatius, familiar with the interrogation procedures of The Apostolic See, was not going to be intimidated. The vision of this overweight prelate, jealous, maybe, of his relative youth and already projecting an air of prejudicial bias, triggered the humanist mindset so recently displacing the younger man's religious indoctrination. Deliberately stirring his coffee for a period longer than necessary, he quietly put the spoon into the saucer, leaned back against the medieval tapestry that cushioned the back of the chair and pursed his lips.

'I take it he refers to the programme on religion and superstition.'

James Dolan scribbled. Joseph Morelli waited.

'Go on.'

'I spoke according to conscience and expressed opinion based on reason. My role, whilst that of presenter, was also open to requests from panel and audience. I answered according to the context of questioners' remarks.'

'Even so, you admitted your status as a Jesuit and any comment you make is bound to reflect on the Catholic and Apostolic Church.'

'Again, I repeat, nothing I said went against the realm of reason.'

'You have a responsibility to consider the wider impact on the Catholic community, even more so on those who would use those remarks to harm the Holy See.'

'You believe the Vatican turning a blind eye to the sexual abuse of minors by priests, and, dare I say it, by bishops and the appalling treatment of unmarried mothers by vindictive nuns over centuries, certainly decades, has not done greater harm? No. Sincerity of belief, honest doubt rather than the garment of ritual pomp, crosiers, chasubles and mitres, commands respect. The world needs some form of religious structure just to maintain social and international stability. But it needs to be a religion free from damnation doctrine. Free from twisted logic deriving nonsensical rules from dubious prophetic pronouncements. Free from biblical contradictions that reveal inconsistent reporting and from belief in charms and debris purporting to effect miracles – splinters from the true cross, fingers from this saint or that saint – ridiculous. That whole aspect is employed as a money-making scam. Look at Lourdes. It raises hope that subsequently turns into disappointment and a bleaker expectation of life than existed before pilgrimage and, on a more prosaic level, the mechanical reciting of countless Hail Marys, as penance after confession, is a reflex action committed as a mindless repetition amounting, almost, to a form of blasphemy.'

'Your disregard for the intercession of Mary, Holy Mother of God, is blasphemy and the women who conceive children out of wedlock deserve harsh treatment for their sin.'

'How can you condemn these women when Mary herself conceived before Joseph married her?'

Cardinal Morelli sat upright, pushed his chair back and thumped the table, his overfed face red with anger, 'This interview is over. Father Dolan, take this heretic out of my sight. Get out. Get out.'

Ignatius leaned towards the fuming prelate, 'He that is slow to anger … .', he knew the unfinished quotation from Proverbs would act as a further sleight to the enraged cardinal but delivered it as a detached but intentionally barbed comment. Delivered more as a cynical observation rather than an act of arrogance. A comment, he hoped, that would trigger this episode in Morelli's mind every time he encountered Proverbs 14.29 in the liturgy.

Getting up he walked to the door, opened it, turned and gave Morelli a contemptuous look, pausing long enough to give added impact before continuing to the anteroom as Father James Dolan sat finishing his notes.

'Prepare a transcript for me immediately. I have decided already, he will be given a choice of an isolated retreat to consider his status or self-excommunication for heresy. A copy also to the Cardinal Secretary of State, with a letter appended, of my recommendations.'

Dolan nodded, 'Yes Monsignor. Do you wish me to send a copy of the discussion to Cardinal Ignatius, in accordance with Canon Law of the Catholic Church?'

Morelli pulled a face. His irritation, at being reminded of procedure, did not go unnoticed by Father Dolan who felt some unwelcome truths had been aired, 'Just the transcript but let me see it first. I will dictate the letter to accompany it, giving my judgement. Dismissed.'

'I will guide you back to the street. You, if I dare say, gave better than you got. Ireland did not disgrace itself today.'

They both laughed. Ignatius understood that little affection existed between Morelli and his secretary. It might prove useful to have an ally at the centre of this dispute should it turn nasty.

33

Cardinal Rochefoucauld arrived with a secretary and an ensemble of flunkies. His status owed more to the influence of wealthy, aristocratic relatives rather than any distinguishing, theological contribution to the Catholic Church.

There was limited guest accommodation at the abbaye. Rochefoucauld and a valet were boarded in guest cells. His secretary, other servants and staff, rooms within the city of Rennes. This proved an inconvenient arrangement for the cardinal but, with some initial objections, he accepted the status quo without further complaint.

'Bring Gabriel de Tregor in. We are ready.'

The refectory had been transformed into a court room of sorts. Francesco Fougères, as an accuser, would normally be expected to attend. Now well beyond medical help and in the advanced stages of sepsis, he lay delirious on his bed. The rabies, masked by the fever, had taken hold of his mind and manifested itself in bouts of incoherent rambling. When the cardinal was finally satisfied with the arrangement of table, seating and witness placement, De Tregor was escorted from his locked cell and placed in a chair before the cardinal. The latter requested the blessing of God on the proceedings and commenced his examination of the captive monk with no further delay.

'You are familiarised with the charges brought against you? Yes or No?'

'Yes.'

Aware his life depended on convincing his interrogator that he was full of remorse, Gabriel spoke with head lowered and with a faint voice. The charges of causing a fire and stealing from the abbot, on their own could result in a death sentence. That of heresy, if proved, would definitely mean the stake.

'Are you responsible for the first two, that of arson and that of theft?

'Yes.'

'What is your explanation for the arson?'

'The abbot, Luc d'Angers possessed some correspondence of mine which he considered heretical. I snatched it from him, set it alight and tossed it behind a screen. In my opinion the contents were not heretical.'

'Who was the recipient? There is no name affixed.'

'A monk in Pisa.'

'His name?'

'Petro di Colenzo.'

'His Order?'

'The Order of St Francis.'

None of this was true. Franciscans were an itinerant order and Gabriel knew there was no way his statement could be verified. Rochefoucauld frowned.

'Why did you steal money from your abbot?'

'To enable me to secure lodging and sustenance.'

177

'You know that theft is a sin?'

'Yes but I took no more than my past labours have generated for the good of charity.'

The oral sparring continued until one of the daily offices of worship acted as a convenient terminator. Convenient, that is, for the cardinal. After only two nights he was already missing the more sumptuous comfort of his Paris quarters.

The Inquisitor looked at his secretary then at the abbot and almoner and finally the two non-clerical members of his itinerary charged with guarding Gabriel.

'Take him back to his cell. I shall give my judgement before leaving after mid-day.'

Assembled for a second time, but this time made to stand, Gabriel tried to read the face of Rochefoucauld. The man had an aquiline nose, possibly broken in some jousting tournament. It gave emphasis to his aristocratic roots. Monk and cardinal were of different cultures and de Tregor's stocky build and undefined features suggested a lineage more of artisan stock and thatched roofs than of chateaux and nobility. Aware of this he didn't rate the outcome to be favourable.

'I have given due consideration to the evidence submitted by the monk, Fougères, in this case. There is no excuse that I can see nor accident of circumstances,' Gabriel wished his interrogator would dispense with the judicial padding and get on with his verdict, 'that justifies

178

the reckless action that resulted in the criminal act of burning property and certainly not the crime of theft. On the issue of heresy, it is my opinion that you, Gabriel de Tregor, have gone against the wisdom of Holy Scripture and derived teachings of Mother Church. On all those counts I can have no option but to pronounce your guilt, in front of these witnesses and sentence you to the cleansing of your soul through fire. To that end you shall be taken to a suitable place and there burnt at the stake. This to take place within three days, the time Our Lord was given between death and resurrection. Take him away.'

The same two heavyweights, assigned to guard Gabriel, marched him back to his cell. Cardinal Rochefoucauld ordered his secretary to lodge a copy of the deposition, verdict and sentence with the Abbot with instructions for Father Pascal to see the sentence was carried out, then to be ready to depart for Paris with no further delay.

34

With the departure of the Cardinal and his entourage, the abbot called Marcel and the apothecary to his private quarters.

'I sense you both feel the fate of our brother Gabriel to be unnecessarily harsh. The man has proved himself a humble and dedicated servant to God, in his time here.'

Pascal Bezier paused, indicating he expected a response.

The apothecary, one Joseph Jouglet, nodded, 'He is more useful to God alive than dead. His service to this abbaye and our brother monks, has been one of humility and of inestimable benefit in giving the miracle of sight back to the older brethren through his knowledge of optics.'

'Fougères, dare I speak of an older brother in negative terms, seems a spiteful, unworthy servant of our Lord. He it is who has pursued a vendetta, it seems, against Brother Gabriel to the point where it has ended in the unfortunate events at our brother's abbaye and his subsequent flight from persecution. I too have benefited from his patient teaching and instruction in the science of optics, the skill of glass making and lens grinding.'

'I have a proposal to make. May God have mercy on my soul for what I wish to propose but I must have your solemn oath of secrecy before you hear it. If you do not agree then no more must be said. If you do concur then understand I am asking you to put your souls in mortal danger but will respect any decision not to take part.'

'I am prepared to listen and accept the condition of secrecy.'

'I too.'

'Good. Our sick visitor is going to die very soon. My experience of past, departed spirits is that he will last for five or six days. No longer. There will be no miracle of survival in his condition. It is a wonder he has lasted thus far but he can serve one fitting purpose before his end. If we substitute Fougères for Gabriel then, in a sense, justice will be served and we shall have saved a good man from agony.'

The two subordinate monks looked at each other, their facial expressions already revealing their response.

The younger monk looked at Father Pascal, his agreement implied in his answer, 'How can it be done without Fougères being recognised?'

'It is the custom in some diocesan sees to invest the condemned heretic with a hooded mask of horns and face of Satan. This we can do. Father Joseph can give him a tincture of archanum but with opium in much greater measure. That will subdue him to a state of passivity. He is unable to walk so we shall have to imply that he has been taken by a condition of apoplexy since incurred by the delayed shock of his intended punishment.'

The three warmed to the atmosphere now engendered by commonly agreed action. For each, the sensation of a dark load removed from their minds.

'We can come to some arrangement over and with Brother Gabriel, as to his future after the event. In the meantime cut the cowl from Fougères habit and fashion it into a mask. We can paint the devil's face with ochre. Red cochineal for the eyes and tongue. Stitched back in place, it won't fall off to reveal his person. Do it now. I will go to see Brother Gabriel.'

Brother Joseph sent his assistants away. Francesco Fougères was beginning to give off the odour of death. Unable to consume his normal intake of victuals, over the time he had been sick, his body was beginning to shrink to the size of the skeleton that supported whatever flesh remained. A coffin, already constructed for his demise, was placed alongside the litter the failing monk lay on. Joseph and Marcel would, that night, fill the container with stones and earth. The burning of Gabriel was posted as taking place the following day. Stooks of straw bedding and faggots of wood had been laid around a granite menhir some distance from the abbaye. A plaited rope from vine cuttings lay loosely looped around the stone pillar that would act as a stake. Space between the piles of wood and straw would allow a struggling victim to be dragged to the menhir with less effort.

Taking a pair of scissors, the apothecary cut the cowl from Foùgères habit. Using a suture, he stitched up the front, facial edge and laid the hood on one of the side benches, ready to be painted. Occasional bouts of delirium alternated with periods of unconsciousness, as the infirmary's only patient saturated the coarse material he was clothed in with copious floods of sweat. He displayed only the symptoms of the sepsis destroying kidneys and other organs. Fortunately for Cabo, evidence of rabies was still masked by the fever caused by the poisons.

Pascal Bezier knocked gently on the locked door of Gabriel's cell and cautioned him to remain silent. It was the time of contemplation when the monks were expected to deepen their faith by meditation and prayer in their cells.

He spoke quietly, just above a whisper, 'I am coming in. We have a plan to save you from the stake tomorrow.'

The abbot unlocked the door and let himself in. He pointed to the edge of Gabriel's bed and both sat side by side.

'Francesco Foùgères is at the point of death. We are going to disguise his person as you and consign him to the flames. In the meantime you must remain in here until nightfall. Do you have any conflict of conscience? We are putting ourselves at risk in doing so but the expectation of discovery is low. The apothecary and your apprentice

Marcel are the only ones who know. I repeat: are you in agreement because if not it will be you and not Fougères who will burn tomorrow?'

Gabriel's shoulders relaxed with a visible exhalation of breath as a wave of tension shuddered from his frame.

'What do you think? I am governed by my conscience. My conscience tells me I have not committed heresy. Because I believe such I do not consider my punishment justified. I thank you with ... ,' Gabriel broke down before he could express his gratitude further and sobbed. Pascal let him weep quietly until he was able to regain composure.

'The arson was unintended. The theft I cannot deny but consider that an unfortunate consequence of the mischief caused me by Francesco Fougères. I thank you with deep gratitude for your merciful intervention.'

The abbot was slightly embarrassed but understood Gabriel or indeed anyone, would find it difficult to express adequately their feelings at being saved from the horrendous fate of being burnt alive.

'You must give some thought as to your future. I suggest you abandon your monastic vocation, if not permanently, certainly until you have established some kind of life outside of the religious. But for the next few hours you will remain hidden here, if not days but that carries risk. Brothers Joseph and Marcel might have some suggestions. I will leave you now. We will meet later to plan your escape.'

Daybreak brought an overcast sky. In the infirmary Joseph placed a number of vessels containing smouldering incense. They helped mask the stench from Fougères' decaying flesh. Despite twice daily cleansing, last thing at night and first thing at dawn and some other perfunctory attention given to the monk's sweat-saturated habit, the smell of putrefaction dominated the room.

Again, during the quiet time, Pascal left his own devotions but this time went to collect Marcel. Fougères needed to be prepared for despatch.

Marcel retched as he entered the room.

'You'll get used to it. Give me some help to raise him up.' The apothecary closed the infirmary door behind abbot and the young monk.

A mixture of brandy and wine with several measures of opium had been prepared by Joseph. When Fougères was sitting upright the contents were patiently fed the monk through a pewter vessel with a spout.

'That'll do. Get the mask.'

Joseph went to a box and selected another length of catgut and needle. Marcel slipped the mask over the heavily drugged cleric as the abbot held him upright. The other stitched the mask back to where it had come from. It was loose enough for him to breathe but no eye holes had been cut to allow him to look out. The grotesque image of the devil's face, together with the three medievally garbed monks, invested the scene with a Hieronymus Bosch-like depiction of the hellscape in his triptych *The Last Judgement*.

Slightly revived by the contents from the flask but totally unaware of his surroundings, the inebriated monk was laid back down.

'Brother Joseph, fetch the hand cart. We will deliver this wretch to his fate, now. It will be a mercy not a crime to relieve him of his suffering. Marcel, muffle the bell. Dusk has fallen. In torch light there will be little risk of the deception being detected. We will summon the brothers to attend the punishment and proceed to the pyre when they have assembled in the courtyard. It is an issue internal to the monastery and not for the entertainment of peasants. So we will conduct the matter in private. No peasant will be at large at this hour. Their fear of witches and goblins will keep them within their homes.'

The procession of monks made its way towards the pyre. Pascal Bezier made it clear that Gabriel was in a state of shock and unable to walk. At the site Fougères was helped from the cart. Assisted by Joseph and Marcel, each under a shoulder, the semi-conscious monk now breathing fitfully, was propelled between the faggots of wood to the menhir. The abbot coiled the plait of vine cuttings around the hooded figure. When he was sure the body was unlikely to slip out of its cocoon of woody fastenings he directed

Marcel and Joseph to place straw, brushwood and faggots of wood around the captive monk. Sprinkling a small flask of cognac on the straw at the feet of the victim he called for a torch, passed it to his left hand, made the sign of the cross.

'In nomine Patris et Filii et Spiritus Sancti, I commend your soul to the mercy of God.'

With one brief moment of hesitation he held the torch towards the mask, then at the unmoving form. He stepped back up, placed his hand on the breast of the pinioned monk. There was no rise and fall of the rib cage. Fougères was dead. The effort expended by the weakened monk had proved too much for a heart fighting to keep a body alive. Most of the vital organs had slowly, one by one, failed.

Stepping back off the pile he muttered a brief few words of relief to himself that he was not putting the torch to a human life. The cognac-infused straw flared. Someone, probably a child, had pushed a sprig of gorse into one of the bunches of brushwood. The dry, beige-coloured needles caught a flame and crackled as they ignited. A child, witnessing the annual, winter burning of gorse would have been fascinated by the incendiary properties of the prickly shrub and the magical spread of the flames up the branches. Here too, as elsewhere in the Breton and Cornish landscapes, the weathered, blackened stalks of the then prickle-free bushes would later be gathered for kindling wood by the peasants.'

It was well after the evening Office of Compline and close to the nocturnal observance of Vigil when the last faggot was thrown onto the centre of the heap. The red, glowing tips, at the ends of blackened lengths of wood, erupted in a shower of embers and sparks. The finer ones were carried by the wind across to patches of heather and became extinguished by the covering of dew that had formed during the night.

Using a long pole with a Y-shaped fork at its end, Joseph pushed, prodded and reformed the pile of burning wood around the granite post. The sickly smell of roasting flesh had long since ceased to hang in the air. Eventually, when it was obvious no physically recognisable part of animal or human bone could have survived the intense heat the assembled monks departed. There was nothing more to be said at the site.

The apothecary supervised the loading of the coffin onto the trolley. A small, wooden cross was all that marked the site of burial of earth and stones purporting to be Fougères. No name, just the cross of Augustine carved at the joint. His death was no surprise to the brethren. They had, over the years, experienced the demise of peasants from infected wounds caused by careless use of axe or digging tool. He was not mourned by the brothers. His part in the delivery, trial and death of Gabriel was resented right from the beginning.

35

Ignatius looked around the studio as the countdown started. The two ex-marines were sitting as members of the audience. So far so good. It was unlikely any disruption would occur before questions had been aired. Receiving the signal from Robyn, he introduced the speakers.

'Good evening ladies and gentlemen. Tonight's topic reflects, perhaps, a more European perspective than one we're exercised by here in the Republic. Certainly less controversial here than in the UK. To that end our panel hosts a polyglot assembly representing a wider, global mix of opinion than usual.

David van Zeeman, presently writer in residence at Trinity, Dublin, is on a sabbatical from Cape Town University. Before turning to writing he was a lecturer in anthropology. His study of inter-tribal conflicts exacerbated by armed interference from outside is documented in his book: *African Diaspora – refugee cultures*. The tome is used by The United Nations in planning aid policy. But it is his fiction for which he is more widely known.

Sandrine Lagarde worked in the French Foreign Ministry as an intern. Completed a doctorate at Yale. Returned to France where she was involved in government administration of DOM-TOMs – for those of you unacquainted with the term, Departements d'Outre Mer et Territoires d'Outre Mer, roughly translated as French, overseas colonies. Now in the French Embassy here in Ireland.

Isaac Karzstein. Documentary film maker and authority on Holocaust History and the Jewish Diaspora.

And lastly but not insignificantly, George Clarke. Ex major of a Gurkha regiment; one-time MP and member of the UK Foreign Office, now enjoying retirement fly fishing on Ireland's rivers.

Right. First question from James Campbell.'

'Should some kind of global birth control be established whereby population numbers are limited? The Earth has only so much space for livestock and an even greater scarcity of fresh water. Is pressure on space and water, by unregulated population growth, causing conflict which in turn is causing the immigration crisis in many parts of the globe? Are we focusing too much on carbon capture and not enough on copulation capture?'

The last comment brought a burst of laughter from the audience. Ignatius waited.

'Plenty there to get the ball rolling. Sandrine, would you like to start us off?'

'Thank you Bill and good evening to the audience. Birth control, it goes without saying, is a difficult political and religious topic to deal with. I'm sure the questioner was aware of this when he posed it. It's the kind of topic I would discuss and have discussed with friends over an aperitif and, to a lesser extent, with colleagues, formally, in government.

Any proposal needs to attempt a prediction of long term, unintended consequences of such a plan or plans. Different circumstances will dictate different actions. Although, sometimes, a universal, blanket action avoids accusations of preferential treatment.

Each zone of the world has different territorial and weather patterns. These influence the supply – or lack of supply - of food: agrarian, animal and that from rivers and oceans. Advances in the science and technology of vegetable and fruit genetics, grain cultivation, fish farming, are leading to new methods of food production. Hydroponics, for example. But there you have a primary consideration, by the very definition of hydroponics: water. There is friction between adjacent countries where a higher source of water is being controlled – dams, watercourse diversion, excessive irrigation – to the detriment of the population downstream. The Colorado River and Mexico, for example.

On an anthropological note, religious and tribal taboos exert pressures to conform. Political coercion, for example: the Chinese one couple one child policy, produced a number of problems. On one level it was a seemingly wise decision. On another, because of a desire to produce a son, it led to the practice of drowning or otherwise, of female babies. Various sociological and demographical issues have arisen, unintended and unforeseen, because of that government injunction and still the consequences are not fully understood or have yet to materialise.

If a global policy were to be proposed I'm pretty certain it to be more difficult to implement and monitor than current attempts by G7 states to achieve consensus over bringing global warming under control, for example.

There is much else I would say but my fellow panel members will, no doubt, express those and different sentiments.'

'David?' Ignatius indicated the 'floor' to his next speaker with a wave of his ball pen.

'Good evening. Let me say how much I am enjoying my stay over here in Dublin. Great city.'

A few cheers and simultaneous clapping greeted van Zeemans' comment.

'Particularly meaningful for me because my maternal great grandmother came from Drogheda. She too was a writer but her great passion was travel. She met my great grandfather in Kimberly. He was a Cornish mine engineer whose skills were in demand, as you can imagine, in the gold and copper rich territories of Africa. Anyway, I digress.

My country - and that declaration of ownership might have a hidden significance since current thinking suggests all Caucasians owe their birthright to Africa - my country or continent, rather, has been plagued by inter-tribal strife for centuries. More recently this has been augmented by inter-religious conflict between Muslims and Christians in Nigeria and elsewhere on the continent, fomented by Al Qaeda and ISIS. Whilst some of that is not all down to population pressures a lot of it is. The net result is an explosion in refugee camps in both hemispheres. Where these camps have been long established their resident population is out-breeding the facilities, such as they are, with little or no hope of being resettled in civilised accommodation.

The resulting exodus from war-torn Angola, what, thirty years or so ago? has led to continuing immigration problems within the continent itself. Waves of economic migrants are flooding into South Africa from other African states like Angola. Every time a building development is planned in some region, coach loads and I mean coach loads, fifty or sixty labourers in forty-seater coaches, are bussed in hoping to find work. As many as two thousand will turn up where there is only work for twenty. What happens to the other one thousand nine hundred and eighty? The coaches have gone. Food and shelter are a priority. Some will go elsewhere but makeshift camps will start to appear. Gradually their wives or other partners trickle in and soon there are babies as well as the extra mouths from their existing children. The local suburban population will experience greater levels of crime and soon camps become townships. Water supplies? Sanitation? Birth control? Not a hope!'

Van Zeeman paused, 'What, even if a global policy was decided, what instrument of delivery are you going to administer it with? Is it going to be forcibly administered or voluntary? Cultures where polygamy is recognised, what happens there? One man, many wives. Can you see any one of his concubines denying themselves the experience of giving birth? Therein lies an inherent problem, a fundamental urge to procreate but allied with that an unjustified sense of entitlement to the 'right' to have children.

Who or what is the authority that posits this 'right'? I know we have laws enshrined in Civil Liberties and Human Rights, enacted to various degrees and in various ways in countries recognising them in some form or other. You might say the various parliaments around the world have approved and passed these laws through the mandate given the elected members by the voting populace. That's fine but so was the case in the Third Reich where the Nazi Party was set up by the German people. There as here, there was a sizeable minority of intelligent people who saw the danger in Hitler but the proletariat sold their souls to this man. The latter are the kind who don't see the creeping danger of Islamisation brought on by the exponential growth of their large families. The ones who will wake up one morning to find a Muslim caliphate ruled by Taliban-like masters peddling terror of medieval proportions akin to that witnessed in the French Revolution. That is one barbaric consequence of, how shall I put it, unregulated family growth encouraged by religious observance. No. Before we devise a system of global, population control and there's an interesting point, control is not the same as contraception, we need to be sure of whom our elected masters are and where their commercial interests lie but that's another issue.'

'Thank you David. Isaac, let's hear from you.'

'Good evening. We have an appreciative audience, I can see. Where to start? Maybe I should clear some misconceptions some might have as to my religious affiliation since my name suggests I am Jewish and the main subject area of my documentary work even more suggestive of that. I am Jewish in the sense of having a fondness for Jewish culture but am not a Jew. My father is but married a Gentile. So because she is not of that faith I am not, merely by accident of birth. A lot of people are unaware that to be born a Jew one's birth mother has to be a Jew. If anything I verge towards some form of Humanism but don't actually belong to any Humanist group or any other religious organisation. Having said that, I do enjoy the liturgy of Jewish Shabbat when invited by friends to celebrate with them in their homes, of a Friday evening.

I am an Israeli and those of us who live there cannot help but be aware of some media disapproval of the so-called Israeli/Palestinian problem. The origin of this friction, if friction is an adequate description, is exacerbated by continued influx of Jewish returnees and others seeking Israeli nationality. It is further exacerbated by the increasing birth rate, particularly in the Palestinian community.

Coupled with too many people chasing too few jobs, the plight of the Palestinians and to a lesser extent for Israelis, unemployment can, by stretching logic, be equated to overpopulation. That is an issue different from a planet being denuded of vegetation by goats, deforestation or water supplies contaminated by untreated sewage coming from an unregulated, Third World population. Lack of proper hygiene through diminishing water supplies leading to transmissible diseases such as cholera. Typhus from a burgeoning rodent population attracted by whatever meagre food scraps they can glean. So numbers don't just apply to people they also apply to animals.

I've presented various scenarios here but offered no solutions. So what to do? Foreign aid to Third World countries should be tied to a number of conditions – birth control being one of them. Their education system, at tertiary level, should be geared to suiting Third World requirements rather than trying to ape Ivy League or Oxbridge University Colleges. I know educational purists will bang the drum of 'education for education's sake' and 'a classical education benefits everyone' kind of mission statement. But that being so, why are the Greeks and Italians, the progenitors of Latin and Greek literature, classical philosophy and geometry, in a decline so evident in their existing, economic status?

It's the Louis Pasteurs, the Humphry Davys, the Christian Barnards of this world who improve the quality of living on this planet. The only people who can afford the luxury to be poets and painters, without earning a living to support themselves, are those already endowed with an income generated by their parents. Plenty of time for poetry later when these budding literary geniuses have also acquired some alternative skill useful to society. St Paul, although a rabbi, stressed the need to engage in fruitful employment. It was he, I think, who counselled, 'He who would study Torah should first find gainful work'. The man himself was a tent-maker by trade.

A different aspect of overpopulation is creating a gene pool of degenerate offspring. This is encouraged or, more accurately, should I say not prevented, by religious doctrine. It is a particular problem now in families of strictly observant, Orthodox Jews who are forced to find a partner within the ranks of their own congregation. They are forbidden contraception. The result is large families of congenitally, degenerate children. One of the signs of this degeneration is the increasingly evident onset of early blindness in later life not to speak of the frustrations associated by the almost equally crippling, poor eyesight from childhood up. Other genetic defects are less evident but perhaps more invidious. You are fighting man-made, religious tyranny. They are conforming to pressures forced on them by elders imposing harmful, religious protocols. Protocols no benevolent god, should one believe in such, would command his subjects to obey. Any naïve populace needs to be disabused of damaging, religious practices that lead to degenerate gene pools. The only way is through sound, rational education. That in itself is a whole can of worms. An opportunity for dictators to exploit educational curricula to further their own ends.

'Bill, I think that sums up my immediate thoughts.'

'Right, thank you Isaac. George, your floor.'

'Well, that's two of us with Irish connections. My mother came from Cork and I have visited relatives there for as far back as I can remember. Now resident - if somewhat itinerant.

I was raised a Catholic. It's sometime since I attended a mass or confession. The issue of contraception is one I would deal with first. Carbon capture or global warming, rather, seems to have plenty of support internationally but birth control? No. Lack of is one of the causes, direct causes, of global warming because population demand is directly correlated with energy consumption.

The issue of contraception was one that used to raise the hackles of some of the military mob I trained and drank with, in the mess. It would occur, mainly, on overseas postings where crippling poverty and disease were starkly manifest. The anger arose when the dire conditions local populations were living in was accompanied by large families forbidden the use of contraception. A major, officer in a Scottish regiment, got really vitriolic about the Pope. Carried on about similar conditions in what he called 'the Catholic ghettoes of Glasgow.' Women, young women not even thirty but looking sixty from bearing a child nearly every year from the age of sixteen. Worn out. Used. As a Catholic I couldn't disagree with him. It has improved there now but not globally.

So? What to do? The latter has been discussed for decades. Contraception and clerical celibacy have competed with each other as topics of Satanic dimension in the eyes of the Vatican. The two, ironically have a common root: the sexual urge. For me the answer is straightforward. Let everyone's conscience answer to whatever god they believe in and not to some despotic pope, ayatollah or cult leader. We have had some enlightened popes but, by god, we've had some who were either weak and allowed themselves to be dictated to by powerful forces or they were autocratic, reversing good decisions or worse, imposing even more damaging doctrine.'

'Thank you George. Let's open up to comments from the floor. Second row; lady with red beads.' Bill waited until she had the mike in her hand, 'Tell us your name.'

'Hello. I'm Mary Crosby. I've listened to the comments and agree, by and large, with most said by all the speakers. One very controversial issue has not been aired – that of abortion. It seems to me resistance to the procedure comes from the religious cohort. Not all but mainly. A resistance based solely on questionable interpretation of biblical literature, a literature not written by the medical profession.

Fine for those who support judgement from a patriarchal elite peddling religious opinion masquerading as indisputable law, because in the end religion is a matter of opinion, of superstitious belief rather than factually derived reason.

I do understand objections that arise from medical personnel who find some procedures distressing. But would those same personnel object to the experience of watching animals being killed in an abattoir yet quite unconcernedly tuck into a steak? I know the animal has no choice but the employees at the abattoir do, they wouldn't work there otherwise. I know the foetus has no choice but the attendant medical staff do, to a certain extent. Perhaps not as open to choice as their opposite number in the abattoir. Perhaps faced with the dilemma of not wishing to force another of their colleagues to replace them. The matter is not as facile to dismiss as that but it is the woman bearing the foetus who is making the choice.

There is a further consequence. Offspring offered for adoption, because abortion is not an option - or worse, abortion refused when circumstances should dictate termination. I am thinking of children born to drug-addicted parents. Parents who should have been sterilised when they have already produced a clutch of feral offspring, are again pregnant and about to deliver yet another, potential delinquent to society. I have seen the harm inflicted on well-meaning people offering themselves as adoptive parents. Emotional and physical harm.

Abortion should never be denied any woman who is not using it as a substitute for contraception, too lazy or careless to take precautions. But even with the latter, termination rather than an unwanted child is, maybe, preferable.'

'Thank you Mary. Interesting viewpoint. What, may we ask is your profession, if you have one?'

'I was a social worker for a while until I studied criminology at college. Then, after getting my degree, I joined the Probation Service. I have to say and I guess it's not a surprise to the audience, I have less sympathy for an unborn foetus than I do for the uncertain benefit - risk is probably a better word - to society of allowing an unwanted child to be born.'

'Your comments are appreciated. I should say the issue of abortion is going to be the subject of a future *Polemic* programme so will leave further comment to that panel and audience.'

'Right, one more from the audience before we hear the next question. Gentleman, hand up at the back.'

'Patrick Kelly. Retired ... ,' before Kelly had time to respond, a burst from a semi-automatic rifle could be heard followed, almost immediately, by a cascade of shots from a set of differently sounding weapons.

36

Glass shattered in what was later to be seen as the remains of the front, double doors of the ground floor of FONT. The two ex-marines jumped up and separated. One secured an exit door from the studio the other ran through the sound-isolation cell then into the sound mixing room.

'Leave that and get into the studio. Lock the entry door behind you. Quick. Don't fuck about.'

The two bemused sound engineers pulled their headphones off and made a dash for the door. Ross Camp, given a key by Robyn as part of the security brief, locked the other door to the sound room, went out to the mezzanine overlooking the atrium. The LED lighting, a somewhat clinical white compared with the warmer tones of fluorescent tubes, reflected off broken glass fronting the wide stairway. The architects, charged with converting the original building, had retained the Georgian era embellishments and managed to conceal the LEDs in bespoke fittings sympathetic to the original.

Drops of blood, he could see them clearly, trailing across the polished, limestone floor, were dripping from a black-clad figure already three quarters of the way up the first flight. As far as he could see the man must have had a flesh wound somewhere in his upper body. His traction wasn't impaired. Another figure, badly wounded - Ross took in the spreading soak of blood darkening the man's hips and his upper torso - had dragged himself towards the relative shelter afforded by a wall and settee placed for the use of waiting visitors. He lay there bleeding out into unconsciousness. The rapidity of his demise an indication of a serious, arterial wound producing the rapidly increasing pool of blood around him.

At an intermediate landing the gunman chose the right hand flight of stairs, one of two opposing pairs. Standing on the first step, behind a pillar he rested his back against it then twisted around offering only a narrow, quarter profile to the entrance. In that brief interval he bounced a couple of shots through the doorway and made a dash up the remaining flight to the three-branched mezzanine.

Camp, by this time, had got the measure of the situation. Expecting the gunman to investigate the various doors on that level, his back would be to the marine or at least not in his line of sight. Ross Camp ducked low and ran for the stairs. Holding the banister he was able to jump the steps three at a time. Soft-soled combat boots made no sound on the Axminster stair carpet. He reached the dying terrorist undetected but at risk of being shot by a member of the armed detail outside. Prising the Uzi from the limp fingers of the dark-skinned figure he was kneeling by, he then placed himself between terrorist and wall. He checked the weapon. It was a conversion. Full magazine of twenty rounds. It hadn't been fired. He put the safety catch off.

With his back against the wall and sitting in a bunched position, he put both feet on the man's torso. Straightening his legs, he pushed the man out towards the open doorway. An involuntary, choking cough left the throat of the victim accompanied by a spurt of blood and froth. Ross continued to push. He kept his legs up clear of the smear of blood and glass painted by what he now suspected was a corpse.

No white flag. No white shirt. He had to pre-empt any attempt to shoot him by the police. He also didn't want to risk drawing attention to himself from the armed man upstairs by shouting to them to hold their fire. Creeping to the edge of the aluminium frame, all that was left of one of the doors, he waved his hand up and down twice, too fast to be shot at. Again he repeated the action. He recognised the faint sound of a Kevlar vest scrape against the sandstone exterior adjacent to the door's hinges. There was someone close enough to hear him if he talked quietly.

'Don't shoot. I'm security. Don't shoot.'

Camp could hear, indistinctly, whoever it was relay what he guessed to be a request for instructions to a senior officer. Within seconds he was challenged.

'Identify yourself. Name.'

'Ross Camp. Ex 42 Commando. Here at the request of FONT. There are two of us. Our names are on the roster the production director gave your chief. My mate is on the first floor in the studio. All locked in. Secure,' he paused, 'for the moment.'

There was again a brief delay as the intel was relayed back.

'Look, we can't wait. One of your targets is wounded but mobile and, my guess, about to shoot the lock off the studio door. The other target, if you take a quick look, is dead, two metres from you. Face down. I've got his Uzi. I'm going up. Either shoot me in the back or cover me.'

All this must have taken less than twenty seconds. Just as Ross finished speaking there was a burst of fire on the floor above. The terrorist had discovered which of the doors he needed to access.

Ross stood, ran across the floor and up the stairs, two at a time. He could hear the officer he must have been talking to running behind him. At the first level, without pausing, he took a quick glance behind. There were now three of them. He grinned and kept going. The door to the studio complex was closed but there were no bullet holes.

'Watch out. He's not accessed the studio complex, he's in one of the side rooms.'

The man had set a trap. Just as he shouted, one of the other doors opened. Ross, instinctively back in combat alert, let off a burst from the Uzi and rolled closed to the wall. In haste the terrorist managed to get only one, short round off but his arms, hindered by the edge of the inwardly opening door, prevented him taking proper aim. He slammed the door shut.

'Is there an exit from where he is? Dave Williams, by the way.' He introduced himself as he helped Ross to his feet. They backed around to one of the less exposed arms of the landing as the other two covered the door.

'I've seen a plan of the layout to all three floors here. As far as I remember the area he's in at the moment is a conference room with only that door. I know the layout of the studio. There are two exits. One down an exterior, steel fire escape the other back through here. That one,' Ross pointed to the still locked door.'

'Right. We know the layout of the studio and location of the fire escape. Already briefed on that. Our coordinating officer will, I guess, be able to contact them. If we can get the 'all-clear' from Control that the back is secure, we can evacuate the studio down the fire escape. Can we make phone contact?'

'Yes and no.'

'What the hell d'you mean, yes and no?'

'There is a phone but it doesn't ring. A light flashes instead so that any recording's not compromised. So it's a matter of whether anyone will notice.'

'OK.' The officer relayed the information to his CO.

'They've already got contact,' he turned to Ross, 'should've known. They're goin' to tell them to evacuate down the escape. Somebody's now covering the window in the conference room in case he susses what's going on and attempts to fire on them from there. Right, I've got the all-clear to flush him out. We want him alive.'

Williams gave instructions to the other two armed men. Both slid along the wall, each stopping a metre either side of the door.

'Technically you're a civilian but you're more use to us here than out of it. I'm going to shoot the glass out of the top of the door. Those two will toss stun grenades through. Shouldn't be any trouble from then on but we don't want him to anticipate that and rig up some shelter, so we're wasting no more time. You stay here and cover us. I'm joining them as soon as I've busted the glass.'

Williams mimed the action of pulling a pin from a grenade to his colleagues, took aim and shot out the rectangular pane forming the top third of the door. The two police, either side of the door, rose to their feet from a crouch, dropped pins and simultaneously tossed grenades in before even the glass had hit the floor. The explosions were a shock even to those outside. One officer took a quick glance through the splintered gap, well clear of the main body of the door. The other, sheltered by the wall, tried the door handle. No obstruction had been put in place, the door moved freely. A burst of gunfire sent a pulse of bullets through the door at waist level. Their target was alert, not incapacitated by the explosions.

'What did you see?'

'He's pushed a small table on its side oblique to the door,' the officer pointed at the wall indicating the location, 'and away from and out of the line of sight of the window. I reckon that shielded him from the blast. You should be able to see, just, a chandelier through the gap from where you're standing. He's more or less under that.'

'Yes. Got it. Did you have time to spot if he might be wearing a suicide vest?'

'No. Too quick and the table covers most of his front, anyway.'

'We can't afford to risk a fight. He might be desperate enough to seek martyrdom, open the door and spray us before we can stop him. I'm tossing in another. That should do it this time.'

Dave Williams unclipped a grenade, pulled the pin, got the nod from the other two and tossed it high into the air in the direction but well above where he guessed the table to be. The trajectory took it over the top of the gunman. It hit the chandelier and dropped, exploding in mid air, showering the man with ignited, magnesium powder. His balaclava and shoulders took the bulk of the pyrotechnic mix. This time the explosion and flash deafened and temporarily blinded the terrorist. The three outside heard his gun clatter to the floor as he staggered to his feet with fists pushed into his eyes.

Williams stood, glanced through the gap, 'He's out of it and his front is too flat to be hiding a vest,' flinging open the door as he was saying it. The first officer to reach the table grabbed its top edge and slammed it upside down onto the conference floor, simultaneously kicking the gun out of reach of the terrorist. The other shouldered the dazed terrorist sideways and flat onto his stomach. Cuffed, the next thing was to extinguish his now smouldering mask and shoulders. The artificial fibres in the balaclava were melting and sticking to his flesh. Pain from these man-made threads was the same as if boiling jam had been spilt on his neck and scalp. Coming out of his daze and realising what must be happening to him, he started to scream. The officer, who put the wrist restraints on, ripped the balaclava from the threshing man's head.

'There's an extinguisher on the wall along the landing, in the corner, that way.' Dave Williams pointed in the direction he was referring to. Ross Camp dashed out and came back fiddling with the plastic loop securing the restrictor to the operating lever. He ripped it out and pressed. A gush of carbon dioxide, fire suppressant hissed out of the flattened, conical nozzle. It extinguished the burning jacket but did nothing to ease the pain. The four men had no sympathy for their target. His hearing was probably totally impaired but the temporary, flash blindness was receding. He could now see his captors and, not surprisingly, his face registered hatred. He spat.

'Do that again. I'll put the mask back on, set it alight and let it burn for a while.'

Their captive uttered a few words in Arabic and lapsed into a sullen but arrogant silence. Williams, satisfied there was no further danger, reported back to his CO. Ross Camp shook hands with the three officers and handed the Uzi over to one of them.

'That's one for the papers tomorrow.'

'Charlie Hebdo visits Dublin. I can see the headlines now.'

'I'm going to unlock the door to the studio complex. Come along to meet my mate.' Dave Williams handed the terrorist over to his two subordinates and followed Ross Camp into the studio and down the fire escape.

37

Gabriel had been hidden for nearly two weeks. The abbot and Marcel had been smuggling food into the visitor's cell and, on the counsel of the former, had let his beard grow. Having not shaven several days before his trial, he was now sporting a beard that would not look out of place on any one of the sea-dogs roaming the seas thereabouts. A good disguise.

Father Pascal Bezier conducted the last Office of the day. The monks retired to their cells for much welcomed sleep. Well after all sounds of activity had ceased, Bezier lit a candle in one of the lanterns and went to the kitchen to prepare a platter of food for Gabriel. It would be the last meal he would eat at the abbaye. He also assembled an assortment of saucisson, cheese, an onion, hard biscuits, figs, a few raisins and put them in a sack.

'Have you got the clothes?' The abbot addressed Marcel as he appeared from the darkened recesses of the adjacent cloister.

Marcel waved a similar lantern to reveal a number of garments folded over his forearm, 'Yes.'

'Good. We should spend a little time in his company, together, after he has eaten. Brother Joseph will also be with us.'

The routine was well established. Gabriel had unbarred his cell ready for the abbot or Marcel to come with his food. Listening out for the very faint footfall of his visitor, this time he could tell there was more than one person approaching. He opened the cell door just a crack and peered through. Relieved to identify his visitors were not other monks, he opened the door to let them through. The abbot held out the plate in both hands with the sack dangling from one of them. Gabriel took the plate and placed it on a small table.

'What's this?' Gabriel, puzzled, took the sack held out to him by Pascal.

'Extra provisions. You are safe now to travel abroad. No one will recognise you with that beard. Even your old abbot would be fooled. I sent Marcel to make enquiries at the port. There is a regular visitation of ships from Cornwall and some, as you hoped, are from Penzance.'

'Thank you Father Abbot. It is time I freed myself from your generosity.'

'Not at all my son. We are just as much indebted to you. We have benefited from your time here. I have already said and we will be sorry to see you leave us. Marcel has found lodgings for you in Saint Malo. He will take you. The auberge is run by a chandler married to a Cornish woman. You can stay there until a suitable boat arrives. Have you given thought to a change of name? It is too risky that you keep your old, as we counselled but it might be that we need to make further contact. The likelihood is doubtful but no harm will come from us knowing.'

'Yes. Since I am bound for Cornwall I shall adopt Piran. He is the saint from Ireland who settled in Cornwall. Hawken, I believe, is an old Cornish family name so Piran Hawken will be my persona nova.'

'Good. Well chosen. It preserves the link to your vocation, without arousing suspicion.'

'What about Cabo? He is getting old. I think it unwise to take him with me.'

'He can stay as last time. His company might be a risk. We like him. The rats don't.'

The little assembly of monks laughed quietly.

'Marcel has a change of garments for you. They fit him. He is of stature similar to you so you should find them to your satisfaction. You have your original utensils in your satchel and there is still room for these provisions. They will last you for your journey. Here also is a small quantity of coins.'

Gabriel started to protest.

'No my son. Your need is no less than that of the poor we dispense alms to. Take it. Eat your meal. We will then spend a little time in communion, since it will be our last meeting together.'

Gabriel finished the food and changed into a pair of leggings and tunic spun from material of the same weft the Benedictine habits were fashioned from. It gave him the appearance of a travelling artisan – which effectively, as a maker of lenses, was what he was going to be, for a while

214

at least. The four of them, Pascal, Marcel, Joseph and Gabriel then knelt for a brief period of prayer.

'Marcel will come for you a candle's width before sun up. Time now for sleep. We will bid farewell then.'

Gabriel watched the three from the cell door as their bouncing shadows receded into the passage and disappeared through to the cloister.

Gabriel slept fitfully to begin with. Some two hours after midnight he heard the chanting of the night-time service of Vigil performed faintly in the chapel. This had a calming effect, stayed the rush of thoughts and myriad images that had been tumbling into his mind. Images unbidden; images of Pisa; images more recent, of his time back at the scriptorium, the root of his present circumstances. He lapsed back into a deep, restorative sleep.

It seemed only moments ago that his mind was fighting attempts to settle into sleep, when he was woken by Marcel knocking gently on the door. He had slept in the clothes he was given and was ready immediately. The abbot and apothecary were with Marcel. Gabriel embraced the two older brothers. It was difficult for him not to weep.

'God keep you safe. Pray for us as we shall for you.'

Pascal Bezier said no more. The four walked quietly to the northern door of the monastery. Again, one more brief embrace, then Marcel and Gabriel set off for Saint Malo, Cabo asleep, undisturbed by the departure.

The abbot returned to his lodgings. There was one more secret task to complete. He placed the lantern on his writing table. A quill and parchment had already been set out ready, the evening before. He wrote with care but at speed; care in content, speed in execution. Satisfied with what he had written he sprinkled the surface with fine sand to hasten drying, read it once more and, finally, signed it. About to get up, he took the quill and added a final sentence, smiling to himself as he added a small stick-image instead of a full stop.

The sheet was yet another document, judicially toxic. A confession. Too dangerous for public scrutiny. Bezier felt relieved yet at the same time a hostage to what he had written. Conscience, the little thorn that lames the foot, was not what had prompted him to write. A sense of history, rather, a premonition of a future reader, made him set down details in the neat handwriting of a monk trained in liturgical script.

Rolling the sheet into a cylinder of diameter little more than two fingers width, he trapped it in a gap between two large pebbles. Taking a candlestick containing the stub of a candle, he held the wick over the open end of the lantern. The heat soon melted the beeswax and ignited the end. A stick of red sealing wax lay in a tray of various implements, a pen knife, a candle snuffer and paraphernalia associated with calligraphy. He held candle and sealant over the midpoint of the exposed edge of the parchment. Molten drops formed an island of red on the beige paper. Before it could set, he pressed the free edge into contact with the main roll of parchment. Satisfied it had set sufficiently, he blew out the candle, picked up the sealing wax and dropped it back onto the tray.

Bezier stood. With lantern and parchment he crossed to a set of three, stone slabs forming a seat beneath the window. The glass looked out on monastery land towards the distant town. Translucent but not totally transparent, during the day it allowed a pleasant light through its green stained panes.

None of the slabs were cemented in place. He put the lantern and sheet on one of the side slabs and tilted the middle one against the sill. Inside, an oak casket sat with other items, some of value, others of sentimental rather than of intrinsic worth. A key was secreted under a small, unsecured stone within the cavity. Lifting out casket then key, he unlocked the lid and placed the document inside. Replacing key and casket, he lowered the stone slab gently into place.

Satisfied, fulfilled even but now tired by the day's or night's events, rather, he retired for a very short rest before the Office of Primes.

38

The local Jesuit Superior called Ignatius to the Chapter House. A second cleric was present in the library, Ignatius' spiritual advisor. Both were older by some three or four decades. The atmosphere was more cordial and informal than his examination in Rome. It should be. His relationship with the Jesuit Superior had always been one of friendship rather than of master/subordinate. The same with his spiritual advisor.

'Whiskey?'

'Thank you.'

Superior and advisor were already sipping one of Ireland's well known malts. Ignatius welcomed this touch of informality in what he knew was an unwelcome task for the two, long-time friends.

The older Jesuit, although not a cardinal, was, in the hierarchy of the Society of Jesus, the senior authority. He motioned Ignatius to sit in one of the smoothly worn but undamaged, leather, wingback chairs that formed a set of six furnishing the room. Ignatius watched him pour a generous measure, took the glass offered him and sat back, waiting.

'We've received the judgement of the Holy See, Rome. You will have received the same document,' he picked up the only item that lay on his desk and dropped it back, 'so we'll dispense with a formal reading. I will just summarise the instructions demanded of the examination so that we can report back without any accusation of breached protocols.

You were instructed to come to a decision as to a period of rustication at a retreat or of self-excommunication. I have to repeat that, formally, as you know and you are to acknowledge that formally with a yes or no. Were you so instructed?'

'Yes.'

'I am also instructed to remind you that excommunication is normally resolved by a declaration of repentance and a profession of the Creed, should a candidate, no longer in a state of grace, recant subsequently. There is no requirement for you to comment on that. As part of Canon Law you will know that.

Cardinal Morelli has sent me a separate communication to the effect that, should you choose retreat, you, nonetheless, should admit to committing a grave offense that caused you to be spiritually separated from the Church and the community of the faithful. Also that even though you have as yet not shown your choice, at this point, that, as an act of faith, you do make a declaration of repentance and a profession of the Creed, together with a renewal of your vows of obedience.

Should you not choose retreat, you understand that by such rejection, you automatically have left the Church on your own accord by committing said offense.'

The old Jesuit gave the folder in front of him a little push with both hands and shook his head, expressing his reluctance at having been forced to caution Ignatius.

'Red tape! Father Dominic, do you wish to add comment?'

'Thank you Father Benedict,' Ignatius's advisor eyed the young cardinal and smiled kindly.

'It's good to meet as friends. There is little else to say. I might have been remiss in not engineering a meeting before all this. I am not surprised but dare I say it, not disappointed in events as they stand. I had detected a change in the direction of your thinking over the last two years or so. A certain development, not so much of doubt but, perhaps, evolution might be a better description, an evolution in your thinking guiding you towards Teilhard de Chardin whom you have mentioned more than once in our meetings. You must make your decision one of conscience, not of coercion. Whatever you decide honestly will be the correct decision. You will have my blessing either way.'

The formalities of this mini Inquisition out of the way, both older prelates could be seen visibly to relax. It seemed clear to Ignatius that Father Benedict was of a benevolently similar mind to Father Dominic. Benedict invited Ignatius to answer.

'The account you have is more or less as I remember events in Rome. I'm afraid I goaded Cardinal Morelli, saying things, maybe, I should have left unsaid.

Conscience, I know, can be misinformed but I spoke, as you counsel me now, from conscience. I will not accept the offer of a retreat but neither will I admit to committing heresy. As for the television programme he comments on, the statements made by the panel are not necessarily right or wrong. In their eyes they merely don't conform to the structure of ethics supported by Morelli and he doesn't have a monopoly on truth.'

Ignatius sat still and waited, watching the two elders.

'Like Father Dominic, I am not surprised at your decision. We are both old priests and shocked by few things these days. Appalled but not shocked, not surprised by the world as it presents itself. We live in uncertain times. For us, at our age, it is wiser to resist evil as we perceive it; to try to ameliorate circumstances; to give good every chance we can afford it. I will report your answer to Cardinal Morelli but with no comment. Whether we will be consulted on further action remains to be seen. It is unlikely the matter will be left to fate. But who knows? Anyway, let us enjoy our time together now.'

'Do you see yourself still conducting any of the sacred offices? Baptism, marriage ... ', Dominic waved his glass at an imaginary host of participants, 'that's if Rome doesn't decree otherwise.'

'Depends whether there are others able to take it on. Whether there is a continuing shortfall in candidates offering themselves for ordination; the perception the congregation might have of my authority to dispense the holy sacraments. I still feel for the pain, the grief of those bereaved. The privilege of being able to offer some kind of comfort. But,' Ignatius paused, to give emphasis to his words, 'I can no longer subscribe to the mechanical observance given to mindless repetition of liturgy or penitential formulae. That is blasphemy, in a way or certainly a showing of disregard for the spiritual meaning behind the words. How I handle that remains to be seen. I, if you've not already been informed, have found ...,' he hesitated, pursed his lips searching for words, 'formed a relationship with one of my ex students. We met solely by accident, during my sabbatical at the Pontifical Gregorian University. She was there researching for her Ph.D.'

'Little escapes the Catholic community in Dublin. Whilst it's not exactly common knowledge it has become part of the gossip in some circles, not in a noticeably condemnatory sense. Maybe it has done the Church some good in an oblique sort of way. Better that than buggering little boys.'

They all laughed. Benedict waved the decanter, 'Top up? Come on, we rarely have the opportunity to let go like this.'

The two older clerics had, in their long vocations, weathered a variety of experiences from war through to missionary service performed with genuine, Christian love in some of the most extreme conditions of danger and poverty. Both had, at some time or other, experienced the emotion and gratification of a romantic attachment. Both had regretted not pursuing such a fulfilment to its conclusion. The meeting lapsed, briefly, into one of reflective silence.

Father Dominic broke the silence.

'I find it increasingly difficult to pass judgement on anyone's behaviour. Uninvited circumstance makes us hostage to opinion. Yes, there are situations where condemnation is justified but where condemnation is the product of a bigoted mindset, judgement, even when by accident it happens to be right, carries with it a tainted license. Thank God we have fewer years ahead of us than went before.' He swallowed a good measure of whiskey. 'You know you can talk to us freely, without fear. We have known each other, now, for some years. Where do you see your work with this new venture taking you?'

'I know where I intend to take it, rather than it takes me. Did you happen to see the first two programmes?'

'Dominic did. I missed them.'

'The panel of speakers is carefully selected in the hope of stimulating controversy.'

'I don't doubt that,' Benedict looked ruefully at Ignatius, 'with the publicity given to the recent attack on the studio I would say you achieved your aim.'

They laughed, 'But, seriously, here in Ireland? I can understand it in England and France, particularly but here ...?' Benedict shook his head.

'The security team suggest the attackers came in on the Fishguard - Rosslare ferry. We've had a lot of support from viewers. Both programmes have been aired in a number of countries. Surprisingly, there have been several emails from enlightened Muslim viewers, thanking us for pointing out the unreality of some Qur'anic narrative. But they're the exception. Most vitriol comes from literate but not over-educated, Muslims. You can tell, somehow, from the character of their message, they lack insight. Motivated by fear and superstition. If not that, some kind of obligation to be recognised as 'good Muslims'. Virtue signalling, broadcasting their protest, notifying their compatriots at the mosque, that, as 'good Muslims', they registered their disapproval through social media.'

'You'll always be up against the bigots, the extremists in any religion or ideology, come to that. The problem is with us in Catholicism no less. But the worst are the glaze-hardened, 'frogs of the holy water basin', as the French term them, the ones who always seem to be polishing the pews. Other religions don't have the monopoly on hypocrisy. At higher levels, in the exercise of power, when doctrine develops into an inflexible, insidious dogma, schism inflicts damage on an otherwise benign belief system. The same in the political arena; instability if it is unchecked. We've seen that as missionaries. Dominic, you see it that way?'

'Difficult not to. A philosopher or social scientist might take us to task for unqualified arguments, opinion unsubstantiated by fact. For all that, an imperfect belief system - if it is not intrinsically harmful and unites in a positively beneficial way, beneficial, that is, to the majority - is preferred to a vacuum. It welds society together. It welds together people with a common interest or culture.'

Ignatius smiled.

'Something amuses you?'

'Yes. We, that is, my parents and friend, had a similar conversation a few months back. We were remarking on the Holocaust and the likelihood that observance of religious protocols enabled some camp inmates to survive the internment. But, on the other hand, there were secular Jews with no religious faith who also survived. Practice of the one group did not negate success in the other. It's interesting to hear it aired here. Practically the same sentiments. It's a bit like both strikers of opposing South American football teams crossing themselves before penalty shootouts – the winning team thinks god was on their side because of the act of the devotional signal. Nonsense!'

'Nothing new. Maybe the general public don't think beyond what gratifies the immediate needs of their search for pleasure or justifies their prejudices. As Jesuits we've been trained in the most rigorous disciplines of logic and reason. Trained in Jesuit seminaries that are the envy of any faculty of philosophy in any university of note anywhere. But that still does not shield us from error. It doesn't deny us the privilege of erroneous opinions served by an instinct similarly misguided. But we have to speak as honestly as our conscience dictates, without fear and without prejudice.'

Ignatius looked at his watch, 'I think I've taken my quota of hours. Time to take leave. I didn't know what to expect but should've realised it wouldn't be the ordeal it could have been. Thank you for companionship, as ever and the whiskey.'

All three stood. All three, with genuine affection, parted with a fraternal hug.

39

'How'd it go?'

'Fine. We've known each other all of my vocational years. Two of the finest priests one could wish to meet.'

Ignatius related most of the outcome from his meeting with Benedict and Dominic, 'So until we get a response from Rome, life carries on as before.'

'Good. Now to change the subject, the site manager wants to know if you've made your mind up about solar cells. He telephoned from Rocky Valley. Two banks of four or five? He reckons we'd be mad not to go for the ten or even three banks of four he's now suggesting. The labour charges are not going to be that much different for either but the energy gain means the studio will be costing us less to power up than we originally budgeted for. A lot less and it'll still be the same cable rating from the main house to the studio whether eight, ten or twelve.'

'I was thinking about it walking back. We might as well go for the twelve. Winter can be pretty rough, especially if we get a blizzard. Few and far between these days but even without snow that north easterly can be a killer. Let's go for that. We can top up the heat from the mains after sundown.'

'I was hoping you would agree. Food! I've not eaten. Shall we walk into town for dinner? Or shall I rustle up an omelette?'

'Let's eat in town. Just fancy some Dublin prawns and a bottle of dry white. A plate of crusty bread and fish soup to follow.'

'Now you're talkin'.'

*

'I want to run a few ideas past you. Stephen is thinking about the next flush of programmes. I also need to knock something up for the column and Janet Hicks wants a meeting about the new, undergrad, philosophy degree.' The waiter arrived with a bottle of wine, 'Just pour it. Leave the cork. We'll take back what we don't finish. Thank you.' Ignatius waited until he'd gone.

'So. Janet Hicks. You were going to say.'

'Right. Hers is easy. I've suggested we have a tie-in with the new Robotics and AI programme. Lot of agro over Big Tech ethics. Combined with the mathematics faculty and IT, we could future-proof the course.'

'In what way?'

'Well, social media problems keep evolving. Response to the ethics issues they present means the course or one aspect of it, can be tailored to reflect changes. We don't want a knee-jerk response to every negative or positive, though, as soon as one presents itself, just a normal course reappraisal every so often. The algorithms are the big one. It's getting to a point where commerce is driving AI in some areas. I've heard you swearing every time an ad comes up on your laptop, directly connected to some search you've made earlier.

OK, the positive side is when the search engines are put to medical or scientific analysis, say but I don't need to tell you that. I know we've talked about unexplored aspects of your research but linguistic theory, linguistic philosophy, applied to search engines and, to a lesser extent, robotics, is an area I reckon will lead to more insightful applications. There almost seems to be a need for a brilliant mind to come along which hasn't been conditioned by prior influences. Why do I say '*almost*'? No 'almost' about it. We need minds that can work ab origine, minds that get on with it without too much dithering. That's why a pipeful of Latakia clears the air.'

'Clears the air, my ass. Although I must confess there are times when I '*almost*' feel like saying, 'pass me the pipe'. But it probably smells better than it tastes. Anyway, Stephen?'

'He's been fazed by the attack. Haven't we all? But he's not going to put the brakes on. Still wants to stir things up. I'm of the same mind, although we're the ones in the firing line.'

'What about *Compensation for the Clearances* as a topic?'

'Which clearances?'

'The Irish, potato famine clearances.'

'God! That's a new one.'

'Well, not exactly new but it's no different from BLM and compensation claims for descendants of slaves. It would generate plenty of heat with an audience.'

'You must be joking and Irish people wouldn't take kindly to any suggestion of voyeurism exploiting the suffering of their forebears if they perceive it as a wind-up for the *'Troubles'*.'

'Never been more serious. It might focus attention on the complexity and dare I say it, the futility of the slavery issue.'

'Not sure about futility. Intractability, more like. There's a counter argument doing the rounds - part of the white supremacy take on the matter. They're raising the subject of the whole cultural evolution of the US; of the industrial and scientific legacy hard won and fought for by pioneering settlers of Caucasian origin. That illegal immigration and an overwhelming black population is swamping an infrastructure devised by the ingenuity, skills and centuries of progress evolved by European minds not achieved by third world civilisations - if civilisations adequately describes some of the primitive conditions huge swathes of their populations still subsist under.'

'Yes but there has been an imbalance of ... , I dunno, equality of opportunity for ethnic minorities.'

'Hang on a minute. There has to be a context for 'equality of opportunity', as you put it. That context has been provided, however unfairly one perceives it to have been acquired, by Caucasian creativity. The moral or ethical conclusions about the fairness or unfairness of qualifications or ethnic status demanded of candidates applying for jobs, surely has to be decided by the generators, the originators offering that opportunity. They're taking the risk. For me, he who pays the piper calls the tune.

I've taught undergraduates who were, no doubt, more intelligent than I but the point is, within the context of that scenario, I, at the time, was in possession of more experience, knowledge and insight than they were privileged to own at that stage of their education and that was why they applied to attend lectures. We're back to the situation of: 'what are the parameters of the argument?' governing our argument now. To give an example: I don't care if there is some quantum physicist with greater insight into my discipline than I've exhibited over my career but he or she, like me, has relied on groundwork prepared by others. That kind of edifying, intellectual property in the public domain is not the same as, bears no analogy to, some African despot taking over a fully working state, kicking out the successful white administrators and the wealth producing element, plundering and degrading the infrastructure as has

229

happened in a number of ex-colonies. In fact, leaving the black workers worse off than they were under the previous regime. No. Entitlement has to be earned. As far as slavery and compensation are concerned, how far back do we go? It's been repeated elsewhere: the shores from Cornwall, Ireland to the Faroes have been raided for slaves by North African slavers in the past. Western civilisation doesn't have a monopoly on the history of slavery nor do African-Americans a monopoly on virtue.'

'God, you're basically a racist.'

'Well yes, possibly, in that context. If a problem exists which has a racial context then it generates rational observations that will be perceived as racist. Unpleasant as truth is sometimes it still remains truth however you categorise it. I'm a pragmatist but I'd rather be perceived as a culturalist if you're going assign any kind of label at all. The same kind of debate applies to compensating the socially disadvantaged through handouts. Some deserve it some don't. Some are undeserving victims of misfortune, others the wilful architects of their own disasters.'

'This doesn't square with the years you've put in on your vocation as a priest. Surely you have some compassion, empathy for the disadvantaged?'

'Maybe I should have said misfits, rather than disadvantaged. I've got cynical. When some journalist, for example, interviews a single mother with two or three kids, they never ask 'where is the father?' or fathers, rather. I know sometimes they are widows or women who have suffered misfortune through no fault of their own but socialism has gone soft. It's rewarding the symptoms of poverty rather than questioning the path that got it there. Paying for tattoos or cigarettes rather than putting cake on the table.'

'We're getting nowhere with this. Truce.'

'We're not fighting and I could do with a top up. Anyway, I'll give *'The Clearances'* a thought. It's likely we'd need a fall back topic. *Clearances* on its own might not be enough. Depends on whether an audience would drag it into present day conflict over Union.'

The two left the business of argument and turned to enjoying a fresh slug of wine and the plates of local sea food.

40

Marcel and Gabriel reached St Malo after two day's travel. The younger monk elected to stay for a further day after a night's rest at the chandlery. Neither man referred to their time together in the monastery at Rennes. Both had agreed to practise using the name Piran during their journey to the coast.

On the morning he was to travel back to the monastery Marcel took a small, suede pouch from the satchel he was carrying, 'I have a gift for you.'

Piran took the beige, purse-like pouch, pulled the flap from the sash securing it and pulled a flat piece of copper-rich pewter from inside. Set into one end was a circular, magnifying lens, the metal surround squared off with five edges, the remaining length tapered to form a comfortable grip for thumb and two fingers. Two words were inscribed on the grip, *'Marcellus Fecit'*, in fine, French script.

'Thank you my brother. This I shall treasure. May God be your constant companion.'

The two monks embraced.

'If you set foot on French soil again get word to us at Rennes. We can meet in safety somewhere. I wish you well in your new life and a safe journey to Cornwall.'

*

It was two weeks before a boat from Cornwall put into the port. As before, the master of the vessel, a cross between a schooner and a ketch, was obliging and willing to take Piran to one of the south west coastal towns. For a tariff similar to his earlier, aborted journey and help with minor duties aboard, the monk embarked with the crew for Penzance. They left an hour or so before sun up.

By midnight, a strong south westerly signalled the approach of wilder weather. The boat took the seas well but her captain, one Moses Hunkin, decided it safer to make for Falmouth.

'She's blowin' up rough. Mount's Bay's too open. We'm makin' for Carrick Roads,' again, a variety of Cornish and Breton words helped the ship's master and Piran to communicate, 'the seas off Lizard are a killer; we daren't risk passage out from the Point.'

The little two-masted boat, no longer fighting the wind, ran with the gale. Well out from the partially submerged ridge of teeth known as the Manacles and now on a north easterly course, the crew enjoyed relief from the head-on battering they had been putting up with. A craft well maintained, the rigging and masts stood up to the punishment meted out by winds that were known to tear spires off churches and fell trees. They reached the mouth of the river Fal just at dawn. The sun, not quite above the horizon, picked out the upper battlements of the grey structure of Pendennis castle high on the promontory of the western bank of the estuary. Piran, used to what might have been termed as inshore fishing in the boat belonging to his monastery, was not sea-sick. Just occasionally the little boat, belonging to the Augustinian brothers, had ventured out into the Baie de Morlaix and got caught in a rough sea. He had not succumbed to the disabling bouts of sea-sickness his brother monks experienced on the rare occasions it occurred. This time was no different.

Moses Hunkin turned to Piran as the vessel entered the relatively calm stretch of water known as Carrick Roads. Lights from torches not yet extinguished, in St Mawes and Pendennis castles, were still evident from the flickering emanating from musket exits so far unchallenged by war. These fortifications, built by Henry VIII, guarded the entrance to the estuary - St Mawes on the east promontory, Pendennis on the west.

'I'm well known in the town. I can put you off here, if you wish it but you're a good hand on deck and welcome to journey back to Penzance with me when we leave. You might even consider a share in this vessel if it takes your fancy. I put out from Penzance so your lodgings would need to be down Marazion, Mousehole or nearer. But no haste. If you stay, there's good lodgings to be had by the harbour and you'd easy find work as a glass maker hereabouts. Ships make regular passage between Falmouth and Penzance. You're sure to find me in port at least every two moons. There's good commerce with the Bishop of Exeter's Cornish deanery further up the Fal, towards Truro. The Dean likes his brandy and claret and turns a blind eye to Customs and Revenue rules. I do the French run when there's a full moon, to service his needs.'

'Thank you Moses. I've enjoyed my time aboard. My skills could take me to Penzance. I know it from my time at the Priory, on the Mount.'

' 'es, look me up boy, if you decide. Just ask for Moses Hunkin. I'm well known down that end. Anyway, for now, we'll tie up alongside Customs House Quay and dine in the Arwenack Arms. The missus there serves up a good fish stew.'

As the boat got close to the little shipbuilding yards clustering the shore line from Pendennis to Penryn, the inviting smell of smoke from ash and oak wafted across the deck. A multitude of ovens and spits were already fired up to bake loaves or roast a carcass of some animal or other. Salted, filleted cod, well out of reach of stray dogs, hung from racks of timber frames. Elsewhere the odd smoke house concealed similar fillets of herring and mackerel. It was from these that the appetising smells of food emanated, blended with that of the smoke and oils released by the heat from the gutted fish.

Scores of boats had taken shelter. Moorings were such that boats were tied up alongside each other at the quay. It was a matter of jumping from one deck to another in order to reach the last boat adjacent to the huge granite blocks it was moored up against. This was a common practice. An unwritten rule amongst the fraternity of sea captains and small boat owners.

Piran, Moses and his crew checked sails were properly furled and no loose gear able to blow through gunnel drainage ports. Moses filled a flask with cognac, 'This'll pay for our meat and drink. We better be gettin' ashore before the inn fills up with dockers, crews and trade from the town.'

The little group clambered across three other vessels of similar rigging. Their deck rails touching midships. Timbers creaked as the boats rode the swells pulsing into the inner harbour. Various halyards and other tightly secured ropes slapped against tall masts as funnels of wind sought out the sisal ties now freed from their job of keeping sails in place. They took great care crossing between craft. Crushed ribs, maimed legs were the price paid by crew returning inebriated and losing footing between decks. It was also the price for haste after a bellyful of rum had been consumed onboard before leaving a ship.

A fair crowd was already gathered in the Arwenack. Clouds of blue smoke from rough twists of tarry tobacco gave the inn a pleasant atmosphere of wellbeing if not of a healthy lifestyle. Coffee had also reached this end of the south west peninsula and the stimulating smell of its over-percolated grains, added to the appeal of lodgings that didn't move with the wind and sea.

Moses, a well known patron over the years, was greeted by the owner of the inn and led to one of the unoccupied tables close to a kitchen with an open door separating it from the main drinking room of the tavern. Handing over the cognac he also produced a package from the large pocket taking up most of the chest area of the tunic he had changed into before leaving the boat.

'Here boy, for the missus.' Again, use of the word boy signified greeting rather than relative age in the Cornish vernacular.

'What is it?'

'Finest French lace. She'll love it. You can do yourself a favour by saying you ordered it 'specially for when I next came.' He winked and Piran with the other two crew members laughed at the implied meaning of the word favour.

'You ol' bugger. She won't take that soft soap from me anymore but she'll be thankful all the same. Now what can I get you?'

'We'd like a jug of ale whilst we wait an' I've been extolling the virtues of your fish stew to our Breton friend, Piran, here.'

Piran, taking the cue, put his hand up by way of salutation.

'He might be looking for lodgings if he decides not to sail down to Mount's Bay with us. You've got a spare bed should he stay in Falmouth? Or can fix him up with some friendly widow hereabouts?'

Again the group laughed.

'I'll see what I can do. In the meantime: jug of ale, four fish stews and a loaf of crusty bread.'

The innkeeper gave instructions to his daughter who went off to fetch the ale. He disappeared into the kitchen. A short while after, his wife appeared and put a loaf of bread and a board with a slab of cheese on the table before embracing Moses and thanking him for the lace.

Some hours later the group returned to sleep on the boat, all except Piran who elected to stay the night at the Arwenack. The events of the previous month had caught up with him. The full realisation that he was now finally free from the horrendous ordeal of immolation suddenly left him drained of energy. The others would set off early the following morning without returning to shore. Piran needed time to reassess his position - his mind and his domestic circumstances. He would stay.

41

The bed was comfortable but Piran rose at dawn. Still governed by the hours of the Sacred Offices, he found it unnatural not to be rising to celebrate Prime at 6am. There were three other occupants in the room. They slept on. He went down the darkened stairway to a freshly burning pile of logs sitting in a bed of last night's recharged embers in the main room of the tavern. The innkeeper's daughter was in the kitchen setting up a spit loaded with freshly plucked and gutted guinea fowl. There was already a pot of coffee simmering by the embers. She took a pewter mug, hanging by its handle from a wooden peg fixed in a beam above her head and pointed towards the pot. He nodded.

Sitting down at the same table the group occupied the previous day, he found the mug of caffeine a welcome treat. A dash of milk took away the bitterness of the over-brewed beverage, giving it a creamy flavour that added further pleasure to his taste buds. The Cornish had always appreciated the rich cream that fortified the milk even if they didn't appreciate the fine drizzle that blessed the lush grass producing it.

He took stock of his circumstances. He was learned in the ecclesiastical sense. Skilled in a number of quasi-scientific disciplines; lens making; processes bordering on the alchemic and a smattering of surgical procedures he had picked up from the apothecaries in various locations. His journey to and back from Italy had permitted him to observe practices that varied from monastery to monastery, province to province. In each village or town he traversed there would be a blacksmith or wheelwright, cooper or bow maker, glass maker or potter, carpenter or mason to be found. Each had a technique unknown to others. He observed and absorbed, storing images in the preparation and execution of various actions that went into producing some item or construction technique. Although he excelled in none of these skills he had an eye for proportion, a feel for materials and could make an acceptable attempt at any number of these activities. The blacksmiths afforded him the greatest interest. From them he picked up knowledge of making iron tools.

The artisans, jealous of their trade secrets, warmed to Gabriel the monk but as Piran the jobbing itinerant, as he now would be, their demonstrations of skill would have been more guarded.

'What's your name?'

'Lamorna Kessel.' The innkeeper's daughter set a bowl and jug of hot milk on the table. She proceeded to cut a square of stale hevva cake into bite sized pieces, dropping them into the bowl.

'My father says you will be staying with us for a time.' She poured the hot milk over the mound of flour and lard-based, cake fragments. The raisins and dried peel, exposed at the surfaces, glistened, washed by the liquid. 'There, that'll do you 'til midday.' She hurried back through the open door to the kitchen.

Piran finished the breakfast. Phep Kessel, the inn keeper, came into the tavern from the street side. On his way to the kitchen he shouldered a sack of freshly baked loaves onto the table by Piran.

'Moses tells me you're a man of letters as well as an artificer in glass. Sir Peter Killigrew, at Arwenack House, is looking for a tutor for his children.'

'This Peter Killigrew, he would pay a fair stipend?'

239

'He pays well and provides lodgings. I've heard no complaints. It will stand you in good stead, were you move to Penzance, to be known as favoured by Killigrew. He is a Royalist, disposed towards High Anglican just short of popery.'

Piran, although now safely away from Catholic jurisdiction, thought it wise to downplay any opinion Catholic.

'Yes, I am familiar with the ancient languages of Latin and Greek and Euclid's geometry. I care very little for these ancient tongues. They have their use in learned congress with others of like mind but the terseness of your English and our Celtic languages is of sharper, more direct communication. As to popery, my sympathies lie with Luther. I completed a novitiate but not my final vows.'

'Best of both worlds. There's many, hereabout, would agree. You'd be best served by putting your case to him as a man of letters. He has a priest who would see you as a threat if you relate your clerical credentials. Anyway, there's lodgings here for as long as you wish but I can fill your bed easy like if you go. Business is brisk, no obligation on your part to stay but you're welcome to take meat with us here whenever and whatever your status.'

Piran, encouraged by this news, held back from committing himself, mentally, to such a post. He was not sure where his mind lay. In his time on the boat with Moses Hunkin, accounts of Penzance had taken his fancy but in the brief number of hours he had experienced in this corner of Cornwall, the attraction of the estuary, the activity around the port had impacted on his senses, giving him a sense of wellbeing and belonging.

'Thank you Phep. I might enquire at the House. I shall need means to pay my way. Your terms, here, suit me. Until I find gainful employment I shall stay with you. Killigrew sounds a worthwhile try.

42

There was no news from Rome. Rome was never in a hurry. It had survived two thousand years. Why should it need to change patterns of protocol established over two millennia of subterfuge, infighting and bloodshed? Continuing power was essential to continuing existence. Permanence took precedence over short term acts of amoral action in the long-term protection of that power.

Ignatius was aware now of possessing a growing, fatalistic attitude to his status, both as a Jesuit and as a possible lay communicant of the Church. He felt no obligation to bear witness to any kind of guilt the Catholic authorities might attempt to impose. It didn't bother him that he might be seen as a Pariah by past congregations who knew him as a presiding officiant at mass, reciting their Hail Marys, genuflecting and crossing themselves feverishly like some kind of plague might descend on them if they didn't do it swiftly or often enough. He did value the spiritual influence and logic of New Testament theology as revealed by St Paul but again, only in so far as it preserved a certain stabilising, civilising influence on society. Not for any non-existent, supernatural magic that led to all kinds of aberration of thought which in turn led to harmful, cultish persecution of those who would not subscribe to such thought. In the end, for him, this theology was only as valid as the initial premise supporting the wisdom of Christ and not from any divine attribute claimed by the writers of the gospels.

The clarity and simplicity of some of the liturgy, the biblical narratives, these were to be appreciated as canons of literature in their own right but their intrinsic value, as far as he was concerned, now lay only in their worth to those it benefitted. Any so-called hidden mysteries the literature might contain, whose existence depended solely on a criterion of faith rather than reasonable instinct, were to be acknowledged but, apart from their moral or ethical value, only as props necessary to maintaining the mental balance of simple, unquestioning minds. He was a sceptic as far as dubiously verifiable miracles were concerned.

'Still no news from Rome?'

'No.' Ignatius looked up from his laptop at Penny. 'I'm inclined to just let it ride. Somewhere, no doubt, there'll be procedure documented to deal with rogue cardinals but there will also be reluctance to invoke action.'

'I think you should initiate some move yourself. It's occupying your mind. Not doing you any good,' she paused, 'but you're in a better position than most clerics who have no second string to fall back on when they've discovered their loss of belief in the existing order.'

'Maybe you're right. Although I say I'm inclined to freewheel on the matter, I have contemplated *'nailing my 95 theses'* on the Vatican's door. It might have a beneficial effect, although small, on the general agenda.'

'General agenda? Like what?'

'Well, give encouragement to the progressives who want to see change. Anyway, we'll see what comes up. Changing the subject, there's a response to my last email to Stephen. He's interested in your suggestion re the potato famine clearances.'

'You told him about that?'

'Yes. He's asking if I would consider you a suitable candidate for the panel. Wants me to put it to you. You'd be an *Independent* so to speak. What d'you think?'

Penny laughed, 'That's a turn up for the books. Not sure I'd match the line-up of previous stars and being obviously English, not seen as independent in Irish Republican eyes.'

'That's as maybe but you have an incisive mind and it won't be inhibited by having to toe a party line. You're not beholden to any cause. A neutral mind even though you have a recognisably, English voice. Your attitude to Mountbatten confirms that, even though you disapproved of the assassination, particularly the killing of the children at the same time.'

'I'll think about it. There's all the matter of prior preparation. I know it's a spontaneous, unrehearsed performance but it still needs some research, anticipation of thorny issues such as raised by *The Troubles*. It's been done to death one way or another over the years. I wouldn't want to make a fool of myself and if it is combined with other topics, I might be perceived as lacking.'

'I understand. I know some appreciation of history over the last two or three centuries is necessary but we're hoping, in the programme, to put a slant on the influence of the Catholic Church in delaying social progress, subsequent to the famine. The obsequious behaviour of civil authorities toadying up to the Church. The sickening, almost Fascist attitude of some of the less intellectually gifted Garda Síochána and civil authorities towards women pregnant out of wedlock and, even more, the convents that have provided shelter to these women. Convents that, in some respects, have been little short of being baby farms

244

or even worse, infant-killing machines. I have no sympathy for recklessly pursued, unprotected sex but there are obscene acts - or have been - of gratuitous tyranny exercised by bigoted, self-righteous nuns. Nuns of limited intelligence. Bovine in their behaviour. Fortunately, there are, in the majority, those who give dedicated service to the various dioceses around the Republic. Nuns who would be and are, ashamed of those lacking basic, human *agápē*.'

'I'd be happy, if that's the right word, giving a female perspective on that, particularly on the abortion issue. There's plenty of mileage in that one.'

'Hello!' A voice, interrupting Ignatius' comments, was followed by the sound of the back door butting up against the wall.

'We've the sliding cover in place. D'you want to come and have a look? Try it out?'

The voice was Patrick Ryan.

'Coming.'

The two followed him to the new building, along a newly laid, concrete path eventually to be enclosed by frosted glass panels. Inside, a concrete base was waiting for wooden flooring to be laid. A stainless-steel clad chimney, hanging through a mezzanine floor, showed the location of a site for a log-burning stove. The open end of the upper floor was supported by a vertical, four-by-four oak strut fixed midway under an equally robust, cross beam.

All three made for the banister-free staircase clinging to the side of the longer, rectangular wall. Upstairs two workman were enjoying freshly poured flasks of tea as they waited for the inspection. A small, lightweight platform below a square cut-out in the roof, showed the intended location of the stellar telescope. Above it a polycarbonate sheet, in an aluminium frame. Designed to be pushed across the roof, rather than up or down, it obviated the need to work against gravity. The low, circular platform was mounted on four free-running castors, two of which could be locked.

Ignatius stepped onto the platform and released the hooked catch securing the cover. The lightweight assembly glided, almost friction-free, along aluminium guides, on two pairs of wheels. He closed it and invited Penny to do the same.

'OK?' Ryan sought approval he knew would be given.

'Excellent. Better than I expected. Penny?'

'Brilliant. All we need now is the telescope.'

Patrick Ryan thanked the two men, 'Good job boys. You's earned your keep.'

He turned back to Ignatius and Penny, 'We'll get the wood down on the floor then connect the stove before the electrician starts on the fittings. Should be out of here by Friday. The electrician reckons he needs two days, possibly less. Then we're all set for the grand opening.'

Ignatius and Penny had not, in their dealings with Ryan, been familiar to the point of intimating any suggestion of a 'grand opening'. They understood his remark as a hint at some kind of celebration that doubled as a non-financial bonus in the form of a free knees-up. The two workmen cast a knowing glance at their employer, hiding smiles behind a simultaneous slug of warm tea from their screw-off, flask cups.

'Maybe we'll need to mark the first day in with some sort of recognition but not sure when that'll be. Got a pretty full timetable over the next few weeks. In fact, we'll have to leave keys with you for the time being. Have to get back to Dublin tonight.'

'No problem. My boys'll leave the place clean and free from any loose bits. Let me know when you're back here. We'll sign off the job then.'

Penny and Ignatius thanked the two workmen and went down, followed by Ryan, to look at the sliding assembly from the outside.

'One thing I wanted to say out of earshot of the two boys. I might have a proposition for the rental of the studio when you're not in residence. Might you be interested?'

Ignatius faced Penny. Gave her a look as much to confirm his earlier comments about the IRA as to signal his intention to handle the matter without her involvement.

'That's a euphemism for saying a discreet meeting place for persons of anonymous identity, if that isn't an oxymoron.'

'Father, I think we understand our obligations to each other.' Ryan's not so cryptic response set the meaning clear.

'I need to discuss it with my partner.' Ignatius was no longer concerned about referring to Penny as someone in obvious contravention of his vows of celibacy. 'Thanks again for completing well ahead of schedule. I think it hardly needs to be said we're both pleased with the work.' Ignatius shook hands then watched Patrick Ryan return to the studio.

43

The dogs heard Piran well before he reached the heavy, oak door to Arwenack House. It opened just as he raised his staff to knock.

'You look too well attired to be a beggar. What is your business here?' He was greeted by a young woman in her late teens. Two wolf hounds, quiet now, pressed up against her hips. Her manner suggested ownership rather than domestic servitude.

'The landlord at the Arwenack Arms tells me Sir Peter Killigrew needs a tutor for his children. I am qualified in Greek, Latin and Geometry and am well versed in the scriptures.'

The girl gave him a further quick appraisal, decided he was to be trusted and told him to wait at the door with the dogs. She returned after a short while.

'Follow me. My father will see you. What is your name?'

Piran was about to say Gabriel, 'Piran Hawken. I have spent time with the monks in Brittany, following a tour of the southern countries but have returned to Cornwall this Easter season.'

'My father will be interested to hear of your travels.'

The girl led him to an upstairs room overlooking a stretch of water harbouring vessels of widely varying size. Small, open-hulled, single masted boats through to ocean-going galleons and two- or three-masted, coastal trading vessels. A carpet from the Levant, doubtless brought in on a trading ship, was anchored beneath a well polished, oak, writing table. A globe stood in a corner beneath a decorative shield bearing armorial insignia. Other fine items of furniture, displaced about the room, suggested pragmatism rather than conspicuous wealth.

'So you think you are qualified to teach my whelps to be civilised? Come over into the light where I can see you.'

In that first moment of encounter, Piran decided a confident but respectful demeanour would make more impression than a grovelling, cap-wringing compliance. The man had a military bearing and carried with it the same command in the tone of his voice. Piran held himself erect and with a slight but, nonetheless, deliberate mark of respect, gave a nod more in the nature of a bow than that of assent.

'It depends on what discipline I am allowed to exact but my first instruction would be given as a friend rather than a despot. If they perceive that as weakness they shall see what anger is. I will not be compromised by disobedience.'

'Hmm. He speaks with confidence. What say you Katherine?'

'Yes father. The twins need discipline. Since our mother died they have become ungovernable.'

'You are schooled in Latin and Greek my daughter tells me. Where did you receive instruction?'

'I was a novice at a monastery in Finisterre but did not complete my vows. Took leave, on pilgrimages, to visit brothers at other priories and abbayes in Christendom as far as Rome and to this island. From them I learnt skills other than just letters. I am skilled in lens making and have passed my time observing the artisans of various trades in the many towns and villages I have stayed in during my travels.'

'You seem to have travelled extensively for one who is not that old. Why did you not complete your vows?'

249

'My sympathies lie with Luther. I cannot give obedience to Rome.'

'Your honesty is commendable.' Sir Peter Killigrew stroked his chin, as though weighing up a proposition. It was some time before he spoke again. The other two waited. 'You would accept the hospitality offered and a stipend of ten florins a week for your services?'

Piran had already assessed the needs he was prepared to subsist under. This was an offer beyond what he'd anticipated. The master of Arwenack was a man benefitting from a port enjoying growing trading links between the Old World and the New. It was not unlikely, Piran guessed, that he operated a privateer making a lucrative income from piracy. Falmouth was the first and last port of call for two-way traffic between the Americas, the North Sea and Channel Ports of Britain. There were plenty of Dutch, French and Spanish ships that carried cargoes worth plundering. A well armed, fast privateer could provide a good income for its owner. Falmouth was well placed to provide protection and opportunity. Benefitting well from such trade, he could afford to be generous in the interests of his family.

'I would.'

'When can you start? My daughter, as you heard, would wish it to be soon. Since my wife died she has had to shoulder responsibility for the running of the household.'

'I am ready to begin as soon as you say.'

'Good. I see no point in delay. You are lodging at the inn, I gather. My daughter will show you the accommodation. You will be here in the main house. The servants are housed in the lower floor where the kitchen and laundry are. The twins

250

will be tutored in the library; one hour in the morning and one after midday. I should expect them to receive instruction in arithmetic as well as geometry but will leave you to organise the order of delivery of all their learning. Katherine will attend some lessons to learn of their progress and response.' Killigrew turned to the window as a way of declaring the interview over.

'Follow me.' Katherine touched Piran's elbow.

Traversing the landings of the upper floor, Killigrew's daughter led Piran to a room at the far side of the house. It too looked out on a seascape. In the distance, above the tops of the trees, Pendennis castle stood out as a warning to hostile ships. Piran stood looking out at the granite edifice. The sun acted like a spotlight, giving the robust walls a steel-like appearance that reinforced the defensive character of the building. He turned back to take in his immediate surroundings.

The room was far better equipped than the many cells, as a monk, he had lodged in. A plain, wooden platform edged by narrow battens, held a mattress stuffed with some kind of flock, probably wool or torn up garments. It felt firm but not hard. Pressing it released the faint odour of lanolin, confirming the presence of wool. Other items of furniture completed an inventory that would ensure his comfort and provide facilities that, as a tutor, he would find useful. A desk and chair. A generous sill, below the window, suitable for storing writing implements, paper and books. A seafaring chest stood under the window. Katherine lifted the lid.

'You can store your possessions in here. I will ask one of the servants to bring blankets. I trust this is to your liking. You have made a favourable impression on my father. I can tell. It will be a relief to him that he has appointed a tutor to my

251

sisters. He does not enjoy the best of health and, since our mother died, has been sombre. The priest brings him no comfort.'

Piran sensed a warning, a dislike in the latter comment. The landlord's remark, earlier at the Arwenack Inn, reinforced his caution but he sensed further that Katherine Killigrew was not intimidated by any threat of hell and damnation the priest might attempt to exercise over her. The critical tone of her voice conveyed more than the words.

'I have, in my novitiate, assisted as a lay priest, ministering to the bereaved. When did your mother die?'

'During Lent. Last year.'

'It is still close, too close in memory. Your father will heal in his own time. No priest can provide comfort of that means.'

The girl looked quizzically into his face, not in a bewildered way, more as though searching for some kind of common identity. This disturbed Piran. He had, as a cleric, encountered nuns and the wives and daughters of the laity in his role as a monk but had not felt challenged or engaged by them. Unsettled, he stood mute, undetermined. She, likewise, caught unprepared by this sudden mood change, looked down at her feet, no longer the confident curator of the house.

'I will guide you through the rest of the house. My father will probably expect you to eat with us rather than the servants. He will, likely, enjoy learned conversation.'

The tour finished, Piran returned for one more night at the Arwenack Inn.

44

The following morning Piran returned to the manor house. Katherine Killigrew led Piran up to his bedroom. Two blankets lay folded on the mattress together with a pillow of duck down. His possessions were simply the satchel containing his usual everyday utensils, a few implements for use in lens making and a small bundle of clean clothing. He dumped the bag onto the window sill. The clothing he put into the chest.

'The twins are waiting in the library with my father. He doesn't expect you to teach today but expects you to give them a brief, oral examination.'

Piran followed Katherine into the library. The girls eyed him with angelic faces but he was not fooled. Having dealt with beggars through to higher orders of the laity, he had acquired a certain skill in reading people's character. These two were a bit too alert, something in their stare. Not malicious. Mischievous.

'Good day to you Hawken. These are my daughters Mary and Martha.'

Piran nodded. An enigmatic expression on his face conveying no signal to the two as to possible challenges they might exploit in his character. He stared back, neither aggressively nor benevolently. Their faces showed a fleeting hint of uncertainty as they stood, obviously instructed previously by their father, to stand in respect of Piran's office as a teacher. Piran smiled.

'Thank you Sir Peter,' not addressing the girls, 'I look forward to giving them instruction.'

'If you would assess their present state of ignorance I would be pleased to observe and hear their responses. There will be time later for you to inspect their writing skills.'

The twins' father expected Piran to act now.

'You may sit down. You may address me as Sir and if during our many lessons you have questions I shall expect you to raise a hand. I will refer to you as Mary or Martha.'

Piran's initial choice of questions surprised them all.

'The timber lining the walls, what tree does it come from? Your garments are wool or linen? By what means are the planks in the hull of a ship sealed. These candle sticks what is the metal? Your father's sword?'

He rotated the globe, 'How many days does it take for the moon to traverse the Earth? How many cases are there in the declension of a Latin noun and what are they? What is the eighth letter of the Greek alphabet?'

The girls responded to this somewhat unorthodox set of questions with a slight air of objection.

Mary put her hand up, 'We're not boys. We're girls. Girls don't do this.'

'If you are to survive in this world you need to be as cunning as an urchin and as refined as a nobleman. The fact that you are females is all the more reason to master knowledge expected of boys.'

Sir Peter Killigrew smiled approvingly.

First game to Piran. Piran carried on, this time with questions more conventional in the opinion of the twins. He wound up the session with a little instruction on estimation. Using the library, as an example, he guided them through a routine that permitted them to estimate the height of the ceiling, using similar triangles and no measuring device other than the foot rule and wooden, forty-five degree set square that lay on their father's desk. This little activity got them out of their seats and with, now, serious intent, focused on the unorthodox approach to learning of their new tutor.

'You can find the distance across a river, using the triangles flat but I will need paper and quill to explain. Another day.'

The twins, by this time, were beginning to appreciate the novel ways of their new tutor.

'Thank you Hawken. Very instructive. I will leave paper and quills on the table,' he pointed to a table in a corner of the library, 'you can carry out your written work with the girls there. There will be no distraction. Katherine, the girls can now leave.'

The older sister took the twins away.

'How do you find your quarters?'

'Very comfortable Sir Peter. Thank you.'

'Good. Perhaps you would join me for a brandy before supper. My daughter will call you. I think she has explained that I would prefer you to dine with me on occasion and when not you can seek refreshment in the kitchen. Katherine will advise you.'

'Thank you. I hope I can measure up to the kind of company you expect of me.'

'The landlord of the Arwenack tells me you are well travelled. I have been to a number of countries but would gladly hear of your experiences in this country and France and Italy.'

Conversation between the two went on until interrupted by Katherine returning, 'The master of the *Raven* is here with a ship full of cargo.'

'Good. He is well overdo. Hawken, I'll see you at table at sundown. Katherine, would you put paper, quill and slates out for the girls ready for tomorrow?' Killigrew left the two and went to meet the captain of his ship.

'I'll show you where the paper and quills are kept. Perhaps now is a good time to meet the servants. Then, if you need to prepare for the twins' lesson, I can leave you in your quarters but I am going to Penryn to order cloth. If you would like to accompany me I can show you the town. You might like then to visit during your free hours and no doubt you might need purchases of your own.'

Piran sensed, as with father like daughter, he was expected to accept. Again, there was an unspoken, even unintended but welcome invitation to closer liaison. Both were party to the attraction each had for the other.

'Yes, I would be pleased to see Penryn. I understand it once had a well-known college of learning, Glasney College but was disbanded by your King Henry.'

'It was. There are a few carved, stone remains still to be found but little else in human memory of the time.'

45

'Good evening. We have an interesting panel for this edition of *Polemic*. On my right is the MEP who represents The Republic of Ireland in Brussels, Paddy O'Rourke. To his right, Penny Lane, currently completing her PhD at Trinity. On my left Dr David Carstairs, Professor of Infant Mortality Studies at the London Children's' Hospital and on his left Eleanor Sullivan, secretary of the local association of Mothers Against Murder of the Unborn, MAMU. As usual, I am chairing this session. My name is Bill Synne.

Tonight's first topic is *Abortion*, followed by *The Clearances*. First question is from Mary Abbott. Mary.'

'Thank you. Does the panel believe there is a disproportionate degree of tyranny exercised over the majority by a tiny minority, from the extreme wings of all the major religions and their political supporters, that is out of all proportion to those that support abortion?'

'Thank you Mary. Paddy.'

'This is a question that affects all societies. In the EU it exercises the electorate in deeply or should I say 'state supported', Catholic countries. For my own part as your representative at Brussels, I try to contribute a constructive argument when challenged about singular aspects of the debate. Most of you here, with awareness of the common arguments that have been with us for decades, centuries even, will, doubtlessly, reflect conflicting viewpoints. I would guess that Professor Carstairs will offer comment on aspects that the rest of us are not privy to, in his capacity as a medic close to the controversy.

Now, as an ordinary member of society, as opposed to my role as an MEP representing an electorate, I have my own opinions informed from the same sources as the rest of you. In the former my view is that a woman should have the last say on the decisions that affect her body. In the latter, as an MEP, I would have to represent the majority view of the electorate that put me there. Fortunately, I have, so far, not been challenged in that capacity. For now, I believe that truthfully expresses my take on the topic.'

'Thank you Paddy. Eleanor.'

'You will all guess where my sentiments lie from the role that I play in MAMU. Whilst the first speaker's observation that any woman should have the last say in decisions that affect her body, the father of the unborn child should, surely, have an equal say in its survival since his living sperm is part of that living foetus.

That Mary, the Holy Mother of God, should have been prevailed upon to use whatever means might have been available at the time, to abort our Lord Jesus Christ, would have been a blasphemy. The role of Joseph, in respecting the rights of his unborn son to life, testifies to the right of a father to refuse the abortion of his unborn child.

Life is sacred. Life is to be treasured. Once destroyed it cannot be resurrected.'

'Professor Carstairs.'

'Thank you questioner. I am faced with dilemmas almost every week. Part of my work is to offer comment. I use the word comment rather than advice, on diagnoses that reveal serious congenital defects affecting foetuses in the womb and also those that do not show up until actual birth.

Before I comment on that area I would like to address the religious aspect of the question.

For those whom one might term as scientifically enlightened as opposed to those who subscribe to a literal interpretation of man-made, biblical texts - man-made in the sense of oral traditions passed down from orator to scribe - I have to side with indisputable, scientific observation. I could elaborate at length on my somewhat sceptical, cynical is probably a better word, attitude to the religious camp. Don't mistake that for a denial of the stability that a religious balance brings to a culture. Religion practised or should I say recognised, as a unifying element in society, is better, maybe, than some kind of destabilising, populist sentiment offering nothing to replace it with. But the populist element has a justifiable argument, sometimes, that should not be dismissed as irrelevant. There is usually a grain of truth in even the most obtuse of viewpoints.

At conferences related to child or infant mortality, the pre-natal condition is debated as an influential parameter. For example, is the mother obese; does she smoke; has she abused her body by drug addiction; is there a predisposition for congenital weakness in the father's genes; is there some condition, such as these, that results in a physical malformation combined with serious cerebral, sub-normality in the developing foetus? Medical science and I'm afraid I have to side with science, is as much interested in prevention, it doesn't need to be said, as cure. An overused cliché I know. Rigid adherence to misguided ethical practices or, perhaps, more accurately, distortions of biblical teaching that preserve the obscenity of a seriously, physically and mentally disabled birth, is a burden society should not have inflicted on it from narrow-minded, religious despots.'

'That is Fascist.' Eleanor almost shrieked the words.

'No. That is Realist. I know of a family with a physically and mentally abnormal child whose mother gave birth to a second child, hoping it would be normal, so that it could look after its sibling when, ultimately, the parents died. You think that is compassionate? What an imposition. I can't think of a more selfishly, inconsiderate thing to do to a child who will face more than enough challenges in its life without it having to care for a mentally and physically incapacitated brother or sister. Perhaps I have said enough for now.'

'Penny. Your floor.'

'I am guessing, in your use of the word tyranny, you are implying ultimate control exerted by states, through its judiciary, over its female population. If not that, then emotional tyranny exerted by extremist sects ostracising any female member who seeks such a termination.

I agree with Mr O'Rourke. A woman should have the final say on decisions that affect her body. That a raped woman should have to carry the ugly little growth that had been inseminated by some ugly, uninvited specimen of a male, because some state law forbids abortion - some law more than likely formulated by a committee of male judges - beggars belief in this enlightened century. Worse, if a woman or women comprised membership of that committee, then the law is doubly damned. Those women are the worst bigots, the worst examples of treachery towards their own kind.

Of course no one wants to see abortion as a form of contraception or a last resort of the sexually careless. But how many women carry that attitude? Issues of an ethical nature need to be freed from decisions made by lawmakers unlikely to suffer the long term consequences of misfortune they had, by definition, not invited on themselves. Further, in a free democracy the law should serve as many of its citizens as is possible within the legal framework. Allowing everyone to act according to their own moral code permits those who want a termination to have it. Those who have moral objection to it, they have the choice of going to full term. If a state makes abortion illegal it is imposing a moral opinion unlikely to be held by the majority. Imposing a sanction associated with repressive regimes rather than manifesting the outlook of a democracy informed by science or the more responsible, less rabid supporters of a caring socialism. The moral fight is between two opposing sides: those who think they're right with those who think they're right - semantic form intended. Irresolvable, opposing opinions.

The religious camp is part of the latter. The medieval attitude of states in bondage to religious dogma is anathema to those who do not subscribe to theocratic tyranny. I don't know what the Taliban attitude is concerning abortion, for example. We only hear about their attitude to trumped-up charges of adultery against women – not the men. My guess is they exert their patriarchal tyranny in such a way that abortion is not even acknowledged as a phenomenon in their society, not even in their vocabulary. You never hear about it. My further guess is that women there experience self-induced termination with agonizing, probably fatal, outcomes because they don't have the luxury even and I say luxury as a term of irony, of so-called back street practitioners. Such practitioners, were they

261

courageous enough to volunteer their services, would probably face even crueller deaths than that of ritual stoning. No. Abortion is little different, metaphorically, from removing an appendix. Emotionally a far different issue but in definition it boils down to a surgical procedure.'

'What a preposterous, monstrous suggestion,' Eleanor Sullivan spat the words out, 'a living being equated to an appendix? A redundant organ with no potential function? How can you believe what you are saying?'

Ignatius glanced quickly at O'Rourke and Carstairs. The looks on their faces confirmed his view that they were of the same opinion: to let these two fight it out.

Penny was not intimidated. Weeks on a North Sea drilling rig, amongst wind and saltwater-hardened riggers, had relieved her of any number of genteel pretensions she might have been conditioned to, pretensions normally associated with 'good ladies of the parish', as she was apt to describe the self-righteous, more interfering members of society – male or female.

'I'm sorry if you see it that way and that you are offended.'

'I am outraged. The foetus must be allowed to go to full term. God has permitted it to exist and there is any number of women eager to adopt unwanted babies.'

'Oh yes and if god is so compassionate why has he denied such women the means to conceive in the first place? Is that not also some part of his universal plan? Logically it begs that question. And as for IVF, that to me is as repulsive and a denial of service to more deserving, life-threatening conditions, by surgeons whose time could be better spent cutting the backlog of scheduled operations. Nature does not appear to be self-regulating. Uncontrolled, exponential population growth is a global fact in too many regions of the planet. The current, negative birth rates, such as we're now seeing in some EU countries, in no way offset the burgeoning birth rates in those other regions. Why add yet more numbers to an already overwhelmed planet?'

Ignatius decided it was time to step in. 'David, Paddy do either of you have further comment?'

Paddy nodded. 'We haven't addressed the matter of nursing staff who find the procedure distressing. I understand that some nurses are unwilling to assist in the action. Not so much for ethical or religious reasons but that they find the outcome visually disturbing. Is that your experience, Professor Carstairs?'

'Not disturbing for me but there are nurses who, after assisting at a termination, request a transfer. As with all of us, some have stronger stomachs than others. That doesn't mean I don't have sympathy for the stress and pain undergone pre and post the abortion procedure. For me, the sadness is when an underage girl submits to the act. Often she will be suffering enormous emotional and mental strain – that's if one can differentiate between the two. Older, mature females are no less likely to be upset but they are usually more prepared mentally, having been longer exposed to the adult world than their young counterparts. I suggest to these girls that they consider the choices and link it with counselling. Keeping the child. Offering it for adoption rather than terminating. But I also, it's risky I know, try to assess the quality of life the child is likely to have with the biological mother. Some families are loving and

263

supportive, others are the pits. You can tell quite reliably and subsequent experience backs it up, if the child will turn out to be a social liability like the rest of its family. Oh, I know the story of the professor lecturing his students: 'Father an alcoholic and has syphilis; mother is consumptive; thirteen children, another on the way, what would you recommend?' Students shout, 'Abort! Abort!' Professor says, 'Congratulations. You've just killed Beethoven or some such notable.'

I might have got the details wrong. The story has been passed down countless times with countless variations but you get my point. However, intuition kicks in and, when I've had misgivings, regretted, later, not recommending termination.'

'Thank you speakers. Let's open the floor to comment from the audience.'

Ignatius gave time to both sides of the debate.

'I think we've given this a good airing. Out of interest, could we have a show of hands? Those in favour of a woman's choice of abortion?' Ignatius made a rough estimate of the proportion in favour and made similar counts for against and for abstention.

'It's interesting that only a few of you abstained but I don't need to comment on the other two. Self evident. Thank you audience. Next question, please.'

46

'Ryan has submitted his final bill. Not too bad, since we asked for those two bunks to be fitted as extras.'

'How much?'

' Less than he previously quoted. He picked up a couple of free-standing ones from an IKEA sale and knocked off the price differential. He's attached the receipt, so it's a genuine discount.'

'Any other news?'

'The usual flood of trivia. Hang on, there's one just in from Stephen. Give me a second to scan it. His contacts have picked up new intel on the FONT shoot-out. Direct quote, '... *avenge our brothers and delete the Kaffirs* ...'. We'll be getting advice from SIS soon. Advises me to take refuge at an undeclared address of my choice, as soon as possible, until security established. He's sent cc to Robyn, our producer, as well so I'll be getting a call from her.'

'Not good. What are you going to do about Trinity? Your first lectures start in the new semester.'

'Have to think that one out. '

'You know where you can stay.' Penny spoke as though she knew Ignatius's answer.

'Yes. I bet you have the same thought.'

'Inisheer?'

'Yes.'

'Better book the ferry right away. We can do a quick shop in Dublin for essentials and then use the little shop on the island.'

'I'll email Ryan. Since he wants to take advantage of Rocky Valley we might as well make use of him.'

'What do you expect from him?'

'He liked the aggressive response of the audience over the *Clearances* topic. Their Fenian sympathies dominated. So, I shall hint, not so subtly, that we get protection and undeclared support from his IRA friends in the way of lookouts.'

'You still don't know for sure he's associated with them.'

'I know.'

'If that's so I still can't reconcile the pastoral element of your vocation with your sympathy for the IRA.'

'I understand your feelings. They have been unnecessarily violent at times but centuries of oppression, without any means by law to redress the injustices inflicted by the English - and the Scots they shipped in - has bred centuries of unrequited hatred. I don't agree with murder but I have to ask 'what other means were available if legal redress was denied by English courts?' I'm totally neutral in terms of otherwise persistent conflict between Northern Ireland, the Republic and unification. They each can put a case for their separate existences but that ensures eternal conflict. But that aside, we might as well make use of Ryan. We wouldn't be asking him to commit any crime.'

'Right. Less said. Let's get going.'

The two packed an assortment of clothing, footwear and basic items to last a month – hoping only to have to stay for a far shorter duration. En route Ignatius phoned his parents and then had a long conversation with Mike, regarding faculty arrangements.

'He's not too happy but understands. I think you've guessed that from my responses. I told him I can fly into Dublin on scheduled flights from the little air strip and be at Trinity sooner than driving from Rocky valley. It'll work. In fact, on the island there'll be fewer distractions. I can get more work done and the same for you.'

47

Sir Peter Killigrew liked to carve his own meat rather than a servant do it for him. Piran had completed a little over a season teaching the twins and had been invited, as he frequently was, to eat with his employer. The two were dining alone. A bell would summon a servant should extra victuals be needed or a fresh bottle of Bordeaux or after dinner Madeira be fetched from the cellar.

'I am impressed by the progress you have made with my daughters but I have a suggestion. Katherine is a sensible girl and it hasn't escaped my notice that she finds you acceptable company,' he laughed as he paused from slicing the haunch of venison, 'and you her.'

Piran blushed.

'No need to be embarrassed. It would please me if you would consider marrying her.' He recommenced carving, 'I also gather from our many conversations that you are experienced, sufficiently, in the ways of handling a boat or certainly no less so than anyone who has completed a voyage across the Sleeve to our neighbours in France. To that end a union with my daughter would ensure our continued prosperity if you took on the handling of my maritime interests. I do not enjoy the best of health and, as a Member of Parliament for this borough, I can discharge my duties with less concern as to my business interests here if you run them for me. I need say no more. Your knowledge of trade practices, incomplete, maybe, from Rouen to Rome and expertise in languages, should make for a good preparation in learning the matters of commerce and shrewd in your dealings with other merchants, particularly in foreign ports. Do I have your assent?'

'It is true I find Katherine's company a refreshing change from the life I formerly enjoyed. I would be pleased to accept and sense she would not object. As for the demands of your business interests, I am ready to face whatever fate or fortune throws at me. I have encountered dangers of a number of kinds in my travels. Whilst my original vocation tempered my anger it did not prevent me using force should I be required to defend myself. As for Katherine, I have great affection for her but refrained from expressing it. You wish me to make the proposal or does she already know your wishes?'

'Not overtly but she will not be surprised, as I have probed, perhaps not so subtly as I might have done. So make your proposal.'

'The twins' education – how will that be handled if I am engaged elsewhere?

'I have enough confidence in Katherine's judgement and yours to let you find and appoint a new tutor. The twins have had three months of your instruction. It is, perhaps, a good time for them to have a break from study and a holiday. That will give time for you to find a replacement and the change, after a few weeks holiday, will not seem so much of a disruption for them.'

Katherine brought the twins for their usual morning lesson and stayed for the duration. Piran found it difficult to concentrate on delivery. He dismissed them with relief at the end of the session, instructing them to put their slates and chalk away and to go to take refreshment in the kitchen. They bounded out, filling the library with high octave, girlish chatter, releasing physical energy pent up from sustained, mental activity.

'Mistress Katherine, would you kindly stay,' as she got up to follow. She sat back down, laid the tapestry she had been working on to the side of her and waited with a quizzical, slightly puzzled look on her face.

Piran, although inwardly excited, presented a calm front, 'Your father has given his permission to ask if you would consent to marry me.'

Given with a total lack of romantic charm it made Katherine laugh, 'That must be one of the shortest, direct proposals of marriage ever delivered to an intended spouse.'

'Well?'

'Of course I'll marry you. On one condition,' she paused, tantalising him, setting an agenda for the rest of their future, 'that you keep the twins in order.'

'Agreed.'

The two, careful in each other's proximity until now, embraced and kissed for a long period, saying little, savouring every minute of their newfound intimacy.

'Your father will be waiting for lunch. Shall we tell him now?'

'Yes.'

The pair made their way to the Long Hall that served as a dining, banqueting and meeting area. Voices indicated Sir Peter was not alone.

'… and, I understand, he has rejected the benediction of ordination.'

'That maybe so but he is a man of letters, firm of conscience and disciplined.'

Katherine cautioned Piran to stop, putting a finger to her lips. They waited, listening to the two men, 'It is Thomas

Melchior, the priest,' she whispered, 'he is of our Protestant faith but inclined towards the ritual of Rome. My father finds him a burden.'

'That you entrust the education of your children to him is folly.'

'And where did you hear of his credentials?'

'News travels by way of those who frequent the inn. I would counsel you to dismiss him before he does irreparable harm and you have later cause to regret his appointment.'

'Father Melchior, let me remind you who is the patron of the church and who it is has the responsibility for its upkeep, the roof, the collection of tithes and your not inconsiderable stipend. I will not be lectured to by a priest in whose grace and favour it is mine to appoint or dismiss. The man is staying. I will hear no more from you.'

At this point Katherine led Piran into the hall. It was obvious to the two men that some, they could not know how much, of the conversation had been overheard.

Melchior glared at Piran, ignored Katherine, wordlessly took his leave from Sir Peter with a slight tilt of his head and strode across the oak floor, through the arched entry, to the reception hall.

'That is my troublesome priest. The words from history were never more apt. Anyway, I was about to take a glass of sack before dining. Now you're here perhaps you will keep this angry knight company and eat with him.'

'Thank you father. We have news you will not be surprised to receive. Piran has asked my hand in marriage and I have accepted his proposal, happily.'

'That is not news that is good news. Master Hawken I welcome you into the family.'

Sir Peter fetched two glasses from a cupboard, looked at Katherine, 'I think, perhaps, you too should now be allowed to take wine,' and returned to fetch another of the goblets.

He poured the pale, almost clear, dry white wine into the glasses and passed one to each of the two.

'Your future happiness and again, welcome to the House of Arwenack.'

*

Lunch over, Sir Peter led Piran into his library.

'As Katherine is the heir to all this, you will have responsibilities I don't doubt you have already foreseen. You already know I have maritime interests. It is my belief that you would be a match for any of my competitors. Trade is good but does not favour the weak. I propose to introduce you to my contacts and members of various guilds hereabout; later, London. In the meantime it is best that we let Katherine appoint and oversee whom she wishes, to plan and organise the wedding. She is a capable girl, maybe I should say woman now.'

Piran listened to further comment without interruption.

'You have observations to make?'

'Of no particular significance concerning my responsibility to Arwenack. I do, however, believe I can add further to your interests, profitably, by setting up an artificer's workshop. My skills in optics can be expanded to the manufacture of nautical telescopes and navigational instruments. There is no end of metal hereabouts. The Cornish are well known for their resourcefulness and engineering skills

272

with the casting and working of metals. It would mean time equipping a foundry and workshops, training apprentices. A busy port like this will have its captains eager to purchase its share of spy glasses and nautical instruments.'

'That is ambitious but I like your style. There is time to explore such an enterprise.'

The two consumed a glass of Madeira after which Sir Peter Killigrew dismissed Piran and went to his bedroom to rest.

48

'We've been here three weeks now. There must be some news of the way things are developing.' Penny loved the island but was beginning to feel frustrated. She needed to access Trinity library and face to face contact with her supervisor. Her thesis was close to completion but needed tweaking.

'Ryan has contacts at Dublin airport. He can fix transfer to the city. Let's risk a visit. I'll email Stephen for news first; then we can take it from there.'

The next scheduled flight from the little island's airstrip saw them land in a grey, drizzly afternoon. They were at the university in a little over an hour after dumping their gear at Penny's apartment.

'So what's the score with Bokowski and SIS?' Mike O'Connor handed a coffee to Ignatius. The two sat alongside the low table.

'Gone quiet. But that, I'm told, signifies either diminishing interest or imminent action. Both seem to think the latter. Stephen's Mossad contacts are inclined to suggest increased vigilance for the next few weeks rather than a relaxation.'

'You know it's Mossad keeping tabs on this?'

'No. Not officially. But I'm pretty sure that's where he gets his intel. SIS are pretty certain to be informed by Mossad. Although there is no guarantee either obliges the other with exchanges. Put Interpol into the equation and you have a jealous mix.'

'I think you're going to have to take a chance on detection and do whatever minimum you can get away with, for the time being. The brutal alternative is a complete revision of your tenure here. I can't keep Senate at bay indefinitely. They're sympathetic to your circumstances but now students - I don't have to tell you – are paying the equivalent of a small mortgage for their courses, they don't want to be short-changed. Senate has been challenged a few times, this last year, by dissatisfied students.'

Ignatius shrugged, 'I really don't know what's best to do. For myself, I'm willing to take a chance. It's Penny I'm concerned about. We don't know how much the group knows about me or if they know about her.'

'If it goes to a high level in ISIS terms, like a fatwa, you might have to consider a total change of identity. I'm not suggesting it can get that bad but these people are demented. There's no telling what's in their minds. The other side of the coin is any one third party wanting to exploit the situation for political gain rather than theological reasons. Anyway let's give it one more week then take stock. Keep the beard. A few more weeks and you'll be unrecognisable.'

'Talking of students, how many have we got from Muslim countries?'

'Enough but it's not necessarily those you need to worry about. It's unlikely they will have heard of you. The home-grown ones are more likely to be the danger. Quite a few from the Midlands and Leeds/Bradford area. None have enrolled for philosophy. They're mainly focusing on engineering, physics and medicine but it's merely enough for them to be on campus. They can easily find your lecture timetable and location. Freshers aren't due until, what, just over two weeks? You've got time on that score at least.'

'OK. I'll chew it over with Penny and contact Bokowski on a daily basis.'

Penny had two plates of ploughman's on the table by the time Ignatius returned.

'That looks good.'

'I've got some cider in the fridge to go with it. I'm starving. Almost ate mine waiting for you.'

'How'd it go with Mike?'

'OK. Will have to make up my mind about risk and decide soon what to do.'

'Whatever you decide I'll go with it. I'm guessing any further absence from Trinity is a no brainer. I can't see we have much choice. Either you elect to continue as though there's no threat or you have to give up here and start new somewhere else. That'll mean a major upheaval. Change of job, change of city, country even. Change of everything.'

'I don't intend to let this beat me. I'm pretty sure personal protection, security, will see us through to some sort of normality.'

'You can't know that. We should have some sort of plan, however nebulous, rather than rely on fate.'

As it happened the problem was taken out of their hands sooner than they expected. Attack came from an unexpected quarter.

Returning to the Jesuit house the following day, to retrieve some items, he was accosted, on exit, by a woman seeking directions. Dressed in what might be described as a garment used by someone mucking out stables, a worn, originally expensive, thornproof, waxed canvas jacket, she drew a kitchen knife from its sleeve and lunged at him. She had been waiting daily, it transpired, for him to appear.

Caught off guard by her apparently innocent question, the blade penetrated his chest below the lower rib. She gave a loud shriek, dropped the knife and ran off laughing insanely. A nearby group witnessing the event, split. One lot went to assist Ignatius, two others chased and caught the woman. An ambulance rushed the wounded victim off to the infirmary, still conscious but bleeding heavily in spite of attempts to staunch it. Ignatius was able to give Penny's number to one of those assisting before losing consciousness.

Two days later papers carried the headline, 'Presenter of Polemic Killed by Mad Woman'. Penny showed a now conscious Ignatius the account of his death. Stephen Bokowski had been quick to exploit the opportunity to disseminate a fake account of the stabbing to news editors, removing threat of further aggression from the jihadists.

It transpired that the woman had been receiving psychiatric treatment for a range of mental illnesses connected with childbirth - pestering doctors' surgeries with claims that turned out to be phantom pregnancies. Her most recent episode had taken a more serious turn: she had walked off with a three-week old child in a supermarket. The mother had turned her back on the child's buggy for a few seconds to search a section of shelves for a particular cooking ingredient. Fortunately her frantic shouts alerted security who stopped the woman before she could escape with the child. That had been several months earlier. The woman had ceased taking medication and had found a new obsession – anger at those facilitating termination of the very condition she imagined herself denied.

His part, as a person of influence, in not overtly disapproving of abortion in the recent *Polemic* programme, led her irrational mind to build a murderous case against him. As a citizen of Dublin, Cardinal Synne's high profile in the city would have been well-known to her. She took up a daily vigil outside the Jesuit house in the hope of delivering the punishment she was convinced he deserved. Her persistence paid off.

'How's it going?' Stephen Bokowski drew a chair up to Ignatius's bed.

'Healing well. Knife was sharp so didn't tear the flesh but bacteria carried into the wound, from my garments, caused an infection. Lucky full-blown sepsis didn't set in. Anyway they're pleased with progress.'

'Penny and I had a chat on the way here. You're going to have to relocate under new names. The medical staff is sworn to secrecy. The only other people you can inform are parents. Applies to Penny too. At least it's not like you're under a witness protection scheme and still known to be alive. The jihadists will be off your back. Your main concern is where to go and what work you can take on. I can get passports for you and, within a limited field, secure employment through any number of global contacts.' Bokowski leaned back in his chair and waited for Ignatius's response.

'I've had time to think a little about it. I don't want to give up academia, that's for sure but neither do I want a lower tier, lecturing job in physics. Beggars can't be choosers, I know but I'd sooner be a gardener somewhere or stonemason or sheep farmer than processing undergraduates in their first year physics.'

'It won't come to that. The new philosophy course you've put together is ground-breaking. I don't want to see that effort wasted. There is any number of universities where I can secure you a professorial appointment along the same lines and where they would welcome funding of such a course. I support other establishments in much the same way as Trinity. The only difference is you would no longer be fronting and co-producing a show like *Polemic* in the media world.'

The conversation continued on a lighter note until Stephen could see Ignatius needed to rest. 'Time for me to leave. I'll give Penny some time with you on your own then drop her off at her flat. In the meantime get fit. Don't worry about future arrangements. I'll ensure things go to your needs. It happened on my watch. It's my responsibility.'

The following day saw further improvement in Ignatius's energy level and no pain. The knife, besides severing blood vessels, had just touched the outer layer of liver. Threat of any kind of Hepatitis strain and other infections had been blocked by a hefty dose of broad spectrum antibiotics. Otherwise, the wound carried no greater danger than an emergency appendectomy. After a few days of observation he would be ready for discharge.

'So, what do you want to do?' Penny supported him whilst she made his pillows more comfortable.

'Get married.'

'Well, that's an abrupt way of putting it.'

'Do I have an answer?'

She just leaned forward and kissed him tenderly on the lips.

'I take it that's a yes.'

She smiled mischievously, 'Yes Holy Father.'

A spasm of pain hit him as he was unable to suppress a laugh that pulled on the injured tissue.

'I don't think acceptance of a proposal of marriage has caused so much pain in a suitor. Don't make me laugh again.' This time his hand supported the muscles over his stomach as again they both laughed.

'But you mean future plans along the lines of career change,' he looked pensively at her then down at the bed sheets for a brief spell, 'I don't know how willing you are to face a real uprooting. New Zeeland, say. There are some good universities over there. Otago, for example.'

Penny shrugged, 'If it must be for our safety there are worse places. I back-packed around there with a friend. Gap year thing. Beautiful country. If Stephen could fix that I would go along with it. But they're tight on immigration. I don't know what strings he could pull at that level.'

'It would take a while to sort out anyway. We've got time to weigh it up. When I'm declared fit I think we should take a proper break away somewhere. Inisheer was fine but we were both working on stuff. You choose a destination. I've got one in mind but I want you to pick one as well – we'll do both.'

'OK. If you've already one in mind we could do that first. I don't want to go to Italy again. Maybe Greece or France, Provence, perhaps. Where are you thinking of.'

'Well, at the back of my mind I've wanted to visit a monastery in Rennes where a monk was condemned to the stake by The Inquisition. Came up in a manuscript I was researching on Cosmology. For some reason it touched a nerve. The Order survived the Revolution and is still populated by a handful of monks. I'd like to see if there are documents recording the event in their archives. It's been niggling at me ever since I read the manuscript. The monastery has a web site. I looked it up once. Is open to the public on certain days. When I get out of here I'll see if I can arrange a visit with the abbot.'

'We'll have to have a suitable cover. You can't go as Cardinal Synne, obviously.'

'I've had plenty of time to think about it lying here. I'll contact the monastery and say I am an archivist researching heresy and came across reference to de Tregor in my searches. We can try it. It should work, especially if I suggest making a donation.'

'That settles it. France. Rennes then Saint Paul de Vence and the Camargues. I'll drive.'

49

'I don't want that officious priest presiding over our wedding. I find his manner obnoxious. He likes to touch. The twins also find him unpleasant.'

'If that is what you wish I will find a suitable replacement. That will be easy to arrange. I believe the Rector of Penryn would gladly officiate. '

'Thank you father.'

'In the meantime I shall see about dismissing Melchior and appointing one more acceptable to us all. He is a man I no longer care about. I will ask the Bishop of Exeter to nominate a candidate but will make it clear we want a pastor not a dictator. The previous bishop recommended him but I believe he was influenced more by his theological credentials than his pastoral skills. I will put him on furlough from today.'

Piran found Katherine ready to visit Penryn to pick up bridesmaids dresses for the twins. The wedding was imminent, due to take place in just over a week.

'I'm going to meet the captain of the *Raven*. News has come in about her arrival. Your father told me it might be due before he returned from Parliament and that I should see to the unloading of the cargo. Will you take the twins with you?'

'No. I shall go on horseback with one of the servants. The twins can stay with cook or play in the garden. I'll be back well before midday.'

The two embraced and Piran set off for Customs House Quay.

The *Raven* was tied up close to the arched storage cellars running beneath the main street, many of their heavy, church-like doors, fronting the busy harbour side, were wide open. Captain Melvill stood in front of one of these ready to direct transfer of Killigrew's cargo.

'Fine day captain. Welcome back. Ready to unship?'

''es boy. I've a gang aboard, ready. There's a small load to go direct back to Arwenack for Sir Peter. A couple of the men and ourselves can manage it when we've locked up here.'

'You had a good voyage then?'

'Better than that, boy. Engaged a Corsair just outside Mullion. On a raidin' party I reckon, lookin for slaves. Knocked out her main mast, slaughtered her crew and towed her back. That's her ridin' against the pier over there. I'm claimin' her. Not letin' his majesty's government take a share. She's war bounty far as I'm concerned.'

'Right. Let's get the cargo off and into the cellars.'

The unloading was brisk. Dockers and crew were eager to finish and get to the Arwenack Arms. Captain Melvill, Piran and two crew shared out a small number of packages and some larger items to take back to the big house.

Back at the manor house Piran gave instructions, 'Those can go down to the kitchen. These we'll put into the library.'

'Hello cook. Some goods from the ship. The twins have been down?'

'Yes but the priest took them, said something about the wedding.'

Piran, knowing of the planned change, reacted immediately, 'Where has he taken them.'

'Don't know. He came from the direction of the stables and went back that way.'

'Come with me.' Piran didn't wait for any comment and took off in the direction of the stables with the other three.

Nearing the main opening to the generously proportioned outbuildings, he cautioned the three to approach silently. Inside, the two young girls were backed up against a mound of hay. The priest was in front, removing a belt from under his cassock, unaware of the group at his back. When the twins suddenly switched their stares from his face to the space behind, he turned.

Hatred and guilt in one fleeting flash was replaced with an expression of contempt. The kind of contempt that a presumptuous intellectual will reserve for those he considers his inferiors.

'How dare you disturb instruction in the faith. I will not countenance this intrusion.'

The four were in no way misled by this blatant attempt to disguise his intentions.

'I will give you instruction. You take us for fools?' Piran advanced with the other three spaced out to block Melchior's escape. 'Twins, go back to cook. We'll deal with master Melchior. Go now.'

The twins needed no further persuasion. Already sensing a threat from the priest before help put in appearance, they were relieved to be freed from his control.

'There is no need to adopt that attitude. I was merely attempting to ensure they were adequately informed of the religious significance of their sister's forthcoming vows.'

'Master Piran,' Captain Melvill spoke, 'what say we offer him to the press gang? Their officer is in the Arwenack

Arms, I am reliably informed by my men. We'll get the king's shilling for our effort.'

Melchior blanched, 'You can't do that. I am an ordinand of the Diocese of Exeter; one of the king's appointed ministers of the church.'

'And I am the Arch Angel Gabriel, one of the avenging angels. Grab him lads.'

The two crew members darted forward. Melchior put up a fight but with Captain Melvill putting him in a neck lock and Piran kicking the priest's legs out from under him, he was soon on the floor, pinned face down with a mouthful of hay fragments and other detritus from the stable, in his mouth.

'Pull the cassock front over his head and secure it with his belt around his arms. We'll get him down to the *Raven,* somehow, unseen and invite the officer of his majesty's navy to offer him employment in one of his majesty's ships.' Said with irony.

The two crew members guffawed at the genteel description of what they knew would be far from a normal contract of employment. Melchior squealed with fear. One of the crew clouted him across the back of his head as he was securing the rope, 'I have daughters you damned spalpeen. You think we don't know how to protect our own from the likes of you?'

'There's a naval chest in one of the cellars he can fit in. With a couple of poles or a pair of oars and a length of rope we can sling the chest between and the four of us get him there in daylight. We'll dose him up with brandy or rum to keep him quiet on the way. One of you come with me.'

A rope cradle was fashioned and a pair of oars fed through a set of loops.

'Right, dose him up with the rum.'

Melchior, twisted his head to and fro, avoiding the cup put to his mouth.

'Keep still,' the captain kneed Melchior in the groin, 'if you don't drink this quiet-like you won't see the inside of his majesty's ship. Your throat'll be cut and you'll come aboard with us and end up as meat for the fish in Mounts Bay. If there's any ruckus from inside the chest, on the way, the same'll happen.'

The priest was forced to drink a generous measure of liquor. When it was obvious he was well inebriated the four men packed him into the chest and set off for the quay. En route a crew member visited the Arwenack Inn. The bosun in charge of the press gang was invited onto the *Raven*. A small bounty was paid, shared between the captain and two crew and a cutter rowed Melchior across to a naval ship anchored out in the estuary. Piran took the little group back to the Inn and treated them to a hearty meal of spit-roasted suckling pig and ale.

'Tomorrow you can bring the chest back with some tobacco and brandy. If anything is said about the priest's disappearance, since cook will know we were concerned, I shall say he escaped from us and was last seen boarding a ship that left for France. The twins won't suspect, nor care, any differently if they're questioned.'

Piran left the captain and returned to Arwenack to deal with arrangements he was responsible for on the impending wedding. On the way back a dog appeared from one of the alleys leading down to the port and followed him for some distance. The creature was malnourished and looked ill-treated. Despite attempts by Piran it refused to be discouraged from following him. It seemed to read Piran's character, seemed aware of an unwritten history of kindness towards animals that the former monk possessed.

'Alright boy. Come home with me. You shall have a refuge from persecution. I shall call you Cabo.'

50

The abbaye at Rennes still, remarkably, possessed the same door it had been hung with in the time of Gabriel. Ignatius and Penny made themselves known to a novice unloading a lump of potter's clay wrapped in damp hessian, from the rear of a 2CV.

'Your abbot, Father Anselm, is expecting us.'

'Ah yes. You must be the archivist he has told us about. Follow me.'

The two were led through the yard to the abbot's study.

'Come in. Welcome.'

Ignatius shook hands with the abbot, 'This is my secretary, Mme Lane.'

Anselm Lenoir took her hand and gave Ignatius an enigmatic look.

'I expect you would like some refreshment after your journey. I have searched our archives. You can examine what I have found after we have eaten. You will be most interested in what they reveal but let us join the brothers in the refectory, first.'

'Thank you Father Anselm. That will be a pleasure.'

In the library, Anselm had already set out a table with a number of manuscripts.

'This first one is a copy of a letter from a Cardinal Rochefoucauld, accepting his invitation to conduct a trial of the accused heretic, Gabriel de Tregor. This,' he pointed to a second, 'is an account of the trial written by one of the monks. The full, official account, by the cardinal's secretary, will, presumably, be held in the archives at the Vatican. How good is your Latin?'

'Well practised. The documents in Rome were all in ecclesiastical Latin.'

'Good.' The abbot gave Ignatius time to scan the documents before presenting him with a third manuscript. 'This will interest you I am sure and will clear up some of the mystery you expressed over your assessment of the event. Read it out aloud. I am sure your secretary will be as interested and as surprised as you to learn of the contents.'

Ignatius started reading and translating simultaneously:

'I Pascal Bezier, abbot of this abbaye, do testify as to the truth of this account and as a confession before God.

Gabriel de Tregor, an Augustinian, came to us in flight from his monastery in Finistere, accompanied by his dog Cabo. De Tregor is a man of conscience and benevolent intent. His assistance at the abbaye was appreciated by all the brothers of our Benedictine Order. In particular his training of our brother, Marcel, in the science and skill of lens making and from it the gift of eye glasses to the older brethren afflicted by failing sight, endeared his presence to us all.

His abbot, Luc d'Angers, assisted by his nephew Francesco Fougères, brought charges of heresy against the Augustinian. The main content of the charges derived from the dispute between Ptolemy and Copernicus and de Tregor's agreement with Galileo's sympathy towards the latter's heliocentric theory. Other comment, unhelpful to his case, referred to the doctrine of the Trinity and its relation to the *kosmos*.

De Tregor was discovered here by Fougères who requested the attendance of Cardinal Rochefoucauld as Inquisitor Designate of the Holy See in Paris. De Tregor was found guilty and sentenced to be burned at the stake.

The monk, Fougères, struck de Tregor before declaration of guilt was established and was attacked by Cabo, bitten in leg and cheek. His wounds suffered sepsis of which he progressed to the point of death.

My confession is that I, aided by un-named assistance, substituted the body of Fougères in place of de Tregor to burn at the stake.

I ask the forgiveness of God in what I believe to be a justified act of mercy in preventing a man innocent of heresy being sent to Hell.

Gabriel has set off, under guise, to foreign parts. His faithful dog Cabo was entrusted to us and remains with us, an excellent catcher of rats [Here Pascal had penned a minute, match-stick cartoon of a dog sitting with tail wagging instead of a full-stop.]

Signed: Pascal Bezier, abbot of this Order.'

Ignatius was mute for some while.

'That is extraordinary. The abbot must have concealed this during his lifetime. It would have been too dangerous to lodge in the library. I am staggered by this, particularly since I felt, when reading the account in the Pontifical Library, that he was a man condemned out of jealousy, notwithstanding the fact that Galileo was right all along. How did it come to light?'

'We needed a new guide for visitors, then decided to do a book. History of the monastery, medieval plans compared with the modern layout, together with various other features of interest. One of the compilers, carrying out investigations, discovered the hiding place when measuring up internal dimensions. Checked a seating recess in the wall below the window in my study. Noticed the slabs under the window were not fixed with mortar. This was ten or more years ago. Underneath was a small, locked chest. A key secreted in the same cavity. We opened it and found this.'

'May I hold it?' Ignatius passed the document to Penny. 'The script is beautiful considering he wrote it in haste.'

'I have had a copy made for you. We have a Greek iconographer here on a commission to produce a modern triptych for the chapel. He has copied it on artificially aged manuscript paper and photocopied the original for you to compare the two.'

'That is generous beyond any expectation I could have had of the visit. Thank you. I have a donation for your monastery.'

'That will be much appreciated by our almoner who looks after all the finances. We need to replace the cultivator for the monastery garden. It will help defray the cost. Perhaps, before you leave, you would sign our visitor's book and leave a comment?'

The abbot slid the already open book towards Ignatius and held out a pen. Taking the pen, an old-fashioned, steel-nibbed implement, Ignatius dipped it into the inkwell and signed:

'Bill Synne, in remembrance of Gabriel de Tregor martyr and sometime visitor and benefactor of this monastery.'

Printed in Great Britain
by Amazon